Molly Elliot Seawell

Throckmorton

A Novel

Molly Elliot Seawell

Throckmorton
A Novel

ISBN/EAN: 9783337001131

Printed in Europe, USA, Canada, Australia, Japan

Cover: Foto ©Andreas Hilbeck / pixelio.de

More available books at **www.hansebooks.com**

THROCKMORTON

A NOVEL

BY

MOLLY ELLIOT SEAWELL

NEW YORK
D. APPLETON AND COMPANY
1890

THROCKMORTON.

CHAPTER I.

IN a lowland Virginia neighborhood, strangely cut off from the rest of the world geographically, and wrapped in a profound and charming stillness, a little universe exists. It has its oracles of law, medicine, and divinity; its wars and alliances. Free from that outward contact which makes an intolerable sameness among people, its types develop quaintly. There is peace, and elbow-room for everybody's peculiarities.

Such was the Severn neighborhood—called so from Severn church. Every brick in this old pile had been brought from green England two hundred years before. It seemed as if, in those early days, nothing made with hands should be without picturesqueness; and so this ancient church, paid for in hogsheads of black tobacco, which was also the currency in which the hard-riding, hard-drinking parsons took their dues, was peaked and gabled most beautifully. The bricks, mellowed by two centuries, had become a rich, dull red, upon which, year after year, in the enchanted Southern summers and the fitful Southern winters, mosses and gray lichens laid their clinging fingers. It was set far back from the broad, white road, and gnarled live-oaks and silver beeches and the melancholy weeping-willows grew about the churchyard. Their roots had pushed, with gentle persistence, through the crumbling brick wall that surrounded it, where most of the tombstones rested peacefully upon the ground as they chanced to fall. Within the church itself, modern low-backed pews had supplanted the ancient square boxes during an outbreak of philistinism in the fifties. At the same time, a wooden flooring had been laid over the flat stones in the aisles, under which dead and gone vicars—for the parish had a vicar in colonial days—slept quietly. The interior was darkened by the branches of the trees that pressed against the wall and peered curiously through the small, clear panes of the oblong windows; and over all the singular, unbroken peace and silence of the region brooded.

The country round about was fruitful and tame, the slightly rolling landscape becoming as flat as Holland toward the rich river-bottoms. The rivers were really estuaries, making in from the salt ocean bays, and as briny as the sea itself. Next the church was the parsonage land, still known as the Glebe, although glebes and tithes had been dead these hundred years. The Glebe house, which was originally plain and old-fashioned, had been smartened up by the rector, the Rev. Edmund Morford, until it looked like an old country-woman masquerading in a ballet costume; but the Rev. Edmund thought it beautiful, and only watched his chance to lay sacrilegious hands on the old church and to plaster it all over with ecclesiastical knickknacks of various sorts.

The Rev. Mr. Morford had come into the world handicapped by the most remarkable personal beauty, and extreme fluency of tongue. Otherwise, he was an honest and conscientious man. But he belonged to that common class among ecclesiastics who know all about the unknowable, and have accurately measured the unfathomable. On Sundays, when he got up in the venerable pulpit at Severn, looking so amazingly handsome in his snow-white surplice, he dived into the everlasting mysteries with a cocksureness that was appalling or delightful according to the view one took of it. In the tabernacle of his soul, which was quite empty of guile and malice, three devils had taken up their abode: one was the conviction of his own beauty, another was the conviction of his own cleverness, and still another was the suspicion that every woman who looked at him wanted to marry him. Mr. Morford reasoned thus:

I. That all women want to get married.

II. That an Edmund Morford is not to be picked up every day.

III. That eternal vigilance is the price of liberty.

On Sundays he scarcely dared look toward the
pew where General and Mrs. Temple sat, with their
beautiful widowed daughter-in-law, Mrs. Beverley
Temple, on one side of them, and Jacqueline Temple, as lovely in her small, kittenish way, on the
other, for fear that one or the other of these young
women would fall hopelessly in love with him. Mrs.
Beverley, as the young widow was called, to distinguish her from the elder Mrs. Temple, had the
fatal charm for the Rev. Edmund that all things
feared and admired have. He believed in his heart
of hearts that widows were made for his undoing,
and that the good old Hindoo custom of burning
them up alive was the only really safe disposition
to make of them. The charm of Judith Temple's
piquant face and soft, shy eyes was somewhat neu-
tralized by a grim suspicion lodged in Mr. Morford's
mind that she was unnecessarily clever. The Rev.
Edmund had a wholesome awe of clever women,
especially if they had a knack of humor, and was
very much afraid of them. Judith had a sedate
way of replying to Morford's resounding platitudes
that sometimes created a laugh, and when he laboriously unwound the meaning, he was apt to find
the germ of a joke; and Judith was so grave—
her eyes were so sweetly serious when she was laying
traps to catch the Rev. Edmund's sluggish wits. But
Judith herself thought of no man whatever, and had

learned to regard the sparkle of her unquenchable humor almost as a sin. However, having got a bad name for cleverness, neither the most sincere modesty nor the deepest courtesy availed her in keeping it quiet. Morford, in his simple soul, thought a clever woman could do anything; and suppose Judith should cast her eyes on—at this the Rev. Edmund would turn pale in the midst of his sermon when he caught Judith's gray eyes fixed soberly on him. Soberness— and particularly Judith's soberness—was deceitful.

Barn Elms, the Temple place, was near to the Glebe and to Severn church. The house was rambling and shabby, and had been patched and pieced, with an utter disregard of architectural proportion that resulted in a curious and unexpected picturesqueness. A room was put on here, and a porch was clapped up there, just as the fancy of each successive Temple had dictated. It was partly of brick and partly of stone. Around it stood in tall ranks the solemn, black-leaved poplars, and great locust-trees grew so close to the house that on windy nights the sound of their giant arms beating the shingled roof awoke superstitious fears in the negroes, who declared it to be the "sperrits" of dead and gone Temples struggling to get in through the chimneys. There was a step up or a step down in every room in the house, and draughts enough in the unnecessary halls and passages to turn a windmill. There was, of course, that queer mixture of shabbiness and luxury about the old place and the mode of living that is characteristic of Virginia. Mrs. Temple had piles and piles of linen sheets laid away with the leaves of damask roses between them in the old cedar chests, but half the rooms and all the stairs and passages were uncarpeted. It required the services of an able-bodied negro to keep these floors polished—but polished they were, like a looking-glass. The instrument used in this process was called a " dry-rubbin' bresh " by the manipulators, and might well have been used in Palestine during the days of Herod the tetrarch, being merely a block of wood covered with a sheepskin, well matted with wax and turpentine. At unearthly hours, in cold winter mornings and gray summer dawns, the monotonous echo of this " bresh " going up and down the hall-floors was the earliest sound in the Barn Elms house. There was a full service of silver plate displayed upon a huge and rickety mahogany sideboard, but there was a lack of teaspoons. Mrs. Temple had every day a dinner fit for a king, but General Temple was invariably behindhand with his taxes. The general's first purchase after the war was a pair of splendid Kentucky horses to pull the old carriage bought when Mrs. Temple was a bride, and which was so moth-eaten and worm-eaten and rust-eaten that when it started out it was a wonder that it ever came back again. The kitchen was a hundred yards from the

house in one direction, and the well, with its old-fashioned bucket and sweep, was a hundred yards off in
another direction. The ice-house and stables were
completely out of sight; while the negro houses, an-
nually whitewashed a glaring white, were rather too
near. But none of these things annoyed General and
Mrs. Temple, who would have stared in gentle surprise at the hint that anything at Barn Elms could
be improved.

General Temple, six feet tall, as straight as an
Indian, with a rich, commanding voice and a lofty
stride, stood for the shadow of domestic authority;
while Mrs. Temple, a gentle, affectionate, soft-spoken,
devoted, and obstinate woman, who barely reached to
the general's elbow, was the actual substance. From
the day of their marriage he had never questioned her
decision upon any subject whatever, although an elaborate fiction of marital authority was maintained between them and devoutly believed in by both. Mrs.
Temple always consulted the general punctiliously—
when she had made up her mind—and General Temple, after a ponderous pretense of thinking it over,
would say in his fine, sonorous voice : " My dear Jane,
the conviction of your extremely sound judgment,
formed from my experience of you during thirty
years of married life, inclines me to the opinion that
your suggestion is admirable. You have my permission, my love "—a permission Mrs. Temple never

failed to accept with wifely gratitude, and, like the general, really thought it amounted to something. This status is extremely common in Virginia, where, as a rule, the men have a magnificent but imaginary empire, and the women conduct the serious business of life.

Brave, chivalrous, generous, loving God and revering woman, General Temple was as near a monster of perfection as could be imagined, except when he had the gout. Then he became transformed into a full-blown demon. From the most optimistic form of Episcopal faith, he lapsed into the darkest Calvinism as soon as he felt the first twinge of his malady, and by the time he was a prisoner in the " charmber," as the bedroom of the mistress of the family is called in Virginia, he believed that the whole world was created to be damned. Never had General Temple been known under the most violent provocation to use profane language; but under the baleful influence of gout and superheated religion combined, he always swore like a pirate. His womenkind, who quietly bullied him during the best part of the year, found him a person to be feared when he began to have doubts about free-will and election. To this an exception must be made in favor of Mrs. Temple and of Delilah, the household factotum, who was no more afraid of General Temple than Mrs. Temple was. She it was who was mainly responsible for these carnivals of gout by feeding the patient on fried oysters and plum-pudding when Dr. Wortley prescribed gruel and tapioca. Delilah was one of the unterrified, and used these spells to preach boldly at General Temple the doctrines of the "Foot-washin' Baptisses," a large and influential colored sect to which she belonged.

"Ole marse," Delilah would begin, argumentatively, "if you wuz ter jine de Foot-washers—"

"Jane! Jane!" General Temple would shout.—"Come here, my love. If you don't get rid of this infernal old fool, who wants absolutely to dragoon me out of my religion, I'll be damned if I—God forgive me for swearing—and you, my dear—"

Sometimes these theological discussions had been known to end by Delilah's flying out of the room, with the general's boot-jack whizzing after her. At Mrs. Temple's appearance, though, the emeute would be instantly quelled. Delilah was also actively at war with Dr. Wortley, as the black mammies and the doctors invariably were, and during the visits of the doctor, who was a peppery little man, it was no infrequent thing to hear his shrill falsetto, the general's loud basso, and Delilah's emphatic treble all combined in an angry three-cornered discussion carried on at the top of their lungs.

Like mistress, like maid. As Mrs. Temple ruled the general, Delilah ruled Simon Peter, her husband, who since the war was butler, coachman, gardener, and man-of-all-work at Barn Elms. Mrs. Temple, however, ruled with circumlocution as well as circumspection, and had not words sufficient to condemn women who attempt to govern their husbands. But Delilah had no such scruples, and frequently treated Simon Peter to remarks like these:

"Menfolks is mighty consequenchical. Dey strut 'bout, an' dey cusses an' damns, an' de womenfolks do all de thinkin' an' de wukkin'. How long you think ole marse keep dis heah plantation if it warn't fur missis?"

"Look a heah, 'oman," Simon Peter would retaliate when intolerably goaded, "Paul de 'postle say—"

. "What anybody keer fur Paul de 'postle? Womenfolks ain' got no use fur dat ole bachelor. Men is cornvenient fur ter tote water, an' I ain' seen nuttin' else much dey is good fur."

Simon Peter's entire absence of style partly accounted for the low opinion of his abilities entertained by his better half. He was slouchy and sheep-faced, and, when he appeared upon great occasions in one of General Temple's cast-off coats, the tails dragged the ground, while the sleeves had to be turned back nearly to the elbow. Delilah, on the contrary, was as tall as a grenadier, and had an air of command second only to General Temple himself and much more genuine. She was addicted to loud, linsey-woolsey plaids, and on her head was an immaculately white "handkercher" knotted into a turban that would have done credit to the Osmanlis.

The war had given General Temple the opportunity of his lifetime. He "tendered his sword to his State," as he expressed it, immediately organized Temple's Brigade, and thereafter won a reputation as the bravest and most incompetent commander of his day. His ideas of a brigade commander were admirably suited to the middle ages. He would have been great with Richard Cœur de Lion at the siege of Ascalon, but of modern warfare the general was as innocent as a babe. It was commonly reported that, the first time he led his brigade into action, he did not find it again for three days. His men called him Pop, and always cheered him vociferously, but pointedly declined to follow him wherever he should lead, which was invariably where he oughtn't to have been. He had innumerable horses shot under him, but, by a succession of miracles, escaped wounds or capture. It was a serious mortification to the general that he should have come out of the war with both arms and both legs; and it was marvelous, considering that he put himself in direct line of fire upon every possible occasion, and galloped furiously about, waving his sword whenever he was in a particularly ticklish place.

Since the war General Temple had found congenial employment in studying the art of war as exemplified in books, and in writing a History of Temple's Brigade. As he knew less about it than any man in it, his undertaking was a considerable one, especially as he had to give a personal sketch, with pedigree and anecdotes, of every member of the brigade. He had started out to complete this great work in three volumes, but it looked as if ten would be nearer the mark. As regards the theory of war, General Temple soon became an expert, and knew by heart every campaign of importance from those of Hannibal, the one-eyed son of Hamilcar, down to Appomattox. A good deal of the money that would have paid his taxes went into the general's military library, which was a source of endless pride to him, and which caused the History of Temple's Brigade to be, in some sort, a history of all wars, ancient and modern.

The pride and satisfaction this literary work of his gave the general's honest heart can not be described. He read passages of it aloud to Mrs. Temple and Judith and Jacqueline in the solemn evenings in the old country-house, his resonant voice echoing through the old-fashioned, low-pitched drawing-room. Mrs. Temple listened sedately and admiringly, and thanked Heaven for having given her this prodigy of valor and learning. Nor, after hearing the History of Temple's Brigade all the evening, was she wearied when, at two o'clock in the morning, General Temple would have a wakeful period, and striding up and

down the bedroom floor, wrapped in a big blanket over
his dressing-gown, declaimed and dissected all the
campaigns of the war, from Big Bethel to Appomattox. Mrs. Temple, sitting up in bed, with the most
placid air in the world, would listen, and thank and
admire and love more than ever this hero, whom she
had wrapped around her finger for the last thirty
years. O blessed ignorance—O happy blindness of
women! which gracious boon God has not withheld
from any of the sex. But there was something
else that made General Temple's long-winded war
stories so deeply, tragically interesting to Mrs. Temple. There had· been a son—the husband of the
handsome daughter-in-law—Mrs. Temple could not
yet speak his name without a sob in her voice. That
was what she had given to the great fight. When
the news of his death came, General Temple, who
had never before dreamed of helping Mrs. Temple's
stronger nature, had ridden night and day to be with
her at that supreme moment, knowing that the blow
would crush her if it did not kill her. She came
out of the furnace alive but unforgetting. She would
not herself forget Beverley, nor would she allow anybody else to forget him. She remembered his anni-
versaries, she cherished his belongings; she, this tender, excellent, self-sacrificing woman, sacrificed, as far
as she could, herself and everybody else to the memory of the dead and gone Beverley. As fast as one

crape band on the general's hat wore out, she herself, with trembling hands, sewed another one on.
As for herself, she would have thought it sacrilege
to have worn anything but the deepest black; and
Judith, after four years of widowhood, wore, whether
willingly or unwillingly, the severest widow's garb.
Jacqueline alone had been suffered, out of consideration for her youth and the general's pleading, to put
on colors. The girl, who was beautiful and simple,
but quite different from other girls, in her heart cherished a hatred against this memory of the dead, that
had made her youth so sad, so encompassed with
death. Jacqueline loved life and feared death; and
whenever her mother began to speak of Beverley,
which she did a dozen times a day, Jacqueline's shoulders would twitch impatiently. She longed to say:
" What is he to us ? He is dead—and we live. Why
can't he be allowed to rest in peace, like other dead
people ? " Jacqueline was far from heartless ; she
loved her sister-in-law twice as well as she had ever
loved her handsome silent brother, whose death made
no gap in her life, but had ruthlessly barred out all
brightness from it. Jacqueline, in her soul, longed
for luxury and comfort. All the discrepancies and
deficiencies at Barn Elms were actually painful to her,
although she had been used to them all her life. She
wanted a new piano instead of the wheezy old machine in the drawing-room. She wanted a thousand

things, and, to make her dissatisfaction with Barn
Elms more complete, not a quarter of a mile away,
across a short stretch of feathery pine-trees, on a
knoll, stood a really great house, Millenbeck by name.
To Jacqueline's inexperienced eyes, the large square
brick house, with its stone balustrade around the
roof, its broad porch, with marble steps that shone
whitely through the trees around it, was quite palatial.
And nobody at all lived there. It was the family
place of the Throckmortons. The last Throckmorton
in the county was dead and gone; but there was another—grandson to the last—a certain Major George
Throckmorton, who, although Virginian born and
bred, had remained in the regular army all through
the war, and was still in it. This George Throckmorton had spent his boyhood at Millenbeck with his
grandfather, who was evil tempered and morose, and
thoroughly wicked in every way. The old man had
gone to his account during the war, and since then
his creditors had been fighting over his assets, which
consisted of Millenbeck alone. Major Throckmorton
had money, and it had been whispered about that,
whenever Millenbeck was sold, this army Throckmorton would buy it. But it was freely predicted that he
would never dare show his face in his native county
after his turpitude during the war in fighting against
his State, and he was commonly alluded to as a traitor.
Nevertheless, at Severn church, one Sunday, it was

2

said that this Throckmorton had bought Millenbeck,
and would shortly make his appearance there.

General and Mrs. Temple, as they sat on opposite
sides of the fireplace at Barn Elms, discussing the matter with the profound gravity that the advent of a new
neighbor in the country requires, to say nothing of
the sensation of having a traitor at one's doors, came
nearer disagreeing than usual. The night was cool,
although it was early in September, and a little fire
sparkled cheerfully upon the brass andirons on the
hearth in the low-pitched, comfortable, shabby drawing-room. Mrs. Temple, clicking her knitting-needles
placidly, with her soft eyes fixed on the fire, went over
the enormity of those to whom Beverley's death was
due. To her, the gentlest and at the same time the
sternest of women, the war took on a personal aspect
that would have been ludicrous had it not been pathetic. Ah! what was that boy that Beverley had left,
what was Judith the young widow, or even Jacqueline,
to that lost son? Nothing, nothing! Mrs. Temple,
still gazing at the fire, saw in her mind, as she saw
every hour of the day and many of the night, the dead
man lying stark and cold; and, as if in answer to her
thoughts, General Temple spoke, laying down his vol-
ume of Jomini:

"My love, what will you do—ahem! what would
you recommend me to do regarding George Throckmorton when he arrives? Speak frankly, my dear,

and do not be timid about giving me your opinion."

A curious kind of resentment shone in Mrs. Temple's face.

" It is not for a woman to guide her husband; but *we* at least can not forget what the war has cost us."

General Temple sighed. He had heard that Throckmorton had got a year's leave and would probably spend it at Millenbeck. How fascinating did the prospect appear of a real military man with whom he could discuss plans of campaign, and flank movements, and reconnaissances, and all the *technique* of war in which his soul delighted! For, although Dr. Wortley had become a great military critic, as everybody was in those days, he had never smelt powder, and was a very inferior antagonist for a brigadier-general, who had been in sixteen pitched battles without understanding the first thing about any of them.

Jacqueline, who sat in her own little chair, with her feet on a footstool, and her elbows on her knees, began in an injured voice:

" And the house is going to be perfectly grand. Mrs. Sherrard told me about it to-day. A whole parcel of people "—Jacqueline was a provincial, although an amazingly pretty one—" a whole parcel of people came by the boat—workmen and servants, and most splendid furniture, carpets, and pictures, and cabinets, and all sorts of elegant things—just for those two men—for there is a young man, too—Jack is his name."

"Yes," said Mrs. Temple, meditatively, as she still clicked her knitting-needles together with a pleasant musical sound, "the boy must be about twenty-two. George Throckmorton I well remember was married at twenty-one to a pretty slip of a girl, so I've heard, who lived a very little while. He can't be more than forty-four now. He is the last man I ever supposed would ever turn traitor. He was the finest lad—I remember him so well when he was a handsome black-eyed boy; and when we were first married—don't you recollect, my dear?"

General Temple rose gallantly, and, taking Mrs. Temple's hand in his, kissed it.

"Can you ask me, my love, if I remember anything connected with that most interesting period of my life?" he asked.

Neither the handsome Judith nor little Jacqueline were at all discomposed by this elderly love-making, to which they were perfectly accustomed. A slight blush came into Mrs. Temple's refined, middle-aged face. It was worth while to coddle a man, and take all the labor of thinking and acting off his shoulders, for the sake of this delightful sentiment. Like his courage, General Temple's sentiment was high-flown but genuine.

"I was about to say," resumed Mrs. Temple, when

the general had returned to his chair, "that when I came to Barn Elms a bride, George Throckmorton was much here. You did not notice him, my love, as I did—but I felt sorry for the boy; old George Throckmorton certainly was a most godless person. The boy's life would have been quite wretched, I think, in spite of his grandfather's liberality to him, but for the few people in the neighborhood like Kitty Sherrard and myself, who tried to comfort him. He would come over in the morning and stay all day, following me about the house and garden, trying to amuse Beverley, who was a mere baby."

Mrs. Temple never spoke the name of her dead son without a strange little pause before it.

"And, my dear," answered the general, making another feeble effort, "can you not now embrace the scriptural injunction?"

"The Scripture says," responded sternly this otherwise gentle and Christian soul, "that there is a time to love and a time to hate."

All this time, Judith, the young widow, had not said a word. She was slight and girlish-looking. Her straight dark brows were drawn with a single line, and in her eyes were gleams of mirth, of intelligence, of a love of life and its pleasures, that habitual restraint could not wholly subdue. When she rose, or when she sat down, or when she walked about, or when she arched her white neck, there was a singular grace, of which she was totally unconscious. Something about her suggested both love and modesty. But Fate, that had used her as if she were a creature without a soul, had married her to Beverley Temple— and within two months she was a widow. The shock, the horror of it, the willingness to idealize the dead man, had made her quietly assume the part of one who is done with this world. And Nature struggles vainly with Fate. Judith, in her black gown, and a widow's cap over her chestnut hair, with her pretty air of wisdom and experience, fancied she had sounded the whole gamut of human love, grief, loss, and joy. Neither Millenbeck, nor anything but Beverley's child and his father and mother and sister, mattered anything to her, she thought.

Jacqueline, however, looked rebellious, but said nothing. Like her father, she was under the rule of this soft-voiced mother. But it was certainly very hard, thought Jacqueline, bitterly, that with Millenbeck beautifully fitted up, with a delightful young man like Jack Throckmorton—for Jacqueline had already endowed him with all the graces and virtues— and a not old man, a soldier too, should be right at their doors, and she never to have a glimpse of Millenbeck, nor a chance for walks and drives with them. Jacqueline sighed profoundly, and looked despairingly at Judith, who was the stay, the prop, the comforter of this undisciplined young creature.

CHAPTER II.

WITHIN a few days Throckmorton and Jack Throckmorton—the traitor and the traitor's son—had arrived at Millenbeck.

Jacqueline could talk of nothing but the dawning splendors of the place. Delilah, who had an appetite for the marvelous scarcely inferior to Jacqueline's, kept her on the rack with curiosity.

"Dey done put Bruskins carpets all over de house," she retailed solemnly into Jacqueline's greedy ears, "an' velvet sofys an' cheers, an' de lookin'-glasses from de garret ter de cellar. An' dey got a white man name' Sweeney—mighty po' white trash, Simon Peter say—dat is a white nigger, an' he talk mighty cu'rus. Simon Peter he meet him in de road, an' dis heah Mis' Sweeney he ax him ef dey was any Orrish gentmans 'bout here. Simon Peter he say he never heerd o' no sich things ez Orrish gentmans, an' Mis' Sweeney he lif' up he stick, an' Simon Peter he took ter he heels an' Mis' Sweeney arter him, an' Simon Peter 'low ef he hadn't run down in de swamp, Mis' Sweeney would er kilt him, sho'! An' he doan' min' blackin' de boots at Millenbeck an' milk de cows, an' den he dress up fine an' wait on de table—an' he a white man, too! He done tell some folks he wuz a soldier an' fit, an' he gwine ev'ywhar Marse George Throckmorton go, ef it twuz hell itself. Things is monst'ous fine at Millenbeck—*dat* dey is—an' all fur dem two menfolks. Seem like God A'mighty done give all de good times ter de menfolks an' all de hard times ter de womenfolks."

"Is that so, mammy?" asked Jacqueline, dolefully, who was simple of soul, and disposed to believe everything Delilah told her.

"Dat 'tis, chile, ez sho'—ez sho' ez God's truf. De menfolks jes' lives fur ter be frustratin' an' owdacious ter de po' womenfolks, what byar de burdens. I tell Simon Peter so ev'y day; but dat nigger he doan' worrit much 'bout what de po' womenfolks has got ter orndure. Men is mighty po', vain, weak creetures —*I* tell Simon Peter dat too ev'y day."

"Dat you does," piously responded Simon Peter.

The windows to Judith's room possessed a strange fascination in those days for Jacqueline, because they looked straight out to Millenbeck. There she stood for hours, dreaming, speculating, thinking out aloud.

"Just think, Judith; there is a great big hall there that mamma says has a splendid dancing-floor!"

"Jacky, stop thinking about Millenbeck and the dancing-floor. It doesn't concern you, and you know that mother will never let you speak to either of the Throckmortons," answered Judith.

"Yes, I know it," said Jacqueline, disconsolately. "The more's the pity. Papa is dying to be friends with them when they come; but, of course, mamma won't let him."

Jacqueline's voice was usually high-pitched, rapid, and musical, but whenever she meant to be saucy she brought it down to great meekness and modesty.

"Major Throckmorton, you know, is a widower. I don't believe in grieving forever, like mamma. Suppose, now, Judith, *you* should—"

But Judith, whose indulgence to Jacqueline rarely failed, now rose up with a pale face.

"Jacqueline, you forget yourself."

Usually one rebuke of the sort was enough for Jacqueline, but this time it was not. She came and clasped Judith around the waist, and held her tight, looking into her eyes with a sort of timid boldness.

"Just let me say one thing. Mamma is sacrificing all of us—you and me and papa—to—to Beverley—"

"Hush, Jacqueline!"

"No, I won't hush. Judith, how long was it from the time you first met Beverley until you married him?"

"Two months."

"And how much of that time were you together?"

"Two—weeks," answered Judith, falteringly.

"And then you married him, and you had hardly any honeymoon, didn't you?"

"A very short one."

"And Beverley went away, and never came back."

There was a short silence. Jacqueline was nerving herself to say what had been burning upon her lips for long.

"Then—then, Judith, he was so little *in* your life—he was so little *of* your life."

"But, Jacqueline, when one loves, it makes no difference whether it is a month or a year."

"Yes, when one loves; but, Judith, did you love Beverley *that* way?"

Judith stood quite still and pale. The thought was then put in words that had haunted her. She no longer thought of answering Jacqueline, but of answering herself. Was it, indeed, because she was so young, so entirely alone in the world, and, in truth, had known so little of the man she married, that it became difficult for her to recall even his features; that she felt something like a pang of conscience when Mrs. Temple spoke his name; that this perpetual kindness to his father and his mother seemed a sort of reparation? Jacqueline, seeing the change in Judith's face, went softly out of the room. Judith stood where Jacqueline had left her. Presently the door opened, and little Beverley came in, and made a dash for his mother. Judith seized him in her arms, and knelt down before him, and for the thousandth time tried to find a trace of his father in his face. But there was none. His eyes, his mouth, his expression, were all hers. Even the little bronze rings of hair that escaped from under her widow's cap were faithfully reproduced on the child's baby forehead. This strong resemblance to his mother was a thorn in Mrs. Temple's side. She would have had the boy his father's image. She would have had him grave and given to serious, thoughtful games, and to hanging about older people, such as her Beverley had been; but this merry youngster was always laughing when he was not crying, and was noisy and troublesome, as most healthy young animals are. Yet she adored him.

The boy soon got tired of his mother's arms around him, and uncomfortable under her tender, searching gaze.

"I want to go to my mammy," he lisped.

Judith rose and led him by the hand down-stairs· to Delilah. The child ran to his mammy with a shout of delight. His mother. sometimes awed his baby soul with her gravity, when he had been naughty. Often he could not get what he wanted by crying for it, and got smart slaps upon his plump little palms when he cried. But with Delilah there was none of this. Delilah represented a beneficent

Providence to him, which permitted naughtiness, and had no limit to jam and buttermilk.

The Throckmortons had at last come, but had kept very close to Millenbeck for a week or two after their arrival in the county; but on one still, sunny September Sunday at Severn church, just as the Rev. Edmund Morford appeared out of the little robing-room, after having surveyed himself carefully in the mite of a looking-glass, and satisfied himself that his adornment was in keeping with his beauty, two gentlemen came in quietly at a side door, and took their seats in the first vacant pew. They looked more like an elder and a younger brother than father and son. Both had the same square-shouldered, well-knit figures, not over middle height—the same contour of face, the same dark eyes. But it was a type which was at its best in maturity. Major Throckmorton was much the handsomer man of the two, although, as Judith Temple said some time after, when called upon to describe him, that handsome scarcely applied to him—he was rather distinguished than actually handsome—and she blushed unnecessarily as she said it. His hair and mustache were quite iron-gray, and he had the unmistakable look and carriage of a military man. The pew they took near the door was against the wall of the church, and in effect facing the Temple pew, where sat all the family from Barn Elms, including little Beverley, who looked a picture of childish misery, compelled to be preternaturally good, until sleep overcame him, and his yellow mop of hair fell over against his mother. Young Throckmorton, whose eyes were full of a sort of gay curiosity, let his gaze wander furtively over the congregation, and in two minutes knew every pretty face in the church. The two prettiest were unquestionably in the Temple pew. Without boldness or obtrusiveness, he managed to keep every glance and every motion in that pew in sight; and Jacqueline, by something like psychic force, knew it, and conveyed to him the idea that no glance of his escaped her. Nevertheless, she was very devout, and the only look she gave him was over the top of her prayer-book. Judith, with her large, clear gaze fixed on the clergyman, was in her way as conscious as Jacqueline. But Throckmorton saw nothing and nobody for a time, except that he was back again in Severn church after thirty years. How well he remembered it all!—the little dark gallery to the right of the pulpit, where in the old times Mrs. Temple and Mrs. Sherrard had sat, and sung the old, old hymns, their sweet, untrained voices rising into the dark, cobwebbed, resonant roof—voices as natural as that of the sweet, shy singing birds that twittered under the eaves of the old church, and built their nests safely and peacefully in the solemn yews and weeping-willows of the burying-ground close by. The September sunlight, as it sifted through the windows on the heads of the kneeling people—even the droning of the honey-bees outside, and the occasional incursion of a buzzing marauder through the windows—made him feel as if he were in a dream. It was not the recollection of a happy boyhood that had brought him back to Millenbeck. He remembered his grandfather as an old curmudgeon, the terror of his negroes and dependents, wasteful, a high liver, and a hard drinker; and himself a lonely boy, with neither mother nor sister, nor any sort of kindness to brighten his boyish soul, except those good women, Mrs. Temple and Mrs. Sherrard. Deep down in his being was that Anglo-Saxon love of the soil—the desire to return whence he came. He knew much of the world, and doubted if the experiment of returning to Millenbeck would succeed, but he at least determined to try it. He had no very serious notion of abandoning his profession, which he loved, while he grumbled at it, but he had had this project of a year's leave, to be spent at Millenbeck, in his mind for a long, long time, and he wanted Jack to own the place. Himself the most unassuming of men, he cherished, unknown to those who knew him best, a strong desire that his name should be kept up in Virginia where it had been known so long. With scarcely a word on the subject spoken between father and son, Jack had the same drift of sentiment. Both had inherited from dead and gone generations a clinging to old things, old forms, that made itself felt in the strenuous modern life, and even a sturdy family pride that native good sense concealed.

The Rev. Edmund Morford, along with his unfortunate excess of good looks, inherited a rich, strong voice, in which he rolled out the liturgy with great elocutionary effect. He saw the two strangers in the congregation, and at once divined who they were, and determined to give them a sermon that would show them what stuff parsons were made of in Virginia. He was much struck by the scrupulousness with which Major Throckmorton went through the service, which the Rev. Edmund attributed partly to his own telling way of rendering it. But in truth, Throckmorton neither saw nor heard the Rev. Edmund. He went through the forms with a certain military precision that very often passed for strict attention, as in this case, but he was still under the spell of the bygone time. Mr. Morford gave out a hymn, and the congregation rose, Throckmorton standing up straight like a soldier at attention. After a little pause, a voice rose. It was so sweet, so pure, that Throckmorton involuntarily turned toward the singer. It was Judith Temple, her clear profile well marked against her black veil, which also brought out the deep tints of her eyes and hair, and the warm paleness of her complexion. She sang quite composedly and unaffectedly,

a few women's voices, Mrs. Temple's among the rest,
joining in timidly, but her full soprano carried the
simple air. Her head was slightly thrown back as
she sang, and apparently she knew the words of the
hymn by heart, as she did not once refer to the book
held open before her.

There is something peculiarly touching in female
voices unaccompanied. Throckmorton thought so as
he came out of his waking dream and glanced about
him. In an instant he took in the pathetic story of
war and ruin and loss that was written all over the
assembled people. Many of the women were in
mourning, and the men had a jaded, haggard, hope-
less look. They had all been through with four years
of harrowing, and they showed it. In the Temple
pew Mrs. Temple and Judith were in the deepest
mourning, and General Temple wore around his hat
the black band that Mrs. Temple would never let him
take off.

Throckmorton's eye rested for a moment in approval on Judith, and then on Jacqueline, but he
looked at Jacqueline the longest.

Then, after the hymn, Mr. Morford began his sermon. It was electrifying in a great many unexpected
ways. Throckmorton, who knew something about
most things, saw through Morford's shallow Hebraism,
and inwardly scoffed at the cheerful insufficiency with
which the most abstruse biblical problems were at-

tucked. Morford's candor, confidence, and perfect good faith tickled Throckmorton; he felt like smiling once or twice, but, on looking around, he saw that everybody, except those who were asleep, took Morford at his own valuation; except the young woman with the widow's veil about her clear-cut face, whose eyes, fixed attentively on Mr. Morford, had something quizzical in their expression. Throckmorton at once divined a sense of humor in that grave young widow that was conspicuously lacking in Jacqueline, who listened, bored but awed, to the preacher's sounding periods.

The sermon was long and loud, and there was another hymn, sung in the simple and touching way that went to Throckmorton's heart, and then a dramatic benediction, after the Rev. Edmund had announced that the next Sunday, "in the morning, the Lord will be with us, and in the evening the bishop. I need not urge you, beloved brethren, to be prepared for the bishop."

Then the congregation streamed out for their weekly gossip in the churchyard. Throckmorton and Jack went out, too. No one spoke to them, nor did they speak to any one. As a matter of fact, there were not half a dozen people there that Throckmorton would have recognized; but he was perfectly well known to everybody in the church, who, but for the uniform he had worn, would have greeted him cordially and generously, recalling themselves to him. But now they all held coldly and determinedly aloof. Throckmorton, who was slow to imagine offense, did not all at once take it in. But he would not lose a moment in speaking to Mrs. Temple, one of the few persons he recognized, and the one most endeared to him in his early recollections. The Temples, possibly to avoid him, had made straight for the iron gate of the churchyard, and stood outside the wall, waiting for the tumble-down carriage. Throckmorton quickened his pace, and went up to Mrs. Temple, carrying his hat in his hand.

"Mrs. Temple, have you forgotten George Throckmorton?" he asked in his pleasant voice.

Mrs. Temple turned to him with a somber look on her gentle face.

"No, I have not forgotten you, George Throckmorton. But you and I are widely apart. Between us is a great gulf, and war and sorrow."

A deep flush dyed Throckmorton's dark face. He was not prepared for this, but he could not all at once give up this friendship, the memory of which had lasted through all the years since his boyhood.

"The war is over," he said; "we can't be forever at war."

"It is enough for *you* to say," she replied. "You have your son. Where is mine?"

"As well call me to account for the death of Abel.

Dear Mrs. Temple, haven't you any recollection of the time when you were almost the only friend I had? I have few enough left, God knows."

Here General Temple came to the front. In his heart he was anxious to be friends with Throckmorton, and did not despair of obtaining Mrs. Temple's permission eventually. He held out his hand solemnly to Throckmorton.

"*I* can shake hands with you, George Throckmorton," he said, and then, turning to Mrs. Temple, "For the sake of what is past, my love, let us be friends with George Throckmorton."

Throckmorton, who in his life had met with few rebuffs, was cruelly wounded. In all those years he had cherished an ideal of womanly and motherly tenderness in Mrs. Temple, and she was the one person in his native county on whose friendship he counted. He looked down, indignant and abashed, and in the next moment looked up boldly and encountered Judith's soft, expressive eyes fixed on him so sympathetically that he involuntarily held out his hand, saying:

"You, at least, will shake hands with me."

Judith, who strove hard to bring her high spirit down to Mrs. Temple's yoke, did not always succeed. She held out her hand impulsively. The spectacle of this manly man, rebuffed with Mrs. Temple's strange power, touched her.

"And this," continued Throckmorton, out of whose face the dull red had not yet vanished, turning to Jacqueline, "must be a little one that I have not before seen.—Mrs. Temple, I can't force you to accept my friendship, but I want to assure you that nothing —nothing can ever make me forget your early kindness to me."

Mrs. Temple opened her lips once or twice before words came. Then she spoke.

"George Throckmorton, you think perhaps that, being a soldier, you know what war is. You do not. I, who sat at home and prayed and wept for four long years, for my husband and my son, and to whom only one came back, when I had sent forth two— *I* know what it is. But God has willed it all. We must forgive. Here is my hand—and show me your son."

Throckmorton, whose knowledge of Mrs. Temple was intimate, despite that long stretch of years, knew what even this small compromise had cost her. He motioned to Jack, who was surveying the scene, surprised and rather angry, from a little distance. The young fellow came up, and Mrs. Temple looked at him very hard, a film gathering in her eyes.

"I am glad you have such a son. Such was our son."

The carriage was now drawn up, and General Temple looked agonizingly at Mrs. Temple. He wanted her to invite Throckmorton to Barn Elms, but Mrs. Temple said not one word. Throckmorton, in perfect silence, helped the ladies into the carriage. He did not know whether to be gratified that Mrs. Temple had conceded so much, or mortified that she had conceded so little.

Jacqueline in the carriage gave him a friendly little nod. Judith leaned forward and bowed distinctly and politely. General Temple, holding his hat stiffly against his breast, remarked in his most grandiose manner : " As two men who have fought on opposing sides—as two generous enemies, my dear Throckmorton—I offer you my hand. I did my best against you in my humble way "— General Temple never did anything in a humble way in his life, and devoutly believed that the exploits of Temple's Brigade had materially influenced the result—" but, following the example of our immortal chieftain, Robert Lee, I say again, here is my hand."

A twinkle came into Throckmorton's eye. This was the same Beverley Temple of twenty-five years ago, only a little more magniloquent than ever and a little more under Mrs. Temple's thumb. Throckmorton, repressing a smile, shook hands cordially.

" Neither of us has any apologies to make, general," he said. " I think that ugly business is over for good. I feel more friendly toward my own unfortunate people now than ever before. Good-by."

The general then made a stately ascent into the carriage, banged the door, and rattled off.

Short as the scene had been, it made a deep impression upon Judith Temple. Throckmorton's dignity—the tender sentiment that he had cherished for his early friends—struck her forcibly. The very tones of his voice, his soldierly carriage, his dark, indomitable eye, were so impressed upon her imagination that, had she never seen him again, she would never have forgotten him. It was an instant and powerful attraction that had made her hold out her hand and smile at him.

Throckmorton, without trying the experiment of hunting up any more old friends, turned to walk home. It was a good four-mile stretch, and usually he stepped out at a smart gait that put Jack to his trumps to keep up with. But to-day he sauntered along so slowly, through the woods and fields with his hat over his eyes and his hands behind him, that Jack lost patience and struck off ahead, leaving Throckmorton alone, much to his relief.

Throckmorton wanted to think it all over. In his heart there was not one grain of resentment toward Mrs. Temple. He thought he understood the workings of her strong but simple nature perfectly well, and he did not doubt the ultimate goodness of her heart. And General Temple—Throckmorton had heard something of the general's magnificent incapacity during the war—the bare idea of General Temple as a commander made him laugh. How sweet were Mrs. Beverley's eyes, and how demure she looked when she dropped them at some particularly solemn absurdity of the clergyman, as if she were afraid somebody would see the tell-tale gleam in them! The little girl, though, was the most fascinating creature he had seen for long. How strangely and how pitifully altered was the congregation of Severn church from the merry prosperous country gentry he remembered so long ago! And how quiet, how still was life there! All his usual every-day life was shut out from him. Within the circle of that perfect repose nothing disquieting could come. He stopped in the country lane and listened. Nothing broke the solemn calm except the droning of the locusts in the September noon. Warm as it was, there was a hint of autumn in the atmosphere. Occasionally the clarion cry of a hawk circling in the blue air pierced the silence.

"This, then, is peace," said Throckmorton to himself, and thought of the year of idleness and repose before him. "Nothing ever happens here," he continued, thinking. "Even the tragedy of the war was at a distance. As Mrs. Temple says, the men went forth, and those that came back will go forth no more."

Then he began to think over the way in which the people had completely ignored him in the churchyard, where they stopped and gossiped with each other, eying him askance. He knew perfectly well the estimate they put upon him. He could have supplied the very word—" traitor." This made him feel a sort of bitterness, which he consoled with the reflection—

" Most men of principle have to suffer for those principles at some time or other."

By this time he was at his own grounds, and Sweeney's honest Irish face, glowing with indignation, was watching out for him.

" Be the powers," snorted Sweeney to the black cook, " the murtherin' rebels took no more notice of the major than if he'd been an ould hat—an' he's a rale gintleman, fit ter dine with the Prisident, as he often has, an' all the g'yurls has been tryin' to hook him fur twinty years, bless their hearts, an' the major as hard as a stone to the dear things, every wan of 'em !"

CHAPTER III.

WITHIN a week or two after, one afternoon Mrs. Kitty Sherrard made her appearance at Barn Elms, with a great project in hand. She meant to give a party.

Party-giving was Mrs. Sherrard's idiosyncrasy. According to the usual system in Virginia, during the lifetime of the late Mr. Sherrard, there was much frolicking, dancing, and hilarity at Turkey Thicket, the Sherrard place, and a corresponding narrowness of income and general behindhandedness. But since Mr. Sherrard's death Mrs. Sherrard, along with the unvarying and sublime confidence in her husband, dead or alive, that characterizes Virginia women, had yet entirely abandoned Mr. Sherrard's methods. The mortgage on Turkey Thicket had been paid off, the whole place farmed on common-sense principles, and the debts declared inevitable by Mr. Sherrard carefully avoided. As a matter of fact, the only people in the county who paid their taxes promptly were the widows, who nevertheless continually lamented that they were deprived of the great industry, foresight, and business capacity of their defunct lords and masters. Mrs. Sherrard gave as many parties in Mr. Sherrard's lifetime as she did after his death; but, since that melancholy event, the parties were paid for, not charged on account.

When this startling information about the coming festivity was imparted, Jacqueline, who was sitting in her own low chair by the fire, gave a little jump.

"And," said Mrs. Sherrard, who was a courageous person, "I'll tell you what I am giving it for. It is to get the county people to meet George Throckmorton. Not a human being in the county has called on him, except Edmund Morford, and I fairly drove him to it. He began some of his long-winded explanations. 'Aunt Kitty,' he said, 'what am I, even though I be a minister of the gospel, that I should set myself up against the spirit of the community, which is against recognizing Throckmorton?' 'What are you, indeed, my dear boy,' I answered. 'I'm not urging you to go, because it's a matter of the slightest consequence what you do or what you don't, but merely for your own sake, because it is illiberal and unchristian of you not to go.' Now, Edmund is a good soul, for all his nonsense."

Mrs. Temple was horrified at this way of speaking of the young rector.

"And I've intimated to him that I'm about to make my will—I haven't the slightest notion of doing it for the next twenty years—but the mere hint always brings Edmund to terms, and so he went over to Millenbeck to call. He came back perfectly delighted. The house is charming, Throckmorton is a prince of hospitality, and I don't suppose poor Edmund ever was treated with so much consideration by a man of sense in his life before." Mrs. Temple groaned, but Mrs. Sherrard kept on, cutting her eye at Judith, who was the only person at Barn Elms that knew a joke when she saw it. Judith bent over her work, laughing. "I met Throckmorton in the road next day. 'So you dragooned the parson into calling on the Philistine,' he said. Of course I tried to deny it, after a fashion; but Throckmorton won't be humbugged—can't be, in fact—and I had to own up. 'You can't say Edmund's not a gentleman,' said I, 'and he is the most good-natured poor soul; and if he had broken his nose, or got cross-eyed in early youth, he really would have cut quite a respectable figure in the world.' 'That's true,' answered George, laughing, and looking so like he did long years ago, 'but you'll admit, Mrs. Sherrard, that he is too infernally handsome for his own good.' 'Decidedly,' said I."

"Katharine Sherrard," solemnly began Mrs. Temple, who habitually called Mrs. Sherrard Kitty, except at weddings and funerals, and upon occasions like the present, when her feelings were wrought up, "the way you talk about Edmund Morford is a grief and a sorrow to me. He is a clergyman of our church, and it is not becoming for women to deride the men of their own blood. Men must rule, Katharine Sherrard. It is so ordered by the divine law."

"Jane Temple," answered Mrs. Sherrard, "you may add by the human law, too; but some women—"

"Set both at naught," answered Mrs. Temple, piously and sweetly.

"They do, indeed," fervently responded Mrs. Sherrard, having in view General Temple's complete subjugation. "But now about the party. The general must come, of course. I wish I could persuade you."

"I have not been to a party since before the war, and now I shall never go to another one."

"But Judith and Jacqueline will come."

At this a deep flush rose in Judith's face.

"I don't go to parties, Mrs. Sherrard."

"I know; but you must come to this one."

Mrs. Temple set her lips and said nothing, but Jacqueline, who sometimes asserted herself at unlooked-for times, spoke up:

"If Judith doesn't go, I—I—sha'n't go."

"You hear that?" asked Mrs. Sherrard, delighted at Jacqueline's spirit. "Stick to it, child; there is no reason why Judith shouldn't come."

Here General Temple entered and greeted Mrs.

Sherrard elaborately. Mrs. Sherrard immediately set to work on the general. She knew perfectly well that he could do no more in the case than Simon Peter could, but she poured her fire into him, thinking a stray shot might hit Mrs. Temple. Judith remained quite silent. She was too sincere of soul to say she did not want to go; and yet going to parties was quite out of that life of true widowhood she had laid down for herself; and life was intolerably dull. She loved gayety and brightness, and her whole life was clothed with somberness. She was full of ideas, and loved books, and nobody in the house ever read a line except General Temple, and his reading was confined to the science of war, for which he would certainly never have any use. She was full of quick turns of repartee, that, when she indulged them, almost frightened Mrs. Temple, who had the average woman's incapacity for humor. Mrs. Sherrard and herself were great friends—and friends were not too plentiful with Mrs. Sherrard, whose tongue was a two-edged sword. Nevertheless, Mrs. Temple and Mrs. Sherrard had been intimate all their lives, and Mrs. Sherrard was one of the few persons who ever took liberties with Mrs. Temple. Mrs. Sherrard was clear-sighted, and she knew what nobody else did—how starved and blighted was Judith's life by that stern repression to which she had set herself; and she had known Beverley Temple, too, and sometimes said to herself: "Perhaps it is better for Judith as it is, for Beverley, brave and handsome as he was, yet was a dreadfully ordinary fellow. Luckily, she was hustled into marrying him so quickly, and she was so young, she didn't find it out; but if he had lived—"

Mrs. Sherrard departed, impressing upon General Temple that she should certainly expect to see him at the party, with Judith and Jacqueline. Simon Peter in the kitchen reported the state of affairs to Delilah, who remarked:

"Miss Kitty She'ard, she know Miss Judy cyan go twell ole missis say so. Ole marse, he got a heap o' flourishes an' he talk mighty big, but missis she doan' flourish none; she jes' go 'long quiet like, an' has her way."

"Dat's so," answered Simon Peter, rubbing his woolly head with an air of conviction. "Missis s'ut'ny is de wheel-hoss in dis heah team."

"An' ain't de womenfolks allus de wheel-hosses? Ole marse he set up an' he talk 'bout de weather an' de craps, an' he specks de 'lection gwine discomfuse things, an' he read de paper an' he know more 'n de paper do, an' he read de Bible an' he know more 'n de Bible do, an' all de time he .ain' got de sperrit uv a chicken."

"De womenfolks kin mos' in gen'ally git dey way," cautiously answered Simon Peter.

"Yes, dey kin; an' dey is gwine ter, 'long as men-folks is so triflin' an' owdacious as dey is."

Jacqueline developed a strange obstinacy about the party. She declared she was dying to go, but she never wavered from her determination not to go without Judith.

"But your sister does not wish to go, Jacqueline," her mother said to this.

"But I want her to go, mamma. You can't imagine how I *long* to go to this party. It is so very, very dull at Barn Elms—and I have my new white frock."

"Judith has no frock."

"Oh, yes she has. She has that long black dress, in which she looks so nice, and she is so clever at sewing she could cut it open at the neck and turn up the sleeves at the elbow."

Mrs. Temple said nothing more. Jacqueline went about, eager-eyed, but silent, and possessed of but one idea—the party. A day or two after this she said bitterly to her mother, when Judith was out of the room:

"Mamma, I know why you are willing to disappoint me about this party. It is because you love your dead child better than your living one."

Mrs. Temple turned a little pale. The thrust went home, as some of Jacqueline's thrusts did.

"And if I don't go, I will cry and cry—I will cry

that night so loud in my room that papa will come in, and you know how it vexes him to have me cry; and it will break my heart—I know it will."

Mrs. Temple went about all day with Jacqueline's words ringing in her ears. That night, after Jacqueline was in bed, her mother went into the room. It was a large, old-fashioned room, and Jacqueline's little white figure, as she sat up in bed, was almost lost in the huge four-poster, with dimity curtains and valance. The fire still smoldered, and the spindle-shanked dressing-table, with the glass set in its mahogany frame, cast unearthly shadows on the floor in the half-light. Mrs. Temple sat down by the bed. Something like remorse came into the mother's heart. This child was the least loved by both father and mother. Jacqueline began at once, in her sweet, nervous voice:

"Mamma, I have been thinking about the party."

"So have I, child."

"And may we go?"

Mrs. Temple paused before she spoke.

"Yes, you and Judith may go," she said presently in a stern voice—ah! the sternness of these gentle women!

Jacqueline held out her arms fondly to her mother, but Mrs. Temple could not be magnanimous in defeat. She went out, softly closing the door behind her, without giving Jacqueline her good-night kiss, but

Jacqueline called after her in a voice tremulous with gratitude and delight, " Dear, sweet mamma ! "

The moment she heard the " charmber-do'," as the negroes called it, shut down-stairs, Jacqueline slipped out of bed and flew across the dark passage into Judith's room to tell the wonderful news. Judith was sitting before the fire, holding her sleeping child in her arms. The boy had waked and had clung to his mother until she lifted him out of his little bed. He had gone to sleep directly, but Judith held him close; he was so little, so babyish, yet so soft and warm and clinging.

" We are going to the party, Judith," said Jacqueline, excitedly, kneeling down by her.

" Are we ? " answered Judith. A gleam came into her eyes very like Jacqueline's.

" And—and—" continued Jacqueline with a sly, half-laughing glance, " we will meet Major Throckmorton again."

" Go to bed, Jacqueline," replied Judith in the soft, composed voice that invariably crushed Jacqueline.

Next morning General Temple showed the most unqualified delight at Mrs. Temple's capitulation. He considered it becoming, though, to make some slight protest against going to the party. He thought, perhaps, with his tendency to gout, it would scarcely be prudent to expose himself to the night air, and—er—

to Kitty Sherrard's chicken salad; and, besides, he really was not justified in postponing the drawings of some maps to illustrate the position of Temple's Brigade at the battle of Chancellorsville; for, like all other dilettanti, General Temple's work was always of present importance and admitted of no delay whatever.

Mrs. Temple did not smile at this, but treated it with great seriousness.

"Quite true, my dear; but now that I have promised Jacqueline, I can not disappoint her. You must go for her sake."

"Rather let me say, my dear Jane, that I go for your sake—your wishes, my love, being of paramount importance."

For a henpecked man, it was impossible to be more imposing or agreeable than General Temple. So on the night of the party he was promptly on hand, at eight o'clock, in his old-fashioned evening coat, the tails lined with white satin, and wearing a pair of large, white kid gloves.

Jacqueline and Judith soon appeared. Jacqueline, in her new white frock, looked her prettiest, albeit it showed her youthful thinness and all her half-grown angles. Judith's beauty was of a sort that could stand the simplicity of her black gown that revealed her white neck, and, for the first time since her widowhood, she wore no cap over her red-brown hair. Deli-

lah and Simon Peter yah-yahed and ki-yied over both
of them.

"Dem little foots o' Miss Jacky's in de silk stock-
in's ain' no bigger'n little Beverley's, hardly, and Miss
Judy she look like de Queen o' Sheba," delightedly
remarked Delilah.

Judith could scarcely meet Mrs. Temple's eyes.
She felt inexplicably guilty. Mrs. Temple examined
them critically, though, and the general was loftily
complimentary.

"And, Delilah," said Judith, gathering up her
gloves nervously, "be sure and look after Beverley.
He has never been left alone in his life before."

"I will look after Beverley, Judith," said Mrs.
Temple, and Judith blushed faintly at something in
the tone.

All the way, going along the country road in the
moonlight, Judith could feel Jacqueline's little feet
moving restlessly with excitement. As they drove
up to the house, and caught glimpses through the
open hall-door of the dancers and heard the sound of
music, Jacqueline began to bob up and down with
childish delight.

Like most Virginia country-houses, Turkey Thicket
had an immense entrance hall, which was not heated
and was of no earthly use the best part of the year,
and for which all the rooms around it were unnecessarily cramped. Mrs. Sherrard's hall was of more use

to her than most people's, owing to her party-giving proclivities, and was brightly lighted up for dancing. As Judith came down the broad stairs on General Temple's arm, a kind of thrill of surprise went around among the guests. Nobody expected to see her. Many of them had never seen her except in her widow's veil and cap. Judith, remembering this, could not restrain a blushing consciousness that made her not less handsome; and, besides, her good looks were always full of surprises. One never knew whether she would be simply pale and pretty, or whether she would blaze out into a sudden and captivating beauty.

They made their way through the dancers, Jacqueline alternately pale and red with excitement, and the general bowing right and left, until they entered the small, old-fashioned drawing-room. Mrs. Sherrard, in a plain black silk, but with a diamond comb in her white hair and a general air of superbness, was delighted to see Judith. It was a victory over Jane Temple. She detained her for a moment to whisper : "My dear, I am dreadfully afraid I shall make a failure in trying to get George Throckmorton accepted here. The girls, who most of them never saw so fine a man before, will hardly have a word to say to him ; the men are a little better, but it isn't a pronounced success by any means. I have been longing for you to come. You have so much more sense than any of the young people I know, I thought you would be a little less freezing to him."

At this a warmer color surged into Judith's cheeks. She could not remember ever to have seen a man who impressed her so instantly as Throckmorton. With her clear, feminine instinct, she had seen at the first glance what manner of man he was. As Mrs. Sherrard spoke to her, she turned and saw him standing by the fireplace, talking with Edmund Morford. Throckmorton could not have desired a better foil than the young clergyman, with his faultless red and white skin, his curling dark hair, his mouth full of perfect teeth, and his character as a clerical dandy written all over him. Throckmorton, whose good looks were purely masculine and characteristic, looked even more manly and soldierly by contrast. Both men caught sight of Judith at the same moment. Morford was thrown into a perfect flutter. He wondered if Judith had put on that square-necked, short-sleeved black gown to do him a mischief. Throckmorton, obeying a look from Mrs. Sherrard, came forward and was formally introduced. Judith offered her hand, after the Virginia custom, which Throckmorton bowed over.

"Mrs. Temple did not present me to you on Sunday," he said, with a smile and a slight flush; "but I guessed very readily who you were."

Judith, too, colored.

"Poor mother, you must not take her too hardly. You know how good she is, but—but she is very determined; she moves slowly."

"Yes," replied Throckmorton, with his easy, man-of-the-world manner; "but I am afraid there are others as unyielding as Mrs. Temple, and not half so kindly—for she is a dear soul! It seemed to me the carrying out of a sort of dream to come back to Millenbeck. My boy Jack—that young fellow yonder—looks rather old to be my son, don't you think?"

"Y-e-s," answered Judith, with provoking dubiousness and a wicked little smile.

"Oh, you are really too bad! I am very tired of explaining to people that Jack is nothing like as old as he looks. Well, the boy, although brought up at army posts, rather wanted to be a Virginian, and to own the old place; you know that sort of thing always crops out in a Virginian."

"Yes," smiled Judith; "I see how it crops out in *you*. You are immensely proud of being a Throckmorton, and you would rather own Millenbeck, if it were tumbling down about your ears, than the finest place in the world anywhere else."

"Now, Mrs. Beverley," said Throckmorton, determinedly, "I can't have my weaknesses picked out in this prompt and savage manner. I own I am a fool about Millenbeck, but I'd have sworn that nobody but myself knew it.   I've got a year's leave, and I've come down here with Sweeney, an old ex-sergeant of mine, who has owned me for several years, and my old horse Tartar, that is turned out to grass; and if I like it as well as I expect, I may resign "—Throckmorton was always talking about resigning, as Mrs. Sherrard was about making her will, without the slightest idea of doing it—"and turn myself out to grass like Tartar.   But my reception hasn't been—a—exactly—cordial—or—"

"I am sorry you have been disappointed," said Judith, gently; "but it seems to me that we are all in a dreadful sort of transition state now.   We are holding on desperately to our old moorings, although they are slipping away; but I suppose we shall have to face a new existence some time."

"I think I understand the feeling here—even that dead wall of prejudice that meets me.   One look around Severn church, last Sunday, would have told me that those people had gone through with some frightful crisis.   I thought, perhaps being one of their own county people originally might soften them toward me, but I believe that makes me blacker than ever."

Judith could not deny it.

Throckmorton, who was worldly wise, read Judith at a glance, besides having learned her history since first seeing her.   He saw that she was under a fixed restraint, and that a word would frighten her into the deepest reserve. He treated her, therefore, as if she had been a Sister of Charity. Judith, who made up for her lack of knowledge of the world by rapid perceptions and natural talents, had seen more quickly than Throckmorton. Here was a man the like of whom she had not often met. Throckmorton knew perfectly well the solitary lives these country women led, and he had often wondered at the singular fortitude they showed. He set himself to work to find out what chiefly interested this young woman, who showed such remarkable constancy to her dead husband, but who gave indications to his practiced eye of secretly loving life and its concerns very much. He had heard about her pretty boy. At this Judith colored with pleasure and became positively talkative. Her boy was the sweetest boy—she would like never to have him out of her sight. Major Throckmorton, with a sardonic grin, confided to Judith that he would frequently be highly gratified at having *his* son out of his sight, because Jack made the women think he, the major, was a Methuselah, and covertly made much game of him, for which he would like to kick Jack, but couldn't.

Judith laughed merrily at this—a laugh so clear and rippling, and yet so rare, that the sound of it startled her. Was Mrs. Beverley fond of reading? Mrs. Beverley was very fond of reading, but there was

nothing newer in the array of books at Barn Elms
than 1840. Major Throckmorton would be only too
happy to supply her with books. He had had a few
boxes full sent down to Millenbeck. At this Judith
blushed, but accepted, without reflecting how Major
Throckmorton was to send books to a house where he
was not permitted to visit.

She also protested that she had read nothing at all
scarcely; but Throckmorton came to find out that, for
want of the every-day modern literature, she was perfectly at home in the English classics, and knew her
Scott and Thackeray like a lesson well learned. He
began to find this gentle intelligence and cordiality
amazingly pleasant after the cold shyness of the girls
and the unmistakable keep-your-distance air of the
older women. They sat together so long that Mr.
Morford began to scowl, and think that Mrs. Beverley, after all, was rather a frivolous person, and with
every moment Judith became brighter, gayer, more
her natural charming self.

Meanwhile Jack Throckmorton had carried
Jacqueline off for a quadrille, and was getting on
famously. First they remarked on the similarity of
their names, which seemed a fateful coincidence, and
Jacqueline complained that the servants and some
other people, too, often shortened her liquid three syl-
lables with " Jacky," but she hated it. Jack, who had
a sweet, gay voice, and was an inveterate joker, which

Jacqueline was not, amused both her and himself extremely.

"Will you look at the major?" he whispered. "Gone on the pretty widow—I beg your pardon," he added, turning very red.

"You needn't apologize," calmly remarked Jacqueline. "Judith *is* a pretty widow, and the best and kindest sister in the world, besides. It is all mamma. Mamma loved my brother better than anything, and wants us all to think about him as much as she does."

Jack, rather embarrassed by these family confidences, parried them with some confidences of his own.

"I shall have to go over soon and break the major up. You see, there isn't but twenty-two years' difference between us, and the major is a great toast among the girls still, which is repugnant to my filial feelings."

Jacqueline listened gravely and in good faith.

"So, when I see him pleased with a girl, I generally sneak up on the other side, and manage to get my share of the girl's attention, and call the major 'father' every two minutes. A man hates to be interfered with that way, particularly by his own son, which doesn't often happen. The major has got a cast in one eye, and, whenever he is in a rage, he gets downright cross-eyed. Sometimes I work him up so, his eyes don't get straight for a fortnight."

"But doesn't he get very mad with you?" asked Jacqueline in a shocked voice.

"Of course he does," chuckled Jack; "and that's where the fun comes in. But, you see, he can't say anything; it is beneath his dignity; but his temper blazes up, although he doesn't say a word. Sometimes, when I've run him off two or three times close together, he hardly speaks to me for a week—not that he cares about the girl particularly, but he hates to be balked."

"What a nice sort of a son you must be!"

Jack laughed his frank, boyish laugh.

"Why, the major and I are the greatest chums in the world. I would do anything for him. And if he ever presents me with a step-mother, I'll do the handsome thing—go to the wedding, and all that. And he's a fascinating old fellow, too—just takes the girls off their feet."

When the dance was over, Jack brought Jacqueline back to Judith, who still sat with Throckmorton. Jacqueline's eyes were shining with childish delight, and she arched her thin white neck restlessly from side to side.

"I have had such a nice dance!" she cried, breathlessly.

Judith, smiling, said, "Major Throckmorton, this is my little sister Jacqueline."

Throckmorton, having once fixed his eyes on

Jacqueline, seemed unable to take them off, as on that Sunday he had first seen her in Severn church. Delilah, who noticed in her primitive way the wonderful power of attraction that Jacqueline had, used to say, "Miss Jacky she allus cotches de beaux." She certainly "cotched" Throckmorton's attention from the first. Something in this slim, unformed, provincial girl was suddenly captivating to him. His genuine but sane admiration for Judith seemed tame beside it. Jacqueline, however, only saw a rather striking man, well on toward old age, in her infantile eyes, and wished herself back with Jack, when Major Throckmorton took her for a little promenade. Morford then made up to Judith, but found her singularly cold and unresponsive, and her eyes and smile were quite far away, over Morford's head, as it were. The truth is, the Rev. Edmund Morford was a considerable let-down from George Throckmorton; and, in Judith's starved and pinched existence, it was something to meet a man of Throckmorton's caliber. So, in place of the charming sweetness Morford had learned to expect from Judith, he received a cold douche of listlessness and indifference. All the rest of the evening people noticed that Judith, who had a good deal of smoldering vivacity under her quietness, was remarkably cold and silent and rather bored, and they supposed it was because of her aversion to anything like gayety. In truth, Judith had realized rather more startlingly than usual the bareness and colorlessness of her life.

Mrs. Sherrard's effort was a strong one, but, as she said, it was scarcely a success. General Temple ostentatiously sought out Throckmorton, and tasted the delights of a discussion regarding the trans-Alpine campaigns of Hannibal, in which Throckmorton was a modest listener, and the general a most fiery, earnest, and learned expounder—a past grand-master of military science. But, on shaking Throckmorton's hand at saying good-night, with solemn but genuine effusiveness, he said not one word about calling at Millenbeck. Throckmorton went home feeling rather bitter toward all his county people, except his stanch friend Mrs. Sherrard; Judith, so gentle, clever, and well-read; and that fascinating child, Jacqueline.

CHAPTER IV.

For a week after the party Jacqueline lived in a
kind of dream. She could do nothing but talk of the
party. The whole current of her life had been dis-
turbed. Since this one taste of excitement there was
no satisfying her. The daily routine was going down
to a solemn breakfast, and then getting through the
forenoon as best she might, with her flowers, and her
pets among the ducks and chickens, and romping with
the little Beverley—for this unfortunate Jacqueline
had no regular employments—and then the still more
solemn three o'clock dinner, after which she practiced
fitfully on the wheezy piano in the dark drawing-
room; then a country walk with Judith, if the day
was fine, coming back in time to watch the creeping
on of the twilight before the sitting-room fire. This
was the happiest time of the day to Jacqueline. She
would sit flat on the rug, clasping her knees, and gazing into the fire until her mother would say, with a
smile :

"What do you see in the fire, Jacky?"

"Oh, endless things—a beautiful young man, and

a new piano, and a diamond comb like Mrs. Sherrard's, and— Oh, I can't tell you!"

"Miss Jacky she see evils, I know she do," solemnly announced Simon Peter. "When folks sits fo' de fire studyin' 'bout nuttin' 'tall, de evils an' de sperrits dat's 'broad come sneakin' up ahine an' show 'em things in de fire."

General Temple, a few days after the party, fell a victim to a seductive pudding prepared by Delilah, and was immediately invalided with the gout. Dr. Wortley was sent for, and at once demanded to know what devilment Delilah had been up to in the way of puddings and such, and soon found out the true state of the case. A wordy war ensued between Dr. Wortley and Delilah, and the doctor renewed the threat he had been making at intervals for twenty-five years.

"Temple," he screeched, "you may take your choice between that old ignoramus and me—between ignorance and science!"

"Ef ole marse was ter steal six leetle sweet 'taters an' put 'em in he pocket," began Delilah, undauntedly.

"Why don't you advise him to steal a wheelbarrowful instead of a pocketful?" retorted the doctor.

"Kase he doan 'quire but six, an' he got ter *steal* 'em, fur ter make de conjurin' wuk. Den ev'y day he th'ow 'way a tater, an' when he th'ow de tater 'way he th'ow de gout 'way, too. De hy'ars from a black cat's tail is mighty good, too—"

"Temple, how do you put up with this sort of thing being uttered in your hearing?" snapped the doctor.

General Temple looked rather sheepish. He had never actually tried stealing six potatoes, or testing the virtue in hairs from a black cat's tail, as a relief from gout, but he had not been above a course of tansy tea, and decoctions of jimson-weed, and other of Delilah's remedies that scientifically were on a par with the black cat's tail. But, being racked with pain, he took refuge in pessimism and profanity.

"Excuse me, Wortley, but all medicine is a damned humbug!—I mean—er—an empirical science. What is written is written. The Great First Cause, that decrees from the hour of our birth every act of our lives, has decreed that I should suffer great pain, anguish, and discomfort from this hereditary disease."

"Marse, ef you wuz ter repent an' be saved—"

"Hold your infernal tongue!"

"An' jine de Foot-washers—"

"Damn the Foot-washers!" howled the general.

"Plague on it!" snarled Dr. Wortley, whirling round with his back to the fire. "If you've got as far as predestination, you're in for a six weeks' spell. I can cure the gout, but I'll be shot if I can do anything when it's complicated with religion and black cats' tails and a constant diet like a Christmas dinner!"

In the midst of the discussion, the doctor's shrill voice rising high over Delilah's, who, with arms akimbo and a defiant air, only awaited Dr. Wortley's departure to get in her innings with the patient, Mrs. Temple, serene and sweet, came in and quelled the insurrection. Delilah at once subsided, Dr. Wortley began to laugh, and the general directed that Mrs. Temple's chair be put next to his.

"As your presence, my love, makes me forget my most unhappy foot," he said.

Mrs. Temple's adherence to either Delilah or Dr. Wortley would have caused victory to perch upon that side; but Mrs. Temple, like the general, had more faith in Delilah than she was willing to own up to. So, between Delilah's feeding him high all the time, while the doctor only saw him once or twice a week, General Temple bade fair to remain an invalid for a considerable time. The attack of gout, though, just at that time, had its consolatory aspects. General Temple really wished to call at Millenbeck, but Mrs. Temple showed no sign of yielding. For the present, however, there could be no notion of his stirring out of doors. As long as the gout lasted there was a good excuse. But General Temple worried over it.

"My love," he said one night, while Mrs. Temple and Jacqueline and Judith sat around the table in his room, where they had assembled to make his evening less dull, "I am troubled in my mind regarding George Throckmorton. It unquestionably seems heathenish for us to have one so intimately connected with our early married life—that truly blissful period—within a stone's throw of us, and then to deny him the sacred rites of hospitality."

Jacqueline gave a half glance at Judith which was full of meaning, and Judith could not for her life keep a slight blush from rising in her cheek.

Mrs. Temple said nothing, but looked hard at the fire, sighing profoundly. She had made herself some sort of a vague revengeful promise, that no man wearing a blue uniform should ever darken her doors. She had yielded first one thing, then another, of that scrupulous and daily mourning and remembrance she had promised herself, for Beverley —but this—

The pause was long. Mrs. Temple, looking at General Temple, was touched by something in his expression—a longing, a patient, but genuine desire. Occasionally she indulged him, as she sometimes relaxed a little the discipline over Jacqueline in her childish days. She put her hand over her eyes and waited a moment as if she were praying. Then she said in broken voice, "Do what seems best to you, my husband."

General Temple took her hand.

"But, my own, I do not wish to coerce you. No matter what I think is our duty in the case, if it does not satisfy you, it shall not be done. I would rather anything befell Throckmorton, than you, my beloved Jane, should be grieved or troubled."

Mrs. Temple received this sort of thing as she always did, with a shy pleasure like a girl.

"I have said it, my dear, and you know I do not easily recede. Like you, this thing has been upon me ever since Throckmorton's return. I have felt it every day harder to maintain my attitude. Now, for your sake, I will abandon it. Have Throckmorton when you like. I will invite him over to tea on Sunday evening."

General Temple fairly beamed. When Mrs. Temple gave in to him, which was not oftener than once a year, she gave in thoroughly.

"Thank you, my wife. It certainly seems unnatural that Millenbeck and Barn Elms should be estranged. It shall be so no longer, please God. And that George Throckmorton is a high-toned gentleman"—General Temple paused a little before saying this, hunting for a term magniloquent enough for the occasion—"no one, I think, will deny."

This was early in the week. The very next afternoon, Jacqueline finding time more than usually hard to kill, went up into the garret and began rummaging over the remains of Mrs. Temple's wedding finery of thirty years before. She dived down into a capacious chest, and brought forth two or three faded silk dresses, the bridal bonnet and veil, yellowed from age; and, among other antiques, a huge muff almost as big as Jacqueline herself. This suddenly put the notion of a walk into her head. Judith was engaged in reading Napier's History of the Peninsular Wars to General Temple, and Jacqueline had only herself for company. So, carrying her huge muff in which she plunged her arms up to her elbows, she started off. It was a raw autumn afternoon. The leaves had not yet all fallen, although the ground was dank with them, and the peculiar stillness of a lonely and low-land country was upon the monotonous landscape. The entire absence of sounds is a characteristic of that sort of country, and it makes a gloomy day more gloomy. Jacqueline, tripping along very fast, did not find it cheerful. She would go as far as the gate of the lane that led into the main road, and then turn back. This lane was also the entrance to Millenbeck, and Jacqueline had some sort of a faint expectation that she might run across Jack Throckmorton. She looked longingly toward Millenbeck, visible at intervals through the straggling fringe of pines. What an infinity of pleasure could be had, if her mother only came round thoroughly regarding the Throckmortons! What rides and dances she could have with Jack, and Judith could talk to the major! "What a dull life Judith must lead!" she thought, stepping lightly along. It was true, Judith liked to read; but Jacqueline, who frankly confessed she could not read a novel through from cover to cover, hardly appreciated reading as a resource. Jacqueline's imagination, with this superstructure to build upon, went ardently to work, and in a few minutes had installed Judith as mistress of Millenbeck, and herself as the young lady of the establishment. To do Jacqueline justice, she longed for Judith's happiness, who, she sometimes bitterly felt, was her only friend. Just as she had arranged this scheme to her satisfaction, she looked up, and saw, not twenty feet ahead of her, Major Throckmorton coming out of the underbrush at the side of the lane. A big slouch hat half concealed his face. His usual trim and natty dress, with that unmistakable "military cut," was exchanged for a shooting suit of corduroy, much stained, and otherwise the worse for wear. His stylish and immaculate hat was replaced by the flapping felt, and his gun and game-bag proclaimed his day's employment. Yet Jacqueline thought she had never seen him look so handsome, and in some way she was not half so much afraid of him in his shooting-togs as in his perfectly fitting evening clothes. Jacqueline's face turned a rosy red. As for Throckmorton, he too felt a thrill of pleasure. This pretty child, as he called her, had been in his mind rather constantly since he saw her at the party.

He quickened his pace, and took his hat off while still some distance away.

"Any more parties in prospect?" he asked, smiling, as he took her little hand in his.

"No, I don't suppose there will be. Delicious parties like that don't happen very often," answered Jacqueline, quite seriously, and not in the least understanding Throckmorton's smile as she said this. "And—and young Mr. Throckmorton—oh, how I enjoyed dancing with him!"

The major did not smile at this. To have "young Mr. Throckmorton" thrust at him by a charming young girl was not particularly pleasing.

"Jack is a very jolly young fellow," he replied, shortly. "We are great friends, Jack and I."

Jacqueline had turned around, and they were now walking together toward Barn Elms.

"I—I should think," said Jacqueline, giving him one of her half-glances from under the dark fringe of her eyelashes—"that J—Jack would be afraid of you."

Throckmorton laughed aloud.

"Why should he be afraid of me?"

"Oh, I don't know. Everybody is afraid of one's father," replied Jacqueline, candidly.

"Jack and I entertain sentiments of mutual respect," laughed Throckmorton again. "The only fault I find with him is that he is unduly filial sometimes. For example, when I am enjoying the society of a charming young lady he thinks too young for me, he behaves as if I were his great-grandfather instead of his father. Jack has a good deal of Satan in him."

Jacqueline did not always follow Throckmorton's remarks, but she noticed he had a rich voice, and he was the straightest, most soldierly-looking man she ever saw in her life. Throckmorton slung his game-bag around and held it open.

"Do you like robins?" he said. They are delicious broiled on toast "—and he took out a bird by the legs and showed it to her.

Jacqueline stood perfectly still. Her eyes dilated and her breath came quickly. She took the bird out of his hand. It had long stopped bleeding, and its little cold head, with half-closed eyes, fell over piteously. Jacqueline took out her handkerchief and wrapped the poor robin in it.

"Oh, the poor bird!" she said, and snddenly two large tears ran down her cheeks.

Throckmorton stood surprised, touched, delighted, and almost ashamed. He had been a sportsman all his life, and could see no harm in knocking over a few birds in the season; but the picture of this tender-hearted child, that could not see a dead bird without weeping, struck him as beautifully feminine. But what could he say? If he was a bloodthirsty brute to shoot a robin, what must all the slaughter of birds he had been guilty of in his lifetime make him? He could only say, half shamefacedly and half laughing, "My dear little friend, you wouldn't have men as squeamish as women, would you?"

But to this Jacqueline only responded by pressing the poor bird's cold breast to her cheek.

Throckmorton, however, with an air of gentle authority, took the bird from her and put it back in the bag.

"If you cry for such things as this, you will have a hard time in life," he said.

Jacqueline's face did not clear up at once.

"I want you to do something for me—to promise me something," she said, gravely.

"What is it?" asked Throckmorton. Jacqueline had laid her charm upon him in the last ten minutes, but he did not forget his caution entirely.

"It is," said Jacqueline, punctuating her words with tender, appealing glances, "that you won't kill any more robins—never, never, as long as you live."

Throckmorton refrained from smiling, as he felt inclined, but it was plainly no laughing matter to Jacqueline. And if he gave the promise—nobody knew the absurdity of it more than Throckmorton—suppose Jack heard of it, what endless fun would he poke at his father on the sly! Nevertheless, Throckmorton, calling himself an old fool, made the promise.

Jacqueline, flushed with triumph, now conceived a

bold design.   She would—that is, if her courage held out—tell him that her mother had at last come round. This delightful information she proceeded to impart.

"Do you know," she said, smiling and showing her little even white teeth, "that mamma has at last agreed to—to let us have something to do with you and Jack?"

"Has she, indeed?" replied Throckmorton, with rather a grim smile.

"Yes," continued Jacqueline, with much serious-ness. "Occasionally she gives papa a little treat. You know she always liked you, and papa has been dying to call to see you. But mamma can't forget the war and Beverley. At last, though—she's been think-ing about it ever since that first day at church—she concluded to give in—and—and—you're to be asked to tea next Sunday evening!"

The way this was told was not particularly flatter-ing to Throckmorton, but he was sincerely grateful and attached to Mrs. Temple, and he knew and pitied the state of feeling that had caused her to intrench herself in her prejudices. She must indeed remem-ber those old days when she was willing to do what Throckmorton suspected she had promised herself never to do. "I want to be friends with Mrs. Temple —that's plain enough," he said, "and if she asks me I shall certainly come."

"Do you know," said Jacqueline, after a pause, in a

very confidential voice, "I sometimes wish—now this is a secret, remember—that papa and mamma would forget Beverley a little—and think—of Judith and me? They seem to expect Judith to wear black all the time, and never to smile or to laugh or to sing, as if Beverley could know. I don't believe the dead in their graves know or care anything about us."

She was on delicate ground, but, her tongue being unloosed, Throckmorton's attempt to check her was a complete failure.

"Judith, you know," she continued, cutting in on Throckmorton's awkward remonstrance, "only knew Beverley a little while. Her father and mother were dead, and papa was her guardian. She came to Barn Elms to live after she left school, and Beverley came home from the war, and they were married right away—almost as soon as they were acquainted. It was so sudden because Beverley's leave was up, and Delilah says that Beverley knew he was going to be killed soon. She says he dreamed it, or something. Do you believe in dreams?"

"No, and you mustn't believe all Delilah tells you."

"Anyhow, he went away, and he never came back. That broke papa and mamma's hearts. And you know—little Beverley—Judith's child—is like her—and not a bit like Beverley, and mamma talks sometimes as if it was a crime on the child's part. She says to everybody, ' Don't you think the child is like his father?' and nobody answers her quite truthfully, and she knows it."

Throckmorton hardly knew how to receive these family confidences, but he could not but admire the color coming and going in Jacqueline's cheeks, and the fitful light that burned in her eyes as she talked.

" And Judith—I do love Judith. It seems hard —now this is another secret—that she should never have any more pleasure in this world. And she is so bright and clever. She understands the most wonderful books. And there's something—I can't help telling you this."

" Perhaps you had better not tell me," said Throckmorton in a warning voice.

" But I can't help it, you are so—so sympathetic: I don't believe Judith cared for Beverley much."

Jacqueline drew off to see the effect of this on Throckmorton. She did not at all suspect him of any interest in Judith; but this family tragedy, that had stalked beside her nearly all her life, she thought was of immense importance, and she wanted to see how it affected Throckmorton. In fact, it only embarrassed him. He said, rather briefly:

" Mrs. Beverley is very handsome—very charming."

" She's the best sister in the world," exclaimed Jacqueline. " Some people think that sisters-in-law

can't love each other.   Sometimes I would throw myself in the river if it wasn't for Judith."

"Why should such a tender little thing as you
want to throw herself in the river?" he asked; and
if Jack had heard the tone in which this was spoken,
he would, no doubt, have found food for ungodly
mirth in it.

"You don't know what sorrows I have," responded Jacqueline, gravely.   And then they were almost
at the gate of Barn Elms, and Throckmorton bade
her good-by, and tramped back home, while Jacqueline scudded into the house to confide the wonderful
adventures of the afternoon to Judith.

In a day or two a note from General Temple came,
inviting Throckmorton and Jack to tea at Barn Elms
the following Sunday evening.   It was rather a letter
than a note, General Temple spreading himself—his
honest soul loved a rhetorical flourish—and containing many references to their early association. Throckmorton accepted, in a reply in which he told, much
more glibly than his tongue could, the grateful affection he had cherished from his neglected and unhappy boyhood toward the whole family at Barn
Elms.   On the Sunday evening, therefore, Throckmorton, with Jack, presented himself, and was effu-
sively received by the general and Simon Peter, who
were not unlike in their overpowering courtesy to
guests.   Judith was cordial and dignified, and Jacque-

line full of a shy delight. No doubt they would be invited to Millenbeck, and she would see with her own eyes the Bruskins carpets and other royal splendors Delilah was never weary of recounting.

General Temple was able to be down in the drawing-room, but Mrs. Temple was not present. Delilah, however, soon put her head in the door, and, crossing her hands under a huge white apron she wore, brought a message.

"Mistis, she say, won't Marse George please ter come in de charmber."

Throckmorton at once followed her. The "charmber" at Barn Elms was a sort of star chamber, and utterances within its precincts were usually of a solemn character. As Throckmorton entered, Mrs. Temple rose from the big rush-bottomed chair in which she sat. Throckmorton remembered the room perfectly, in all the years since he had been in it—the dimity curtains, the high-post mahogany bed, the shining brass fender and andirons, the tall candlesticks on the high wooden mantel. He remembered, with a queer, boyish feeling, sundry moral discourses gently administered to him in that room on certain occasions when he had been caught in the act of fishing on Sunday, or poking a broomstick up the chimney to dislodge the sooty swallows that built their nests there in the summer-time, and other instances of juvenile turpitude. And he well recollected once, when Mrs. Temple was ill, he had hung about the place, a picture of boyish misery; and when at last he was admitted into the room where she lay, white and feeble, on the broad, old-fashioned lounge, how happy, how glad, how honored he had felt. He went forward eagerly and raised Mrs. Temple's hand to his lips.

"George Throckmorton, this is nearer forgiveness than I ever expected to come," she said.

"Dear Mrs. Temple, don't let us talk about forgiveness. Let us only remember that we are friends of more than thirty years' standing—because I can't remember the time when I was a boy that I didn't love you."

"And I loved you, too—next to my own Beverley. I sent for you here that I might tell you my trouble as you used to tell me yours so long ago. Often you have sat on that little cricket over there and told me of your grandfather's cruel ways to you—he was a godless man, George."

"He was indeed," fervently assented Throckmorton.

"And now I want to tell you of *my* sorrows, George."

Throckmorton listened patiently while she went over all of Beverley's life. She told it with a touching simplicity. Throckmorton well saw how that still stern unforgiveness might rankle in her gentle but

immovable mind. Then he told her of his marriage
—something he had never in all his life spoken of
to any one in that manner; but the force of sweet
and early habit was upon him—he could talk to Mrs.
Temple about the young creature so much loved and
so long dead. Mrs. Temple, who knew what such re-
vealing meant from a man of Throckmorton's strong
and self-contained nature, was completely won by
this. An hour afterward, when they came into the
drawing-room, and found Jack and Jacqueline in a
perfect gale of merriment, with Judith looking smil-
ingly on, Mrs. Temple laid her hand on Throckmorton's shoulder, and said to General Temple, with
sweet gravity, "He is the same George Throckmorton."

Judith was leaning a little forward in her chair,
with her arm around her child. The boy was a beautiful, manly fellow, and gazed at Throckmorton with
friendly, serious eyes. Throckmorton, whose heart
was tender toward all children, smiled at him. Beverley at this marched forward and climbed upon Throckmorton's knee, his little white frock, heavy with embroidery worked by Judith's patient fingers, spreading
all around him. The boy immediately launched into
conversation, eying Throckmorton boldly, although
his eyes usually had the shy expression of his mother's.
He wanted to know if Throckmorton had a gun, and
could he beat the drum; also, if he could ride a horse.

Sometimes grandfather would take him up and let him ride as far as the gate. Throckmorton answered all these questions satisfactorily, and then told about a pony he had at Millenbeck—a pony that had been Jack's, when Jack was no bigger than Beverley, and that was now too old and slow for any but a very little boy. While Throckmorton talked to the child, Judith listened with a smiling look in her eyes. Throckmorton could not but be struck by the pretty picture the young mother and her child made. He saw the resemblance between them at once, and when he told of a tragic adventure Jack had with the pony, falling through a bridge, both pairs of large, soft eyes grew wide with grave amazement. Unconsciously Judith assumed the child's expression. Beverley seemed determined to monopolize his new acquaintance, but presently Judith with a little air of. authority sent him off with Delilah. Beverley paused at the door to say:

"You come again and bring the pony."

Presently they went into the dining-room, and the old-fashioned tea was served. There was enough to feed a regiment, and all of the best kind, but nothing approaching vulgar display. Mrs. Temple put Throckmorton at her right, and every time she spoke to Jack she called him George. Throckmorton had forgotten nothing of the old days, and he not only began to feel young himself, but he made General and Mrs. Temple feel that time had turned backward. Jacqueline, on the opposite side of the table, smiled at him and talked a little. In her heart she could not quite make out Throckmorton. He had arrived at an age that seemed to her almost venerable; yet he quite ignored the fact that he ought to be old, and certainly was not old, nor could anybody say that he was young. Jack's boyish fun she understood well enough, but Throckmorton's shrewd humor, his confident, experienced way of looking at things, was rather beyond her. And as the case had been, whenever Throckmorton saw her, he had to exercise a certain restraint, lest everybody should see how strangely and completely she magnetized him. If anybody had asked him to compare Judith and Jacqueline, he would have given Judith the palm in everything—even in beauty; but Jacqueline's young prettiness in some way caught his fancy more than Judith's deeper and more significant beauty.

But Judith had her charm too for him. She captivated his judgment as Jacqueline captivated some inner sense to which he could give no name. Judith's talk was seasoned with liveliness, and Throckmorton, who possessed a dry and penetrating humor of his own, could always count on a responsive sparkle in Judith's eye.

When they returned to the drawing-room, Mrs. Temple said:

"Judith, my dear, sing us some of your sweet hymns."

Judith sat down to the piano and in her clear and bell-like soprano sang some old-fashioned hymns, so sweetly and unaffectedly that Throckmorton thought it was like angels singing. The sound of the simple music, the soft light of fire and lamp, the atmosphere of love and courtesy that seemed to breathe over the quaint circle, had a fascination for him. It was the poetry of domestic life. He had often dreamed of what "home" might be, but he had never known it, for that brief married life of his had been too short, too flickering; they were boy and girl lovers, and, before the new life had had time to crystallize, he was left alone. But here he saw the sweet privacy of home, the repose, the family nest, safe and warm. He sighed a little. Money could not buy it, else he would have had it at Millenbeck, comfortable handsome country-house that it was. But here, at this shabby old Barn Elms, it was in perfection, in all its naturalness and simplicity. After all, women were necessary to make a home; even money, with a Sweeney as presiding genius, couldn't do it.

It was late when they left. Mrs. Temple's parting was as solemn as her greeting:

"I have done that which I never expected to do, and all because in my heart I can't but love you, George Throckmorton!"

Throckmorton's keen pleasure showed in his dark eyes.

"I always knew, if you would only listen to that dear, kind heart of yours, you would forgive the Yankees," he laughed.

CHAPTER V.

Miracles usually happen in cycles. They unquestionably did in the Severn neighborhood. Before the hurricane of talk over Throckmorton's arrival, Jack's audacity, and Sweeney's brogue had fairly reached a crisis, a letter came one day to General Temple, from his nephew, Temple Freke, announcing his intention of paying a visit to his dear uncle and aunt at Barn Elms.

General Temple handed the letter to Mrs. Temple with a sort of groan.

"This is he— I mean, my love, this is most discomposing."

At this Mrs. Temple shook her head in a manner expressing perfect despair. The problem whether Throckmorton should be admitted within the doors of Barn Elms was a mere nothing compared with this. Both of them firmly believed in a personal devil; and Temple Freke, with his extravagance, his vices, his unprincipled behavior, stood for Satan himself. This Freke was very unlike the conservative, home-keeping type of a gentleman that prevailed in Virginia. He was born and brought up in Louisiana, and was fifteen years old when, by the death of his father, General Temple became his guardian, and he was brought to Barn Elms to lead the staid Beverley into all sorts of scrapes, and to torment General Temple's honest soul almost to madness. The elder Freke, perhaps, knowing the boy's disposition, had made General Temple's guardianship to extend until Temple Freke's twenty-fifth birthday.

Of the horrors of that guardianship, nobody but the kind and simple-hearted general could tell—of Freke's extravagance, of his gambling and betting and drinking, and one frightful scene, when Freke, with a loaded pistol in his hand, swore that, unless a certain debt of honor was paid, he would kill himself on the spot; and General Temple, who was not easily frightened, promptly paid it, with the conviction that the young fellow was quite capable of carrying out the threat. Immediately after this, General Temple shipped him off to Europe, but apparently it made bad worse. For six whole years was General Temple commanding, entreating, praying, and wheedling to get Freke back to Virginia. It was true, he might have cut off supplies, but Freke made no bones of saying that, if he couldn't get his own money, he would contrive to get somebody else's; so the poor general, with groans and moans, would cash Freke's drafts on him as long as money could be screwed out of the Louisiana sugar plantations to do it with.

But, as Mrs. Temple often said, Freke was unquestionably a gentleman; he was mild-mannered to a degree, and his very impertinences were brought out with a diffidence that frequently hoodwinked General Temple. He was not nearly so handsome as Beverley, being much shorter and sandy-haired, in contrast with Beverley's blonde beauty; but Mrs. Temple always felt in the old days, with a little pang of jealousy, that this ordinary-looking boy, with his exquisite manners—not the least affected or effeminate, but simply the perfection of personal bearing—could put Beverley at a disadvantage. The two had little in common, and had never met after their school-days, when General Temple, in the innocence of his heart, had sent Freke abroad, to reform, until the very time of Beverley's death. Freke, whose courage was as flawless in its way as General Temple's, had come home during the war and enlisted in the Southern army. A strange fate had placed him close to Beverley when he was killed. He had held Beverley's dying hand, and to him were intrusted the last messages to the mother and the young wife, who waited and prayed at Barn Elms. Nothing on earth but this could have brought Mrs. Temple to tolerate Freke at all, after the sensational career which had begun with the pistol scene. Moreover, to increase the abnormal conditions about this unregenerate being, as the Temples considered him, he was perfectly irresistible. How it was, General Temple gloomily declared, he didn't know, but Freke had the most extraordinary way of insinuating himself into the good graces of both men and women —not by any affectation of goodness, for there was a frankness about his wickedness that was peculiarly appalling to General Temple. Freke was no handsomer as a man than as a boy; he had been steadily making ducks and drakes of his fortune since he was twenty-five; yet, somehow, Freke always seemed to have a plenty of friends, solely by the charm of his personality. The most serious escapade that had come to General Temple's knowledge since Freke was of age was his running away with a Cuban girl in New Orleans, and afterward getting a divorce by some hocus-pocus, and thereafter, with serene confidence, he bore himself as an unmarried man. Now, divorce was practically unknown in that old part of Virginia, and the Temples regarded it as in the category with murder and arson; so that this final iniquity of Freke's would have quite put him beyond the pale, but for those hours he spent kneeling on the ground with the dying Beverley.

General Temple had a sort of Arab hospitality that would not have begrudged itself to the Evil One himself, and to tell Freke that he was not welcome under the roof of Barn Elms, where his grandfather and his grandfather's father had lived, was an enormity of which he was not capable. And Mrs. Temple was no manner of use to him in the case. In vain he tried to shuffle the decision off on her. Mrs. Temple would not accept it. Like the general, she sighed and groaned, and turned it over in her mind; but always came back that picture of Beverley lying bleeding and dying, and Freke risking his life to stay by him. So at last, after a week of mutual misery, one night, in the privacy of the "charmber," Mrs. Temple, watching the general stalking up and down during one of his fits of midnight restlessness, said, tremulously:

"My love, we must let Freke come. We can not refuse it—for—for Beverley's sake."

So the next morning a letter was dispatched to Freke, written by General Temple with considerably less cordiality than usual, and very feeble rhetorically, expressing the pleasure his uncle and aunt felt at the prospect of a visit from their nephew.

The next day, as soon as the direful news of his coming was made known to Jacqueline, she rushed off, as she always did, to give Judith the startling information.

Judith heard it with a strange feeling of repulsion, which she at first imagined was that infinite disapproval she felt for Freke; but, if he came, all of that terrible story about Beverley would have to be told over. Judith had not yet come to a clear understanding of herself, but she had begun to shrink from that dwelling on Beverley which seemed to give Mrs. Temple such exquisite comfort.

"Everything that looked at Freke fell in love with him," announced Jacqueline. "Of course, he is as handsome as a dream—something like Mr. Morford, I dare say."

There were two or three faded photographs of him at Barn Elms, and none of them gave the idea of great beauty; but protographs in those days were not very artistic reproductions.

Judith laughed a little uneasily.

"I wish he wern't coming, Jacky," she said. "He is too—too startling a person for quiet people like ourselves. There is one comfort, though: he will soon get tired of us."

Within a week or two came a very well-expressed letter from Freke, thanking his uncle and aunt for their hospitable invitation, and saying that on a certain day he would land from the river steamer at Oak Point. Jacqueline was immensely taken with the letter, which was written on paper the like of which she had never seen before, and was sealed with a crest.

Two immense trunks arrived in advance of the expected visitor. Mrs. Sherrard happened to be at Barn Elms when the luggage appeared. Mrs. Temple's face expressed her misery.

"Jane, you have my sympathy. A more unmitigated scamp than Freke doesn't live," was Mrs. Sherrard's remark.

"Kitty," feebly protested Mrs. Temple, "he is my husband's nephew."

"The more's the pity."

As a rule, the reputation of incalculable wickedness hurts nobody, in the opinion of the very young. The more Mrs. Temple preached and warned, holding on to that one saving clause, Freke's devotion to Beverley in his dying hours, the more attractive he seemed to Jacqueline. At last one afternoon, when the carriage returned from Oak Point Landing with the much-talked-of Freke, Jacqueline, who had been curling her hair and prinking all day for the visitor, came down into the drawing-room, and the expression of acute disappointment on her face said loudly:

"Is this all?"

For Freke was neither surpassingly handsome nor any of the superlative things Jacqueline had fondly imagined him to be. He was not even as handsome as Throckmorton, and Jacqueline thought *him* no beauty. Freke was under middle height, and his hair was as sandy as of old, and not too abundant. His features were ordinary; and Jacqueline, not being a physiognomist, did not take in the piercing expression, the firmness and intelligence that redeemed them from commonplaceness. He did look unmistakably the gentleman, Jacqueline grudgingly admitted. *This* the adorable, the irresistible, the— But Jacqueline was too disgusted to continue.

Freke, who read Jacqueline like an open book, and suspected the advance impression she had received, could hardly keep from laughing out aloud at the girl's air and manner. He talked a little to her, somewhat more to Judith, but chiefly to Mrs. Temple.

It was late in the afternoon when he had arrived, and tea was soon announced. Directly it was over, Mrs. Temple marshaled a solemn procession into "the charmber" to hear Freke's description of Beverley's last hours. She went first with Judith, followed by Freke and General Temple. Mrs. Temple had tried to get Jacqueline to come, too, but Jacqueline, who had a horror of weeping and tragedies, begged off; and Mrs. Temple, who really attached but little importance to the girl at any time, did not press the point. The door of the room remained closed for two hours. Jacqueline, who had got tired of Delilah's company and the cat's, went up-stairs early, but not to bed. She waited until she heard Judith's door open, and then went and knocked timidly at the door.

"Come in," said Judith, in an unfamiliar voice. Judith was sitting before her dressing-table, and had already begun to unbraid her long, rich hair. But

her eyes were fixed with a hard, staring gaze on her
own image in the glass. The mother had wept at
Freke's recital; the widow had remained pale, tearless,
and turning over in her troubled mind the imma-
turity, the transitoriness of that first girlish love-affair that had resulted, as so few first loves do, in a
sudden marriage—a quick widowhood. And she had
a terrifying sense that she had betrayed herself to
Freke. There was one particular point in the narra-
tive, when he described how the dead man had got
his death-wound. Beverley had run across a small
body of Federal cavalrymen, himself with only an advance guard, and, *à la* General Temple, had immediately dashed at them, as if a cavalry scrimmage would -
affect one iota the great fight that was impending
the next day. Beverley himself had engaged in a
hand-to-hand tussle with a Federal officer—both of
them had rolled off their horses, and the struggle between them was more like Indian warfare than civilized warfare—and Freke described, with cruel par-
ticularity, how the two men fought in the underbrush, and crushed the wild rose and hawthorn
bushes, each one trying vainly to draw his pistol—
and at last a shot rang out, and Beverley turned
over on his face with a wild shriek and a death-
wound. The Federal officer had got his arm en-
tangled in his bridle-reins, and Freke thought every
moment the excited horse would trample the wound-

ed man to death; and then, a squad of Confederates coming up, the Federals had made off, the officer mounting his horse and getting out of the way with nothing worse than a few bruises. All the time he was telling this he was eying Judith, who did not shed a single tear. Mrs. Temple wept torrents, and even so did General Temple. For poor Judith, whose reading of Freke was not less keen than his reading of her, it was misery enough to feel that, after all, her widowhood was not very real, and that the mourning, the entire giving up of the world, the devotion to Beverley's parents, was, in some sort, a reparation; but that it should escape her—for Judith with the eagerness to make amends, of a generous nature, had readily adopted Mrs. Temple's view—that it was a crime not to mourn for Beverley.

Jacqueline slipped down on her knees beside Judith, and, nodding her head, gravely said :

"Mamma didn't get *me* into the room. Ah, Judy, dear, why won't they let us forget him—"

"Jacqueline !" cried Judith, turning a pale, shocked face on her.

"I say," persisted Jacqueline, who had one of her sudden fits of courage, "why do they trouble *us* to remember him? I hardly knew him; he was always off at college, and then in the war; why won't they let us mourn decently for him? And then—and then —everybody wants to forget griefs. I do."

Judith rose and shook her off impatiently. "I wish Temple Freke had never come here," she said.

"I do, too," answered Jacqueline, getting up. "I am afraid of him. O Judith, what two poor creatures are we!"

"I know I am," suddenly cried Judith, breaking into a storm of tears. "I know there is no peace for me anywhere!—" Judith stopped as suddenly as she had begun. How could she put it in words, the ghastliness of this perpetual reminder of that which in her heart she longed to forget—this feeling that had been growing on her for so long, that she ought to feel more remorse for marrying Beverley Temple than grief at losing him—that all this solemn mourning for him was like those state funerals, where there is a great service, a catafalque, a coffin, mourners—everything except a corpse? And to her candid soul how wicked, heartless, and unnatural it seemed! Jacqueline's eyes, so full of meaning and fixed on her, troubled her. She got up after a minute and walked over to the window. The red glow of the fire and the dim candle-light did not prevent her from seeing clearly into the moonlight night. She drew the old-fashioned white curtains apart and looked out. The somber trees loomed large and black, but up on the hill, a quarter of a mile away, the light from Millenbeck gleamed cheerfully. From two windows on the lower floor and two on the upper, as well as the great fan- and side-lights of the hall-door, a ruddy glare streamed steadily. Presently Jacqueline came and stood by Judith, timidly.

"Do you know," she said, "it seems queer that three strangers should come into our lonely lives—in this quiet life here? And the one I like—the one I like best—is Jack Throckmorton. I can't talk to the others."

Judith, who had got back a little of her composure, smiled at this.

"You talked away fast enough with Major Throckmorton."

"Oh, yes, but I didn't feel at home with him. Jack and I understand each other. I know what he means when he talks to me. I don't always understand Major Throckmorton. Judith, is my cousin Freke a very wicked man?"

"So people say," replied Judith in a subdued voice, which had not altogether overcome its agitation.

"He isn't handsome enough to be very—very attractive," said Jacqueline after a pause.

But the rule of contrary seemed to suddenly prevail at Barn Elms then. Within a week everybody in the house had succumbed more or less to Freke's charm. General Temple found him invaluable in the preparation of the History of Temple's Brigade; and Freke, who had a store of military knowledge among his great fund of general information, easily

persuaded the general that he was a military histo-
rian of the first order. When the general began his
evening harangues, Freke always had an example
pat of a certain occasion when Prince Eugene, or the
Duke of Marlborough, or some equally distinguished
leader had successfully pursued General Temple's
tactics. All this General Temple laboriously tran-
scribed in his manuscript. Judith, who very much
doubted whether Freke were not making it up as he
went along, had her suspicions confirmed when Freke
would occasionally turn his expressive face on her and
actually wink with appreciation of the general's simplicity. Judith was indignant, but she could not
help laughing at Freke's genuine humor. Mrs. Temple showed her regard for the returned prodigal by
taking him into the "charmber" one day and reason-
ing in a motherly way upon Freke's duty to return to .
his wife. Judith was astounded after a while to hear
Mrs. Temple's gentle but intense laughter making
itself heard outside the room. Freke, with the most
good-natured manner in the world, sitting in the rush-
bottomed chair, with one foot over his knee, began to
tell Mrs. Temple some of his marital experiences with
his Julia. Mrs. Temple at first put on her severest
frown and fairly groaned aloud at his declaration that
he didn't know whether he was married or not in Virginia, as his divorce was got in one of the Northwestern
States; but, divorce or no divorce, he wouldn't tempt

Fate again in another matrimonial venture even with a creature as beautiful as Helen, as wise as Portia, and with a million in her own right. Then he began to tell of the adventures between Julia and himself which had led to their separation, winding up with a description of their final scene, when Julia threw a dish at him and he in turn threw a bucket of ice-water over Julia. Before this, though, Mrs. Temple's laughter had been heard. Freke issued from the room the picture of innocence, and at peace with himself and all the world. Mrs. Temple, on the contrary, was an image of guilt. Never had she before in her life been beguiled from a moral lecture into unseemly laughter—and laughter on such a subject! Mrs. Temple's conscience rose up and fought her, and she began to think that all her moral foundation was tottering.

Surprises were the order of the day. One night, just after family prayers, when the gout, and the doubt whether anybody at all was to be saved, had caused General Temple to make a more pessimistic, vociferous, and grewsome prayer than usual, in which he called the Deity to account for so grievously afflicting the Temple family, Freke, whom Judith had caught smiling in the midst of General Temple's most telling periods, quietly announced that he had that day bought Wareham, a place within two miles of Barn Elms.

It was not much of a place, being at most about

three hundred acres, with a small, untenanted house
on it—and property went for a song, anyhow, in that
part of the world—but, nevertheless, the news was
paralyzing to General and Mrs. Temple. Judith,
who was developing a certain dislike and distrust of
Freke that grew daily, could hardly forbear laughing
at the mute horror of General and Mrs. Temple over
this unlooked-for news. Freke went on to say that
a very little would make the place habitable for him,
and he liked the fishing and shooting to be had
—especially the shooting, as the birds had had four
years' rest during the war. Then he said good-night
pleasantly, and went off to bed.

"This is the dev—I mean this is most unfortunate, my love," remarked General Temple, dismally, to Mrs. Temple, at two o'clock in the morning following this, as he paraded up and down the
"charmber," declaiming against Freke's iniquities.

Next day, Mrs. Sherrard came over, and the direful news was communicated to her by Mrs. Temple,
with a very long face. Mrs. Sherrard's eyes danced.

"Now you'll know what it is to have a nephew
that one would like to be entirely unlike what he
is. That's my trouble with Edmund Morford. You
know, I hate a humbug—and Edmund is a good
soul, but a dreadful humbug."

"Katharine!" exclaimed Mrs. Temple. "A minister of the gospel—"

"Go along, Jane Temple! You have no eyes in your head where ministers of the gospel are concerned. Edmund is perfectly harmless—that's one comfort."

" I wish I could say the same of Temple Freke," Mrs. Temple rejoined, dolefully.

It would be a week or two yet before Freke could take possession of Wareham. Some beds and tables and sheets and towels had to be procured, and meanwhile he stayed on at Barn Elms. It would not have taken a very astute person to see what the charm was. It was Judith.

When the knowledge first came to these two people—to Judith, that Freke's eyes followed her continually; that, as if by some power beyond his will, his chair was always next hers, his ear always alert to catch her lightest word—to Freke, that this young countrywoman, with her spirited, expressive face, her untutored singing—for music was one of his weak points, or strong ones, as the case might be—her gentle sarcasm when he essayed a little sentiment, pretty and tender enough to please a woman who knew twice as much as she; that at first sight, without an effort, she had conquered his bold spirit—it is hard to say which was the most vexed and disgusted. Judith found it easy enough to play the inconsolable widow where a man who aroused a positive antagonism like Freke was concerned, and denounced him in her own mind as a wretch for daring to fall in love with her. And Freke — after New York women and Creole women, French, Spanish, Russian, English, and Italian women—to have been loved and petted, and virtually made free of women's hearts; that this unsophisticated Virginia girl, who had never seen six men in her life, should simply take him off his feet, and that, without knowing it—was simply infuriating. In the privacy of his bedroom, as he smoked his last cigar before turning in, he swore at himself with a self-deprecation that was thoroughly genuine. What did he want to marry again for, anyway? Hadn't he had all he wanted of that pastime? And, of course, being a divorced man, Judith would see him chopped into little pieces before she would marry him—and then the staggering thought that, even if he were not divorced, the odds were against her marrying him at all —it was altogether maddening. But he did not lose his head completely. Judith's indifference—nay, dislike —saved to him his discretion. But had she warmed to him for one little moment—Freke, in thinking over this sweet impossibility, lay back in his chair and watched the smoke curling upward, and was lost in a delicious reverie—when suddenly, the utter preposterousness of it came to him, and he threw the cigar into the fire with a savage energy that nearly wrenched his arm off. No, the little devil—for he was not choice of epithets in regard to this woman—would throw him away with as little conscience and remorse as he threw that cigar away! Like all men of many love-affairs, he regarded love-making as an æsthetic amusement; and while it was absolutely necessary for its perfection that the woman should be desperately in earnest—for Freke did not mind a tragic tinge being given to the matter—it was nonsense for a man to permit himself to be drawn into heroics—and yet— but for the indifference of this girl, who was always half laughing at him—he would not answer for any folly he might commit.

Then there was Jacqueline. She exactly suited him as a victim to his charms, sardonically expressing it to himself. She, too, was not particularly impressed with him as yet, but that was due to her ignorance. He could easily enlighten her, and she would be led like a slave by him; he could make her believe anything. So, in default of Judith, he might as well amuse himself with Jacqueline; and, by resolutely concealing his gigantic folly, he would in the end overcome it. But he felt like a man who, having a head to stand champagne and brandy and absinthe and every other intoxication, comes across something that looks as harmless as water, but which sets his brain on fire and makes him a madman.

The general and Mrs. Temple saw nothing; a man might have made love to Judith and have run away with her under their very noses before they

would have realized that it was possible for any man
to dare falling in love with Beverley's widow; and if
Jacqueline's eyes saw anything, she kept it wisely to
herself.

Freke certainly added a new and picturesque element to their lives; even Judith could not deny that,
although she habitually denied Freke the possession of
any of the graces as well as the virtues. But that
Freke was a wonderful, a gifted, a fascinating talker,
she was forced to admit. His conversation was
quite different from Throckmorton's manly plainness
of speech, who, with more brains than Freke, had not
them as readily soluble in talk. Judith was acute
enough to see the difference between the two men—
one the man of conversation, and the other the man
of action. Throckmorton knew many things, and one
thing surpassingly well—his profession. Freke excelled in conversation; what he knew was imposing,
but what he could do was not. However, he had not
only traveled, but he had observed as well as read.
He never made himself the hero of his own stories;
and there was a sparkle in his eyes, an animation that
gave a deeper tone to his voice, and Judith, in her
dull and colorless life, could not but feel the charm of
it. Nevertheless, it was not all charm. Judith felt
as strongly as ever the incongruity of Freke with his
surroundings.

So, some days more passed. Judith found that

in finesse she was no match for Freke. Indifferent to him as she might be, he could always place himself where he wanted—he managed to have a great deal more of her society than she would willingly have given him; but she reasoned shrewdly with herself—women being naturally clever in these things: "He will soon give it up. The game is not worth the candle." And so it proved; for in a little while he began to shadow Jacqueline, and Jacqueline succumbed like a bird to the charmer. If Freke was present, Jacqueline, who was wont to be impatient when not noticed, would sit quite quietly by her sister-in-law's side, sewing demurely, or walk beside her gravely, not opening her mouth but listening intently, as her changing color showed. One day, when Jacqueline went into the gloomy, darkened drawing-room to play, Freke followed her. Jacqueline sat down, and began some short familiar piece, but she could not render it. She missed notes, became confused, and finally gave up and left the piano in mortification.

"It is because you are here," she said to Freke, with a child's resentment.

"Is it, little girl?" he asked.

He was sitting quite at the other end of the room and did not come near her, but something in his tone made Jacqueline halt, and brought the ever-ready blood into her cheeks. Freke, after a moment, rose and sauntered toward her. As he came up to her he took a stray lock of hair that had escaped, in curly perversity, from the comb; and, just as he stood with it in his fingers, the door opened and Simon Peter announced:

"Walk right in, Marse George. Mistis, she count-in' de tuckeys in de coop, but Miss Judy, she be 'long pres'n'y. Hi! Here Miss Jacky!"

Throckmorton walked in. His eye, which was as quick as a hawk's, caught the whole thing in an instant, and a sort of jealousy sprang into life. Of course, he did not display the smallest symptom of it. He shook hands pleasantly with Jacqueline, and also with Freke, whom he had met several times. With his easy, worldly judgment, he by no means ranked Freke as the chief of sinners, but, without regarding him as a model citizen, found him extremely good company, which Freke certainly was. Jacqueline looked painfully embarrassed, but Freke's coolness was simply indomitable. The two men made conversation naturally enough, while Jacqueline, awkwardly silent, sat and twisted the unlucky lock of hair in her fingers until a diversion was created by Judith's entrance, with little Beverley clinging to her skirts. A faint, girlish blush came into Judith's face when she met Throckmorton; and for his part he felt always the charm, the refinement, the sprightliness, more piquant because subdued, that exhaled like a perfume wher-ever Judith was. Beverley made for Throckmorton, and, before his mother could interpose a warning hand, was perched on the arm of Throckmorton's chair, whence both of them defied her. Jacqueline made but one remark. She asked Throckmorton, timidly:

"How is young Mr. Throckmorton?"

At which the major scowled, but responded carelessly that Jack was all right, as far as he knew.

Young Mr. Throckmorton! and from those lovely lips!

Presently there was a grinding of wheels, and a commotion at the front door.

"Mrs. Sherrard, I know!" said Judith. "She always begins her salutations at the gate."

Sounds were distinguishable.

"Mistis be mighty glad ter see you an' Marse Edmun'. She down at de fattenin'-coop countin' de tuckeys, 'kase we didn't have no luck wid de tuckey--aigs lars' season, an' de wuffless hen-tuckeys—"

So much for Simon Peter, when Delilah's voice broke in:

"Miss Kitty, 'twan' de hen-tuckeys 'tall. Ef de gobblers wuz ter take turns, like de pigeons, a-settin' on de aigs—"

"I allus did think dem he-pigeons look like de foolishest critters *I* ever see a-settin' on de nes' while de she-pigeons hoppin' roun' de groun' 'stid o' miudin' dey business—"

"You are right, Simon Peter," answered Mrs. Sherrard, still invisible. "I wonder that Delilah hasn't profited by Mrs. Temple's example. You've got visitors. Whose hat is this?"

"Marse George Throckmorton's an' Marse Temple Freke's. I gwi' tell mistis you here. Marse c'yarn leave de charmber yet, he gout so bad."

Mrs. Sherrard marched in, followed by Edmund Morford. She wore her most commanding and hostile air. She had poohpoohed Mrs. Temple's dread of Freke, but she meant to give him to understand that his goings on, and particularly his matrimonial difficulties, were perfectly well known in the Severn neighborhood, and properly reprobated. So she shook hands all around, followed by the Rev. Edmund, who never trusted himself at Barn Elms, with those two pretty young women, alone and unprotected.

"I understand you have bought Wareham," remarked Mrs. Sherrard, tartly, to Freke.

"I have," answered Freke, very mildly.

"You'll repent it."

"Not if you make yourself as agreeable as you ought," answered Freke.

The impudence of this tickled Mrs. Sherrard.

"I hear you are an entertaining fellow," she said. "Come and talk to me."

Just then Mrs. Temple entered, but Mrs. Sherrard kept fast hold of Freke. In half an hour he had won her over.   Judith, responding with an intelligent glance to a rather cynical smile on Throckmorton's part, saw it.   Not satisfied with winning Mrs. Sherrard over, Freke applied himself to Morford, and that excellent but guileless person fell an instant victim to Freke's tact and power.   Mrs. Sherrard was so pleased with her morning's visit, that she invited them all over to Turkey Thicket to spend the following Thursday evening.

CHAPTER VI.

In the few days that followed, Judith saw more
plainly that Freke was deliberately casting his spell
over Jacqueline, and, from the soft and seductive flat-
tery he had tried on her, Judith, at first, he exchanged
something like sarcasm. He would discuss constancy
before her, Judith meanwhile keeping her seat resolutely, but she could not prevent the tell-tale color
from rising into her face. But when, as Freke generally did, he surmised that all the so-called constancy in
this world wasn't exactly what it purported to be, she
grew pale beneath his gaze. He watched her intently whenever she was with Throckmorton, and the
mere consciousness of being watched embarrassed
while it angered her. Freke, whose perceptions were
of the quickest, saw far into the future, and often repeated in his own mind the old, old truth that all the
passions of human nature—love, hope, despair, jealousy, and revenge—could be found within the quietest
and most peaceful circle.

The very next evening after Mrs. Sherrard's visit,
Freke appeared in the dusky drawing-room, where

Jacqueline sat crouched over the fire, and Judith, with her child in her arms, sang him quaint Mother Goose melodies. When Freke came within the fire's red circle of light, Judith observed that he had a violin and bow under his arm. Jacqueline jumped up delightedly.

"Oh, oh! do you know any music?"

"I can fiddle a little," answered Freke, smiling.

He settled himself, and, in the midst of the deep silence of twilight in the country, began a concerto of Brahms. The first movement, an *allegro*, he played with a dainty, soft trippingness that was fit for fairies dancing by moonlight. The next, a *scherzo*, was full of tender suggestiveness—a dream told in music. The third movement was deeper, more tragic, full of sorrow and wailing. As Freke drew the bow across the G-string, he would bring out tones as deep as the 'cello, while suddenly the sharp cry of the treble would cut into the somber depths of the basso like the shriek of a soul in torment. A melody like a wandering spirit appeared out of the deep harmonies, and lost, yet ever found, would make itself heard with a sweet insistence, only to be swallowed up in a tempest of sound, like a bird lost in a storm. And presently there was an abatement, then a calm, and the music died, literally, amid the twilight dusk and gloom.

As Freke, with strange eyes, and his bow suspended, tremblingly, as if waiting for the spirit to return, ceased, there was a perfect silence. Jacqueline, who had never heard anything like it in her life, and who, all unknown to herself, was singularly susceptible to music, gazed at Freke as the magician who had made her dream dreams, and after a while cried out:

"Why do you play like that? I never heard anybody play so before."

In answer, Freke again smiled, and played a wild Hungarian dance, fit for the dancing of bacchantes, so full of barbaric clash and rhythm, that Jacqueline suddenly sprang up and began to dance around the chairs and tables. Freke half turned to glance at her; he retarded the time, and softened the tones, when Jacqueline, too, danced slowly and dreamily— until presently, with a storm and a rush of music, *fortissimo* and *prestissimo*, and a resounding blare of chords that sounded like the shouts of a victorious army, he stopped and lay back in his chair, still smiling.

But, although Judith had twice Jacqueline's knowledge of music, with all her feeling for it, Freke was piqued to see that she did not for a moment confound his music with his personality. She seemed to take a malicious pleasure in complimenting him glibly, which is the last snub to an artist. Freke was so vexed by her indifference, that he began to play cats mewing and dogs barking, on his fiddle, to frighten little Beverley, who looked at him with wide, scared eyes.

"Never mind, my darling," cried Judith, laughing. "Be a brave little boy—only girls are scared at such things."

Beverley, thus exhorted, summoned up his courage and proposed to get grandfather's sword to defend himself. Judith's laughter, the defiant light in her eyes, the passionate kiss she gave the boy as a reward for his bravery, annoyed Freke. His vanity as an artist, however, was consoled by hearing Simon Peter's voice, in an awed and solemn whisper from the door, through which his woolly head was just visible in the surrounding darkness:

"I 'clar' ter God, dat fiddle is got evils in it. I hear some on 'em hollerin' an' cryin' fur ter git out, an' some on 'em larfin' an' jumpin'. Marse Temple, dem is spirits in dat fiddle. I knows it."

"They are, indeed; and, if I go down to the grave-yard at midnight and play, all the dead and gone Temples will rise out of their graves and dance around in their grave-clothes. Do you hear that?" said Freke, gravely.

"Lord God A'mighty!" yelled Simon Peter, "I gwi' sleep wid a sifter" (a sieve) "over my hade ev'y night arter dis. Sifters keeps away de evils, 'kase dey slips th'u de holes." And, sure enough, a sieve was hung up over Simon Peter's bed that very night, with a rabbit's foot as an additional safeguard, and a bunch of peacock's feathers over the fireplace was ruthlessly thrown into the fire to propitiate "de evils."

When Thursday evening came, General Temple was high and dry with the gout, and Mrs. Temple, of course, could not leave him alone to fight it out with Delilah.

" Ole marse, you gwi' keep on havin' de gout twell you 'w'yar a ole h'yar foot in yo' pocket. I done tole you so, an' I ain' feerd ter keep on tellin' you so," was Delilah's Job-like advice.

" That's true," snapped the general. " Gad, if I had had a thousand men in my brigade as little ' feerd ' as you, I'll be damned if I ever would have surrendered at Appomattox! God forgive me for swearing."

" I hope and pray He will, my darling husband," responded Mrs. Temple, with calm.piety.

Jacqueline was in a fever of delight, as she always was when there was any prospect of going from home. She danced up and down, romped with little Beverley, and, hugging him, told him in a laughing whisper that she would see "somebody" at Turkey Thicket, and " somebody had beautiful black eyes, and was only twenty-two years old."

Judith, too, felt that pleasurable excitement of which she began to be less and less ashamed. A few words dropped meaningly by Throckmorton, full of that sound sense which distinguished him, made her look differently at life. His philosophy was not Mrs. Temple's. He reminded Judith that we should accept peace and tranquillity thankfully, and that it was no sin to be happy; and everything that Throckmorton said commended itself to Judith. For the first time in her narrow and secluded life she enjoyed with him the pleasure of being as clever as she wanted to be. He was no timid soul, like Edmund Morford, to fear a rival in a woman. It never occurred to Throckmorton to feel jealous of any woman's wit. One of his greatest charms to Judith was that he was not in the least afraid of her. Her quick feminine humor, her natural acuteness, her knack of pretty expression in speech and writing, appeared in their true light, as mere accomplishments, contrasted with Throckmorton's firm and masculine mind. The conviction of his mental grasp, his will-power, all that goes to make a man fitted to command a woman, had in it a subtile attraction for Judith, like the spell that beauty casts over a man. He was the only man in all her surroundings whose calm superiority over her was perfectly plain to her. It was only necessary for him to express an opinion, that Judith did not at once see its force. She sometimes differed courteously with him; but it began soon to be a perilous pleasure to her to find that usually Throckmorton was infinitely wiser, more liberal, more just than herself.

8

When the Thursday evening came, only Judith, Jacqueline, and Freke were to go. It had turned bitterly cold. Simon Peter, sitting in solitary magnificence on the box, handled the ribbons over the Kentucky horses, who dashed along so briskly that the carriage, which was in the last stage of "befo' the war" decrepitude, threatened to tumble to pieces and drop them all in the road.

Going along, Jacqueline sat back in the carriage, very quiet and silent. Freke, with his back to the horses, talked to Judith. Occasionally in the darkness, by a passing gleam, he could see Jacqueline's eyes shining.

"What do you think of Major Throckmorton," he asked Judith.

Although not versed in knowledge of the world, Judith was not devoid of self-possession. The question, though, embarrassed her a little.

"I—I—think he is most interesting, kind—and—"

"Military men are, as a rule, rather narrow, don't you think?"

"I never saw enough to judge. I should think they ought to be the other way."

"Every time I see Throckmorton, the consciousness comes to me that I have seen him before—seen him under some tragical and unusual circumstances. If I didn't know that those who have good consciences, like myself, should be above superstition, I should say that in some previous state of being I had known him; however, I am too strictly orthodox in my beliefs to tolerate such notions. But some time or other—perhaps to-night—I intend to find out from Throckmorton himself if we haven't had the pleasure of meeting in another cycle or state of being. There is, by the way, an ineffable impudence in Throckmorton returning to this county now."

Judith suspected that Freke's peroration was made with the intention of provoking a reply.

They were driving along an open piece of the road, and it was comparatively light in the carriage, although there was no moon. Freke glancing up to see the cause of Judith's silence, caught the gleam of her white teeth in a broad smile. She was laughing at him. It certainly was delicious to hear Temple Freke commenting on anybody's having impudence in returning to the county. Freke, who hated to be laughed at, promised himself he would be avenged. "I'll make you wince, my lady!" he thought to himself. Presently, though, Judith said, in a tone with a sharpness in it, like one who has been wounded:

-"I can't imagine anybody applying the word impudence to Major Throckmorton. He is very reserved —very dignified."

" Throckmorton, I see, has an advocate.—And little Cousin Jacky, what do you think of the other Jacky—Jacky Throckmorton ?"

"I think he's perfectly delightful," assented Jacqueline, after a pause.

Freke said no more about the Throckmortons. The women were evidently against him there; and soon they were driving up to the door at Turkey. Thicket, and going up the hall stairs to take off their wraps, very much as on that last evening, when Mrs. Sherrard took occasion to rehabilitate Throckmorton in the good graces of the county people, as she was now trying to do with Freke.

When Judith and Jacqueline came down the stairs, Freke met them at the foot. Jacqueline had pleaded hard to wear a white dress, but Mrs. Temple was inexorable. She might catch cold; consequently, she wore a little prim, Quakerish gown of gray. Judith, as usual, was stately in black.

Throckmorton was standing on the rug before the drawing-room fire, talking gravely with Mrs. Sherrard. Edmund Morford was there and Dr. Wortley, who, with Jack Throckmorton, constituted the company. Mrs. Sherrard drew Judith into the conversation that she had been carrying on with Throckmorton. He said to Judith:

"I will continue what I was saying—but I assure you it is something I could speak of to but few people. It is this absolute barring out on the part of the county people toward me. Not a soul except Mrs. Sherrard and Mrs. Temple has asked me to break bread. I thought I knew Virginians—I thought them the kindest, easiest, least angular people in the world; but, upon my soul, anything like this cold and deliberate ostracism I never witnessed! Why, half the county is related to me—and I've been to school with every man in it—and yet, I am a pariah!"

"You don't look at it from their point of view," replied Mrs. Sherrard, with more patience than was her wont. "Think how these people have suffered. You see yourself, never was there such ruin wrought, and then remember that you are associated with that ruin. Can't you fancy the dull and silent resentment, the cold anger, with which they must regard all—"

"Blasted Yankees?" cheerfully remarked Throckmorton, recovering his spirits a little.

"But you know," said Mrs. Sherrard, whose ideas on some subjects were rudimentary, but speaking kindly though positively, "you mustn't wear your uniform down here."

Throckmorton laughed rather harshly.

"As I'm not going to be married or buried, I can't see what chance I would have to wear it. But what you say disposes me to put on my full-dress uniform, with sword and chapeau, and wear it to church on Sunday."

Then Mrs. Sherrard went off after her latest passion, Temple Freke, and left Judith and Throckmorton standing together.

"I think *I* understand you," said Judith, with her pretty air of diffidence. " But, as you know, the people here have one principle which stands for honor, and you have another. You have got power and—and—victory out of *your* principle, and we have got nothing but ruin and defeat and wretchedness out of *our* principle. How can you hold us to a strict account?"

"I do not—God knows I do not!—but I want a little human kindness. I get it from a few. Dr. Wortley, who was my tutor at my grandfather's, and has licked me a hundred times—and Morford, and the families at Turkey Thicket and Barn Elms—but none of them, I think," continued Throckmorton, looking into Judith's eyes with admiration, " exactly understand how *I* feel as well as you. What kept me in the army was, as you say, a principle of honor. It was like a knife in 'me, every Southern officer who resigned. I respected them, because I knew, as only the naval and military men knew, that they were giving up not only their future and their children's future, for what they thought right, but that they knew the overwhelming odds against them. I don't believe any one of them really expected success—they knew too much—it was a sacrifice most disinterested. I could not go with them ; but I had to face as much obloquy among my people by staying in the army as they had to face in going out. But I swear I never gave one thought to the advantage to me of staying where I was! I stayed because I could not, as a man of honor, do otherwise. I thought my own people would recognize this—that by this time the bitterness would be over."

"Never mind," said Judith, with a heavenly smile, " it will come—it will come."

A little later, Mrs. Sherrard whispered to Throckmorton :

" Are not my two beauties from Barn Elms sweet creatures? "

" Very," answered Throckmorton, a dark flush showing under his tan and sunburn. " Little Jacqueline is a charming creature."

" Oh, pooh! Jacqueline. You mean Judith."

" Mrs. Beverley is most dignified, charming, and interesting ; but little Miss Jacky—"

" I should think she would be a nice playmate for your Jack," remarked Mrs. Sherrard.

Throckmorton looked awkward, not to say foolish. Had he forgotten his forty-four years, his iron-gray hair, all the scars of life? Jacqueline and Jack were inseparable from the start, and their two heads were close together on the deep old-fashioned, sofa, at that very moment.

" The major stole a march on me the other day, going over to Barn Elms," remarked Jack, confidentially. " However, I'll get even with him yet."

"Oh, how can you talk so about your own father?"

"Why shouldn't I talk so about my own father?"

"Because it's not right."

"Look here, Miss Jacky. Nobody thinks as much of the major as I do—he's the kindest, noblest, gamest chap alive—but you see, I'm a man, and he's a man. When he got married at twenty-one, he took the risk of having a son in the field before he was ready to quit himself."

"Do you—do you remember your mother?" asked Jacqueline, in a low voice.

"No," answered Jack, fixing his dark eyes seriously on Jacqueline. "I have a miniature of her that my father gave me when I was twenty-one. He keeps her picture in his room, and on the anniversary of her death he spends the day alone. Once in a great while he has talked to me about her."

Jacqueline glanced at Throckmorton with a new interest. He was still talking to Judith. The pleased look on the major's face aroused the mischievous devil in Jack. In five minutes Jacqueline, to her disgust and disappointment, found herself talking to Dr. Wortley, while Jack had established himself on the other side of Judith. Neither Throckmorton nor Judith was pleased to see him.

"You ought to hear my father tell about some of his campaigns 'way back in the fifties," remarked

Jack. "It's a good while ago, but the major isn't sensitive about his age like some men."

Perhaps the major was not, but Jack's observation was received in grim silence.

"I am sure Major Throckmorton can tell us a great many interesting things," answered Judith, smiling involuntarily—"particularly to us who lead such quiet lives, and who know so little. I sometimes wonder how I shall ever be able to bring up my boy; I have so few ideas, and they seem to be all rusting away."

"I thought you were a great reader," said Throckmorton.

"I like to read, but—"

"My father is a Trojan of a reader," continued Jack, "and his eyesight is really wonderful."

At this the major, with the cast in his eye very obvious, rose and walked over to where Jacqueline was sitting. Jack had accomplished his object, and ran his father out of the field. But Judith felt a sense of bitter disappointment. However, with the sweetness of her nature, she overcame her resentful feelings toward Jack, and, in spite of his boyish disposition to make people uncomfortable, really began to like him.

Throckmorton, though, was not ill pleased on the whole. It was by an effort that he had kept away from Jacqueline until then. But, after talking with her awhile, he was not quite so well satisfied. Her childishness was pretty, and the acuteness of her remarks sometimes surprised him, but there was nothing to her—she talked and thought about herself. Throckmorton tried once or twice to get her into the channel of rational conversation, but Jacqueline rebelled. She acknowledged with a pretty smile that she hated books, and that she was poor company for herself. Throckmorton felt a tinge of pity for her. What would become of her twenty years hence—so pretty, so charming, so inconsequent?

Freke had in the mean time completed his conquest of Mrs. Sherrard. Presently he went to the piano and trolled out songs in a rich barytone, playing his own accompaniments. This musical gift was a revelation to Mrs. Sherrard. It was not comparable, though, to his violin-playing. Nevertheless, it was enough to turn Jacqueline's head a little. Freke sang a sentimental song, with a tender refrain, and every time he sang this refrain he cast a glance at Jacqueline.

Gradually the blood mounted to her face, until, when he stopped, she was as rosy as the morning. Then Freke sat down by her, and after that Jacqueline had no eyes for anybody else—not even Jack.

Throckmorton saw it, with a strong disgust for Freke, and with that same strange pang of jealousy he had felt before. Judith's angry disapproval burned within her, but she made no attempt to circumvent Freke until, looking around after a while, she missed him and Jacqueline both.

Judith, watching her opportunity, slipped out into the hall, and there found the culprits. Jacqueline made a little futile effort to pretend that they were looking at some prints by the light of a solitary kerosene-lamp; but Freke, who at least had no pretence about him, held on boldly to Jacqueline's hand, until she wrenched it away.

"Jacqueline, dear," said Judith, trying to speak naturally, "it is cold out here; come in!"

"I'm not cold," answered Jacqueline after a pause.

"But it is not polite to run away like this," urged Judith, casting an angry look at Freke, who, with folded arms, was whistling softly.

"I can't help that, Judith," answered Jacqueline, pettishly. "Why do you want me in that stiff drawing-room with old Dr. Wortley and Mrs. Sherrard, and—"

"But Jacqueline, *I* want you!"

There was no mistaking that tone.

"Go along, Jacky," said Freke, with cheerful submission. "You'll be liable to catch some dreadful moral complaint if you breathe the same atmosphere with me too long. I am a sinner of high degree, I am."

Jacqueline turned and sullenly followed Judith

back, while Freke, smiling and unruffled, walked by her side. And then supper was served, but Jacqueline was perfectly distrait and could not keep her eyes off Freke, who was the life and soul of the party. The supper was after the Virginia order—very good—and so profuse it could not all be got on the table.

On the drive home there was perfect silence. Freke made one or two observations to Judith, but her cold silence convinced him that it was useless. He was not afraid of her, but he saw no good in pretending to placate her. When they reached Barn Elms and were standing in the cold hall, Judith said to Jacqueline:

"Go on. I shall be up in a moment."

"I'll wait for you," replied Jacqueline, doggedly.

"You may wait, but I wish to speak to Freke privately. I shall take him into the drawing-room."

At this, Jacqueline went slowly and unwillingly up the stairs.

Judith picked up the lamp and went into the dark drawing-room. The fire still smoldered dimly in the great fireplace. Freke took up the tongs and made a vigorous attack on the fire, and in two minutes the flames were leaping around the brass firedogs. Then he settled himself comfortably in the corner of the sofa.

Judith, although her determination was made, yet felt timid, and her heart beat.

"What excuse can you give," she asked in an unsteady voice, "for your behavior with that child to-night?"

"None whatever," answered Freke, coolly. "I am not bound to justify myself to you, nor do I admit there was anything to be excused."

"You are right in saying you are not bound to justify yourself to me," said Judith; "but can you justify yourself to her father and mother? You see how she is. You know what they—what we all —think of you. You are a married man, remember."

"Am I?" asked Freke, laughing. "By Jove, I wish I knew whether I was or not!"

"What right have you to fill Jaqueline's head with dreams and notions? The child was well enough until you came. Why can't you go away and leave her in peace?"

Freke smiled at this. "I don't feel like going away," he said, "and particularly now that I see you wish me to go. I have rather different plans in view now that I have bought property here. It doesn't look well for a man to be cast off by his relations; and I intend to have, if I can, the backing of the Temples."

"But how long, think you, could you stay, if the child's mother knew of your behavior to-night?"

"That I don't know. But I wish to stay, Madam Judith; and, since you are so prudish, I will promise you not look at Jacqueline again. Will that satisfy you?"

"I will first see how you keep your promise. But I warn you, Freke, if you remain here much longer, I shall use all the influence in my power to get you out of this house. You are no advantage to the child. It would be better for her if you went away and never came back."

Freke had been sitting all this time, while Judith, standing up, pale and disdainful, spoke to him. But now he rose.

"Now," he said with sudden seriousness, "since you have expressed that hospitable intention concerning me, let me tell you something—something very interesting, that I have suspected for some time, but only found out to-night. You remember I told you of that death-struggle of Beverley's with an officer—how they rolled over and over and fought."

"Yes—yes—"

"And how the officer's horse, held by the bridle, I thought every moment would trample—"

"Yes—yes—yes!" cried Judith.

"Well," said Freke, coming up close to her, "Throckmorton was that officer!"

Freke had meant to give her one fierce pang; it was a delicious thing to him to strike her through Throckmorton; but he was quite unprepared for the result, for Judith, although young and strong, after standing for a moment gazing at Freke with wild eyes, swayed and without a sound dropped to the floor in a dead faint.

Freke, cursing his own folly, ran to her and called loudly. His voice echoed through the midnight silence of the house. It brought Mrs. Temple, frightened and half dressed, into the room, followed by Delilah, struggling into her petticoats, and Simon Peter, scratching his wool and but half awake.

Freke had raised Judith on his arm. Something strange, like pity, of which he knew but little, came to him as he looked at her pallid face.

"You git 'way, Marse Temple," said Delilah, with authority. "Me an' mistis kin manage dis heah.—Hi, Miss Judy! Open yo' eyes, honey, an' tell what de matter wid you."

Mrs. Temple, who never lost her head in emergencies, in five minutes had Judith in a fair way of coming to herself. Freke said truthfully that he never was so surprised in his life as when Judith fell over. Mrs. Temple could not account for it either, and proposed to leave the solution to Dr. Wortley when he should be sent for in the morning. In a few minutes more Judith came to and sat up. Almost her first conscious glance fell on Freke. She gazed at him steadily, and in an instant the conviction that what he had said was mere wanton cruelty came to her. Freke himself avoided her glance uneasily.

"Honey, tell yo' ole mammy wh'yar hu'ts you," pleaded Delilah, anxious to take charge of the case in advance of Dr. Wortley.

"Nowhere at all. I only want to get to bed.— Mother, I hope father wasn't waked."

"My dear, nothing short of an explosion would wake him."

Mrs. Temple wisely refrained from tormenting Judith with questions. Her fainting-fit was certainly unaccountable, but Mrs. Temple remembered once or twice in her own early days when she had done the same thing. So she merely gave Judith some brandy-and-water, and in a few minutes, with Delilah's help, got her on the old-fashioned sofa.

While Mrs. Temple and Delilah were stirring about the room, shutting up for the night and raking the fire down, Freke came up to Judith. Revenge was familiar to him, but not revenge on women, and remorse was altogether new to him.

"What I told you," he began, awkwardly, "the facts in the case—"

"Say no more about it; I don't believe you!" answered Judith in a low voice, but scornful beyond description.

Freke's rage blazed up under that tone.

"You don't believe me? Then I'll make Throckmorton tell you himself. I can find it out from him without his suspecting it, and I'll make him tell you how he killed your husband."

Judith drew back and gave him a look that was equivalent to a slap in the face. Just then Mrs. Temple and Delilah went out into the hall to make fast the door.

"Well, then, if by any accident you have told me the truth, it was the fortune of war—"

"Yes, but the hand that killed your husband! Ah! do you think I don't see it all—all—all—not only what has happened, but what is happening now?"

Judith rose slowly from her sofa, forgetting her weakness. At that moment Freke thought he had never seen her look so handsome. Her eyes, usually a soft, dark gray, were black with indignation; her cheeks burned; she looked capable of killing him where he stood. She opened her lips once or twice to speak, but no sound came. She had no words to express what she felt at that moment. Freke felt a sensation of triumph. At last he had brought this proud spirit to book; and Throckmorton—at least if she scorned himself, Freke—she was forever out of Throckmorton's reach. There was a gulf between them now that nothing on earth could bridge over. He stood in a calm and easy attitude, his face only less expressive than Judith's. Nobody who saw Freke then could say, as Mrs. Temple sometimes had said,

" What is there so interesting in Freke's face ? " It was full of power and passion.

It seemed an age to each as they stood there, but it was really only a few moments. Mrs. Temple and Delilah came back. Judith nodded to Freke, and walked off, disdaining Delilah's arm. She felt pride in showing him her strength and composure. She even glanced back at him, and gave him a smile from her pale lips.

" You have a spirit like a man ! " he cried after her, involuntarily. Mrs. Temple thought he meant because Judith had rallied so quickly from her fainting-fit.

" Rather a spirit like a woman ! " answered Judith, in a loud, clear voice, as she went up the stairs.

It was some little time before she could get rid of Mrs. Temple and Delilah. But presently the door was locked, and she was alone.

Some power beyond her will drew her steps to the window that looked toward Millenbeck. The moon had gone down, and a few clouds scurried across the pale immensity of the sky, whipped by the winds of night. There was enough of the ghastly half-light to distinguish the dark masses of the trees and even the outline of the Millenbeck house. From the window which she knew well enough belonged to Throckmorton's own den the cheerful light still streamed. He was sitting there, reading and smoking, no doubt.

She could imagine exactly how he looked. His face, when he was silent, was rather 'stern, which made the charm of his smile and his words more captivating by contrast. And what horror she ought to feel of this man!—for, in spite of that first involuntary protest that she did not believe Freke, the heart-breaking conviction came to her every moment that he was telling the truth. But did she feel horror and hatred of Throckmorton? Ah! no. And when she tried to think of Beverley, the feeling that he was dead; that he would trouble her no more; that he was forever gone out of her life, filled her with something that was frightfully like joy.

But when she remembered that an open grave lay between her and Throckmorton, it was not something like anguish she felt—it was anguish itself. Here was a man she might have loved—a man infinitely worthy of love—this much she acknowledged to herself; and yet Fate had married her to a man she never could have loved. For at that moment she saw as by a flash of lightning the falseness of her marriage and her widowhood. She dared not think any longer; she could only throw herself on her bed, and try and stifle among the pillows her sobs and cries. And, remembering Beverley and Throckmorton and Freke, and his words to her that night, this gentle and soft-hearted creature sounded all the depths of grief, love, shame, hatred. She tried to pray, but her prayers—

if prayers they could be called—were mere outcries against the inexorable and unpitying God. "Dear Lord, what have I done to thee that I should suffer so?"

The night wore on, the candles burned out, the fire was a mere red glow of embers. Anguish and despair, like other passions, spend themselves. Judith had ceased to weep, and lay on her bed with a sort of icy torpor upon her. Little Beverley, who rarely stirred in his sleep, waked up and called for his mother; but even the child's voice had no power to move her. The little boy, finding himself unnoticed, crawled out of his small bed and came to his mother's side. The sound of his baby voice, the touch of his little warm, moist hands, awakened something like remorse in her. She tried to help him up on the bed, but her arms fell helplessly—she, this strong young woman, was as weak as a child with the conflict of emotions. The boy, however—a sturdy little fellow—climbed up alone and nestled to her. She covered him up and held him close to her, and kissed him coldly once or twice. "My child, he killed your father," she said to him, thinking of Throckmorton, and that perhaps, for the child's sake, she might arouse some feeble spark of regret for the father—some dutiful hatred of Throckmorton. But she could do neither the one nor the other.

At last, as a wet, miserable, gloomy dawn approached, she fell into a wretched sleep. Judith's unexpected fainting-fit was a very good excuse for her keeping her room for a day or two—a merciful provision for her, as, along with other new experiences, she found for the first time that her soul was stronger than her body, and that grief had made her ill. She expected, in all those wretched hours that she lay in her darkened room, that every time the door opened it would be Mrs. Temple coming with a ghastly face to tell her the dreadful thing that Freke knew; and the mere apprehension made her heart stand still. She, this candid and sincere woman, rehearsed to herself the very words and tones that she would express a grief and horror she did not feel. But when several days passed, and the explosion did not come, she concluded that Freke, for his own reasons, meant to keep it to himself.

For Freke's part, he had no intention of telling anybody except Judith. He had no mind to bring about the storm that would follow his revelation. He meant to show Judith that gulf between Throck-morton and herself, and that was all. He would have been unfeignedly sorry had the hospitable doors of Millenbeck been no longer open to him.

When Judith came down-stairs, he felt a great curiosity to know how she would meet him. He himself was perfectly easy and natural in his manner to her; and she, to his enforced admiration, was equally self-possessed with him, although she could not always control the expression of her eyes. " What a Spartan she is! " thought Freke to himself. " She could die of grief and chagrin with a smile on her lips, and with her voice as smooth and musical as the velvet wind of summer."

CHAPTER VII.

The autumn crept on. Freke had gone to Wareham, to Judith's delight, but she found that she had rejoiced too soon, for he was at Barn Elms nearly every day. The still, silent enmity between Judith and himself showed itself, on her part, by a certain fine scorn—an almost imperceptible raising of her narrow brows, that was infuriating to Freke. Still, he could not shake her self-possession. She even listened to his talk, and to his captivating violin-playing, with a cool and critical pleasure. When, as often happened, his step was heard in the hall at twilight, and he would walk into the drawing-room or the dining-room, as if Barn Elms were his home, with his violin in his hand—for he kept one at Barn Elms—and seating himself would begin to play in his masterly way, Judith would listen as closely as Jacqueline. But the spell was merely the spell of the music. She could listen to the celestial thrilling of the strings, the soft lamenting, without in the slightest degree succumbing to the player—not even when Freke, playing a wandering accompaniment, like another air

from the one he was singing, would sing some of
Heine's sea-songs, in which she could almost hear the
sound of the wind as it rose and wailed and died upon
the waves. When the music stopped, and Freke would
look at her piercingly, she was no more moved by
it emotionally than General Temple was, who pronounced it " uncommon fine fiddling, by George !
Some of the tunes haven't got much tune, though."
This unbroken resistance on Judith's part piqued
Freke immeasurably; but quite naturally, as it often
is with men of his temperament, as he could not
please her, he determined to spite her—and he did it
by a silent, furtive courtship of Jacqueline. Of this,
neither General nor Mrs. Temple suspected anything.
In one sense, the girl had suffered from neglect.
Beverley had been the favorite of both parents. He
had been the conventional good son, the comfort of
his parents' hearts, while Jacqueline was more or less of
a puzzle to both of them. In vain Mrs. Temple tried
to interest her in household affairs; Jacqueline would
have none of them. She shocked and mystified her
mother by saying that she hated Barn Elms—it was
so old and shabby, and there were not enough carpets
and curtains in the house ; and the hair-cloth furniture in the drawing-room made her ill. Mrs. Temple,
who excelled in all sweet, feminine virtues, who would
have loved and bettered any home given her, thought
this sort of thing on Jacqueline's part very depraved.

The mother and the daughter did not understand each other, and could not. Judith's superior intelligence here came in. Jacqueline loved her, and, while she obeyed her mother from sheer force of will on Mrs. Temple's part, she rebelled against being influenced by her. Judith, on the contrary, without a particle of authority over Jacqueline, could do anything she wished with her. Mrs. Temple could only command and be obeyed in outward things, but Judith ruled Jacqueline's inner soul more than anybody else.

The county people, outside of the Severn neighborhood, still held perfectly aloof from Throckmorton. This angered him somewhat, although, as a matter of fact, the people who did recognize him supplied him with all the company he wanted; for Throckmorton was always enough for himself, and depended upon no man and no woman for his content. He had bought Millenbeck and come there for a year, and a year he would stay, no matter what the Carters and the Carringtons and the Randolphs thought about it. Then he really had enough of company, and all the books and cigars he wanted, and plenty of the finest shooting, although he never killed a robin after that absurd promise he made to Jacqueline, but he never saw one without giving a thought to her and a grim smile at himself. And so the quiet autumn slipped away. Throckmorton felt every day the charm

of exquisite repose.   In his life he had known a good
deal of excitement—the four years of the war he had
been in active service all the time—and this return to
quiet and a sort of refined primitiveness pleased him.
He was charmed with the simplicity of the people at
Barn Elms—the simplicity of genuine country people,
whose outlook is upon nature.   He had often heard
that country people never were really sophisticated,
and he began to believe it.   Even in the stirrings of
his own heart toward the place of his boyhood, after
the lapse of so many busy and exciting years, he recognized the spell that Nature lays softly upon those
'whose young eyes have seen nothing but her.   Throckmorton, in spite of a certain firmness that was almost
hardness, was at heart a sentimentalist.   He found
content, pleasure, and interest in this lazy, dreamy life.
Of happiness he had discovered that, except during
that early married life of his, he had none, for he was
too wise to confound peace and happiness.   At forty-
four, when his dark hair had turned quite gray, he
acknowledged to himself that nothing deserved the
name of happiness but love.   But all these dreams
and fancies he kept to himself, and revolved chiefly in
his mind when he was tramping along the country
roads with a gun over his shoulder, or stretched
before a blazing wood-fire in the library at Millenbeck smoking strong cigars by the dozen.   He managed to keep his sentimentalism well out of sight,

not because he was ashamed of it, but because he respected it.

Freke was a positive acquisition to him. Throckmorton had that sort of broad, masculine tolerance that can find excuses for everything a man may do except cheating at cards. Freke came constantly to Millenbeck, much oftener than Throckmorton went to Wareham.

Millenbeck, though, was a pleasant place to visit. Throckmorton had left the restoration and fitting up of the place to people who understood their business well; and consequently, when he arrived, he found he had one of the most comfortable, if not luxurious, country-houses that could be imagined. His fortune, which at the North would have been nothing more than a handsome competence, was a superb patrimony in the ruined Virginia, and with ready money and Sweeney anybody could be comfortable, Throckmorton thought. The Rev. Edmund Morford also gave him much of his (Morford's) company, and obtained a vast number of household receipts and learned many contrivances for domestic comfort from Sweeney.

"Be jabers, the parson's more of an ould woman than mesilf," Sweeney would remark to his colored coadjutors. "He can make as good white gravy as any she-cook going, and counts his sheets and towels every week as reg'lar as the mother of him did, I warrant," which was quite true. But the parson's good heart outweighed his innocent conceit and his effeminate beauty with Throckmorton. Morford tried conscientiously to get Throckmorton into the church, but with ill success.

"Sink the parson, Morford," Throckmorton would laugh. "Perhaps I'll get married some day, and my wife will pray me into heaven, like most of the men who get there, I suspect."

Nevertheless Throckmorton had a reverent soul, and, although he would have turned pale and have been constrained by an iron silence had he got up and tried to open his mouth on the subject of the inscrutable problems that Morford attacked with such glib self-sufficiency, he revered religion and did not scoff even at the callowest form of it.

Both Jack and himself got to going over to Barn Elms often; Throckmorton, however, being an old bird, exercised considerable wariness, so as not to collide with Jack at these times. Jack kept up a continual fire from ambush at his father, regarding which of the young women at Barn Elms the major would eventually capitulate to; but Throckmorton treated this with the dignified silence that was the only weapon against Jack's sly rallying. As for General Temple, he regarded all of Throckmorton's visits as particularly directed toward himself, for the purpose of acquiring military knowledge; and Throckmorton heard more of the theory of war from General Temple

at this time than he ever heard in all his life before.
While the general, who had all campaigns, modern
and ancient, at his finger-ends, declaimed with sonorous confidence on the mistakes of Hannibal, Cæsar,
Scipio, and other well-known military characters,
Throckmorton listened meekly, seldom venturing an
observation. General Temple indicated a faint surprise that Throckmorton, during his career, had never
undergone any of the thrilling adventures which had
actually happened to General Temple, who would have
been a great soldier after the pattern of Brian de Bois
Guilbert; nor could Throckmorton convince him
that he, Throckmorton, conceived it his duty to stay
with his men, and considered unnecessary seeking of
danger as unsoldier-like in the highest degree. Throckmorton, however, did not argue the point. In place
of General Temple's innumerable and real hair-breadth
escapes, and horses shot under him, Throckmorton
could only say that the solitary physical injury he received during the war was a bad rheumaticky arm
from sleeping in the wet, and a troublesome attack of
measles caught by visiting his men in the hospital.
But General Temple knew that Throckmorton had
been mentioned half a dozen times in general orders,
and had got several brevets, while General Temple
had narrowly missed half a dozen courts-martial for
being where he didn't belong at a critical time. The
fact that he was in imminent personal danger on all

these occasions, General Temple considered not only
an ample excuse, but quite a feather in his cap.

Occasionally, though (during the general's disqui-
sitions), Throckmorton's eye would seek Judith's as
she sat under the lamp, with a piece of delicate embroidery in her hand, stitching demurely, and something like a smile would pass between them. Judith
understood the joke. The mingled softness and arch-
ness of her glance was very beautiful to Throckmorton, but it had not the power over him of Jacqueline's
coquettish air. Throckmorton was rather vexed at the
charm this kittenish young thing cast over him. He
had always professed a great aversion to young fools,
who invariably turn into old bores, but he could not
deny that he was more drawn to sit near Jacqueline
in her low chair, than to Judith sitting gracefully
upright under the lamp. That Jacqueline was not
far off from folly, he was forced to admit to himself
every time he talked with her, but the admission
brought with it a slight pang. Then he never lost
sight of the disparity in their years; and this was
painful because of the secret attraction he felt for her.
Sometimes, walking home from Barn Elms, across
the fields in autumn nights, he would find himself
comparing the two women, and wishing that the older
woman possessed for him the subtle charm of the
younger one. Any man might love Judith Temple—
she was so gentle, so unconscious of her own superi-

ority to the average woman, so winning upon one's reason and self-respect — and then Throckmorton would sigh, and stride faster along the path in the wintry darkness. Suppose—suppose he should seriously try to win Jacqueline? How long would he be happy? And what sort of a life would it be for her, with that childish restlessness and inability to depend for one moment on herself? And Throckmorton knew instinctively that, although he possessed great power in bending women to his will, it was not in him to adapt himself to any woman. He might love her, indulge her, adore her, but he could not change his fixed and immutable character one iota. It would be a peculiar madness for him to marry any woman who did not possess adaptability in a high degree; and this Throckmorton had known, ever since he had grown hair on his face, went only with a certain mental force and breadth in women. He had the whole theory mapped out, that the more intellectual a man was, the less adaptable he was, while with women the converse was strikingly true— the more intellectual a woman was, the more adaptable she was. He also knew perfectly well that in women the emotions and the intellect are so inextricably involved that a woman's emotional range was exactly limited by her intellectual range; that there is nothing more commonplace in a commonplace woman than her emotions. Nay, more. He remem-

bered Dr. Johnson's thundering against female fools:
"Sir, a man usually marries a fool, with the expectation of ruling her; but the fool, sir, invariably rules
the man." But all this went to pieces when he saw
Jacqueline. She was to him as if a figure of Youth
had stepped out of a white Greek frieze; and whén-
ever he realized this charm of hers, he sighed to himself profoundly.

People are never too old or too sensible to commit
follies, but people of sense and experience suffer the
misery of knowing all about their follies when they do
commit them.

To Freke, who was incomparably the keenest ob-
server in all this little circle, the whole thing was a
psychic study of great interest. He had the art in a
singular degree of getting outside of his own emotions; and the fact that he had been guilty of the
egregious folly of falling in love with Judith at
first sight made him only keener in studying out the
situation. He took an abstract pleasure in partly con-
fiding his discoveries to Mrs. Sherrard, who was a
bold woman, and had become an out-and-out partisan
of his—the only one he could count on, except Jacqueline, under the rose. It was a subject of active
concern why Freke ever bought Warcham in the beginning, and still more so why he should continue to
stay there. When pressed on the subject by Mrs.
Sherrard—they were sitting in the comfortable draw-

ing-room at Turkey Thicket, the blazing wood-fire making the dull wintry afternoon, and the flat, monotonous landscape outside more dreary by contrast— Freke declared that he had settled in the country in order to cultivate the domestic virtues to advantage.

"Pooh!" said Mrs. Sherrard.

Freke then hinted at a possibility of his marrying, which, considering his divorced condition, gave Mrs. Sherrard a thrill of horror. He saw in an instant that this divorce question was one upon which Mrs. Sherrard's prejudices, like those of everybody else in the county, were adamantine, and not to be trifled with; so he dropped the obnoxious subject promptly and wisely.

"The fact is," he said, standing up with his back to the fire, and causing Mrs. Sherrard to notice how excellent was his slight but well-knit figure, "I've got to live somewhere, and why not here? I don't know whether I've got anything left of my money or not— anything, that is, that my creditors or my lawyers will let me have in peace—but there's excellent shooting on the place, and it only cost a song. I think I can stay here as long as I can stay anywhere; you know I am a sort of civilized Bedouin anyhow. And then I own up to a desire to see that little comedy between—between—Millenbeck and Barn Elms played through. It's an amusing little piece."

Mrs. Sherrard pricked up her ears. Freke's repu-

10

tation as a conquering hero had inspired in her the interest it always does in the female breast. Was it possible that he shouldn't be making love to either Judith or Jacqueline?

"I'll tell you what," he cried, smiling, "they are the most precious pack of innocents at Barn Elms! There's my uncle—a high-minded, good-natured, un-terrified old blunderbuss—the most unsophisticated of the lot. Then my aunt, who belongs properly to the age of Rowena and Rebecca—and Judith."

Here Freke's countenance changed a little from its laughing carelessness. His rather ordinary features were full of a piercing and subtile expression.

"Judith fancies, because she has been a wife, a mother, and a widow, that she knows the whole gamut of life, when actually she has only struck the first note correctly a little while ago—no, I forget—that young one. But that's very one-sided, although intense. She loves the child because he is her own, not because he is Beverley's—rather in spite of it, I fancy."

Mrs. Sherrard, in the excitement of the moment—for what is more exciting than unexpected and inside discoveries about our neighbors?—got up too.

"I knew it—I knew it!" she answered, her sharp old eyes getting bright. "I saw Judith when she was a bride, and she wasn't in the least rapturous. And the next time I saw her she had on that odd widow's cap she wears, and that blessed baby in her arms; and if ever I saw secret happiness painted on any human countenance it was hers; and all the time she was trying to imagine herself broken-hearted for Beverley Temple."

"Fudge!" almost shouted Freke. "It's my belief she'd have traded off six husbands like Beverley for one black-eyed boy like that young one."

"Beverley," began Mrs. Sherrard, delighted, yet fluttered by this plain speaking, "you remember, was a big, handsome fellow—rode like a centaur, danced beautifully, the best shot in the county—as polite as a dancing-master or—General Temple—as brave as a lion—"

"Oh, good God, don't talk to me about Beverley Temple! He was the most wooden-headed Temple I ever knew, and that's saying a good deal, ma'am!" responded Freke, with energy.

"*You* are no fool," said Mrs. Sherrard, as if willing to argue the point.

"Yes, but you couldn't any more take me as a type of the Temples than you could take Edmund Morford as a type of the Sherrards. Lord, Mrs. Sherrard, what an ass your nephew is!"

"Isn't he, though? But he is a good soul," was Mrs. Sherrard's answer.

Was it Judith or was it Jacqueline that Freke was trying his charms on, thought Mrs. Sherrard, taking

her afternoon nap over the fire, after Freke left.
Freke, however, really could not have enlightened
her. For Judith his admiration increased every day
—her very defiance of him was captivating to him.
He well knew that she hated every bone in his body,
and he had made up his mind, as a set-off to this, to
get a description of a certain scene during the war
out of Throckmorton some time in her presence. It
was a species of vivisection, but she deserved it—deserved it richly—for had she not brought it on herself by the way she treated him, Temple Freke? And
then Jacqueline—she was certainly a fascinating little
object, though not half the woman that Judith was
—this Freke magnanimously allowed, riding briskly
along the country road in the wintry twilight.

The family at Barn Elms had never yet dined
with Throckmorton, owing to General Temple's continued wrestle with the gout, that had now made him
a prisoner for four long weeks. Mrs. Temple, who
every day got fonder of George, as she called Throckmorton, had promised to dine at Millenbeck when the
general was able to go; but, as she invested all their
intercourse with Millenbeck with the solemnity of a
formal reconciliation, she delayed until the whole
family could go in state and ceremony. At last Dr.
Wortley, having gained a temporary advantage over
Delilah, and brought General Temple to observe his
(Dr. Wortley's) regimen, instead of Delilah's, a week

or two marked a decided improvement. The general's Calvinism abated, his profanity mended, and he became once more the amiable soldier and stanch churchman that he was by nature.

"Now, Mrs. Temple," said Throckmorton one evening as he was going away, "if you will keep the general out of mischief for a day or two longer, you will be able to pay me that long-promised visit. Let me know, so I can get Mrs. Sherrard and Dr. Wortley—and Morford and Freke; but you, my dear friend, will be the guest of honor."

Mrs. Temple blushed like a girl, with pleasure—Throckmorton's way of saying this was so whole-souled and affectionate.

"You say right, my dear Throckmorton," remarked General Temple, putting his arm around Mrs. Temple's waist, "the tenderest, sweetest, most obedient wife"—at which Simon Peter, putting wood on the fire, snickered audibly, and Throckmorton would have laughed outright had he dared.

So it was fixed that on the following Friday evening they were all to dine at Millenbeck, Mrs. Temple promising to watch the general, lest he should relapse into gout and gloom—and a promise from Mrs. Temple was a promise. She went about, a little surprised at the complete way that Throckmorton had brought her round. Here was one Yankee whom she loved with a genuine motherly affection—and he was a

Virginia Yankee, too—which she esteemed the very worst kind.

Jacqueline, as usual, was off her head at the notion of going, and Judith's suppressed excitement did not escape Mrs. Temple's eye. Both of them, provincials of provincials, as they were, felt a true feminine curiosity regarding the reputed splendors of Millenbeck, which was, in fact, destined to dazzle their country-fied eyes.

On the Friday evening, therefore, at half-past six, they found themselves driving down the Millenbeck lane. General Temple had begun, figuratively speaking, to shake hands across the bloody chasm from the moment he started from Barn Elms. He harangued the whole way upon the touching aspect of the reconciliation between the great leaders of the hostile armies, as typified by his present expedition. Going down the lane they caught up with Mrs. Sherrard, being driven by Mr. Morford in a top buggy.

"Jane Temple, are we a couple of fools?" called out Mrs. Sherrard, putting her head out of the buggy.

"No, Katharine Sherrard, we are a couple of Christians," piously responded Mrs. Temple.

General Temple thrust his bare head out of the carriage-window, holding his hat in his hand, as it was his unbroken rule never to speak to a woman with his head covered, and entered into a disquisition respecting the ethics of the great civil war, which lasted until they drew up to the very door of Millenbeck.

A handsome graveled drive led up to the door, and a *porte-cochère*, which was really a very modest affair of glass and iron, had been thrown over the drive; but, as it was the only one ever seen in the county, all of them regarded it with great respect. Throckmorton, with old-time Virginia hospitality, met them at the steps. Like all true gentlemen, he was a model host. As he helped Mrs. Temple to alight, he raised her small, withered hand to his lips and kissed it respectfully.

"Welcome to Millenbeck, my best and earliest friend," he said.

"George Throckmorton," responded Mrs. Temple, with sweet gravity, "you have taught forgiveness to my hard and unforgiving heart."

Within the house was more magnificence. The inevitable great, dark, useless hall was robbed of its coldness and bleakness by soft Turkish rugs placed over the polished floor. There was no way of heating it in the original plan, but Throckmorton's decorator and furnisher had hit upon the plan of having a quaint Dutch stove, which now glowed redly with a hard-coal fire. The startling innovation of lighting the broad oak staircase had likewise been adopted, and at intervals up the stairway wax-candles in sconces shed a mellow half-light in the hall below.

General Temple was exuberant. He shook hands with Throckmorton half a dozen times, and informed him that, strange as the defection of a Virginian from his native State might appear, he, General Temple, believed that Throckmorton was actuated by conscientious though mistaken notions in remaining in the army after the breaking out of the war.

"Thank you," laughed Throckmorton, immensely tickled; "I haven't apologized for it yet, have I, general?"

Up-stairs, in a luxurious spare bedroom, the ladies' wraps were laid aside. Here, also, that perfect comfort prevailed, which is rare in Virginia country-houses, although luxury, in certain ways, is common enough. As they passed an open door, going down, they caught sight of Throckmorton's own room. In that alone a Spartan simplicity reigned. There was no carpet on the spotless floor, and an iron bedstead, a large table, and a few chairs completed the furnishing of it. But it had an air of exquisite neatness and military preciseness in it that made an atmosphere about Throckmorton. Over the unornamented mantel two swords were crossed, and over them was a pretty, girlish portrait of Jack's mother. Judith, in passing, craned her long, white neck to get a better look at the portrait, was caught in the act by Mrs. Temple, and blushed furiously.

She had a strange sensation of both joy and fear in coming to Throckmorton's house. In her inmost soul she felt it to be a crime of great magnitude; and, indeed, the circumstances made it about as nearly a crime as such a woman could commit. More than that, if it should ever be known—and it was liable to be known at any moment—the deliberate foreknowledge with which she went to Millenbeck, she would never be allowed to remain another hour under the roof of Barn Elms: of that much she was perfectly sure. This, however, had but little effect on her, although she was risking not only her own but her child's future; but the conviction that it was absolutely wrong for her to go, caused her to make some paltering excuse when Throckmorton first asked her. He put it aside with his usual calm superiority in dealing with her scruples about going to places, and she yielded to the sweet temptation of obeying his wishes. She took pains, though, to tell Freke herself that she was going—a risky but delicious piece of braggadocio—at which Freke lifted his eyebrows slightly. Inwardly he determined to make her pay for her rashness. She was the only woman who had ever fought him, and he was not to be driven off the field by any of the sex.

Judith's blush lasted until she reached the drawing-room, and made her not less handsome. There the gentlemen were being dazzled by still further splendors. This room, which was large and of stately proportions, was really handsome. Throckmorton, who cared nothing for luxury, and whose personal habits were simplicity itself, was yet too broad-minded to impress his own tastes upon anybody else. Since most people liked luxury, he had his house made luxurious; and his own room was the only plain one in it. Jack's was a perfect bower, " more fit," as Throckmorton remarked with good-natured sarcasm, " for a young lady's boudoir than a bunk for a hulking youngster." In the same way Throckmorton managed to dress like a gentleman on what Jack spent on hats and canes and cravats; but nobody ever knew whether Throckmorton's clothes were new or old. His personality eclipsed all his belongings.

Jacqueline was completely subdued by the luxury around her. No human soul ever loved these pleasant things of life better than she loved them. Comfort and beauty and luxury were as the breath of life to her. She had hungered and thirsted for them ever since she could remember. Going down the stairs she caught Judith's hand, with a quick, childish grasp. The lights, the glitter, almost took her breath away; and when she saw a great mound of roses on the drawing-room table, got from Norfolk by the phenomenal Sweeney, she almost screamed with delight.

"God bless my soul, this is pleasant!" remarked Dr. Wortley, rubbing his hands cheerfully before the drawing-room fire, where the gentlemen, including Morford and Freke, were assembled. "Here we are all met again, under Millenbeck's roof, as we were before the war. Let by-gones be by-gones, say I, about the war."

"Amen," answered Mrs. Temple, after a little pause, piously and sweetly.

Sweeney, who could make quite a dashing figure as a waiter, now appeared, dressed in faultless evening costume of much newer fashion than Throckmorton's, and announced dinner. Throckmorton, with his most graceful air—for he was on his mettle in his own house, and with those charming, unsophisticated women—gave his arm to Mrs. Temple; the general, with a grand flourish, did the same to Mrs. Sherrard; Judith had the doctor of divinity on one hand and the doctor of medicine on the other and Jacqueline brought up the rear with Jack Throckmorton and Temple Freke. Judith, when she saw this arrangement, comforted herself with the reflection that, if anybody could counteract Freke's influence over Jacqueline, it was Jack Throckmorton, whom Jacqueline candidly acknowledged was infinitely more attractive to her than the master of Millenbeck.

But Jacqueline needed no counteraction. Freke, who read her perfectly, was secretly amused, and annoyed as well, when he saw that Jacqueline was every moment more carried away by Throckmorton's wax-candles and carved chairs and embroidered screens and onyx tables, and glass and plate. He felt not one thrill of the jealousy of Throckmorton, where Jacqueline was concerned, that Throckmorton sometimes felt for him, because he was infinitely more astute in the knowledge of human and especially feminine weaknesses and follies ; and he saw that the chairs and tables at Millenbeck were much more fascinating to Jacqueline than Throckmorton with his matured grace, his manly dignity. Freke, too, having long since worn out his emotions, except that slight lapse as regarded Judith, for whom he always *felt* something—admiration, or pity, or a desire to be revenged —had an acute judgment of women which was quite unbiased by the way any particular woman treated or felt toward him. Judith, although she hated him, and he frankly admitted she had cause to, he ranked infinitely above Jacqueline. He had seen, long before, that Jacqueline, if she ever seriously tried, could draw Throckmorton by a thread, and it gave Freke a certain contempt for Throckmorton's taste and perception. Any man who could prefer Jacqueline to Judith was, in Freke's esteem, wanting in taste ; for, after all, he considered these things more as matters of taste than anything else.

The dinner was very merry. When the general

had told his fifth long-winded story of his adventures and hair-breadth escapes during the war, Mrs. Temple, with a glance, shut him up. Freke was in his element at a dinner-table, and told some ridiculous stories about the straits to which he had been reduced during his seven years' absence in Europe—" when," as he explained " my laudable desire to acquire knowledge and virtue threatened to be balked at every moment by my uncle getting me home. However, I managed to stay." He told with much gravity how he had been occasionally reduced to his fiddle for means of raising the wind, and had figured in concert programmes as Signor Tempolino, at which stories all shouted with laughter except Mrs. Temple and the general—Mrs. Temple sighing, and the general scowling prodigiously. Edmund Morford, who was afraid that laughing was injurious to his dignity, tried not to smile, but Freke was too comical for him.

Amid all the laughter and jollity and good-cheer, Jacqueline sat, glancing shyly up at Throckmorton once in a while with a look that Nature had endowed her with, and which, had she but known it, was a full equivalent to a fortune. She had never, in all her simple provincial life, seen anything like this—endless forks and spoons at the table; queer ways of serving queerer things; an easy-cushioned chair to sit in; no darns or patches in the damask; and the aroma of wealth, an easy income everywhere. The de-

sire to own all this suddenly took possession of her.
At the moment this dawned upon her mind, she actually started, and, opening her fan in a flutter, she
knocked- over a wine-glass, which Jack deftly replaced without stopping in his conversation. Then
she began to study Throckmorton under her eyelashes. He was not so old, after all, and did not have
the gout, like her father. And then she caught his
kind eyes fixed on her, and flashed him back a look
that thrilled him. Jack was talking to her, but she
managed to convey subtly to Throckmorton that she
was not listening to Jack, which pleased the major
very much, who had heretofore found Jack a danger-
ous rival in all his looks and words with Jacqueline.

Freke, telling his funny stories, did not for one
moment pretermit his study of the little comedy before him—Jacqueline and Throckmorton and Judith.
It was as plain as print to him. Judith, in her black
gown, which opened at the throat and showed the
white pillar of her neck, and with half-sleeves that
revealed the milky whiteness of her slender arms, sat
midway the table, just opposite Jacqueline. Usually
Judith's color was as delicate as a wild rose, but to-
night it was a carnation flush.

"Is Throckmorton a fool?" thought Freke, in the
midst of an interval given over to laughter at some of
his stories, which were as short and pithy as General Temple's were sapless and long drawn out; for

Throckmorton, who did nothing by halves, and was constitutionally averse to dawdling, returned Jacqueline's glances with compound interest. Before they left the table, two persons had seen the promising beginning of the affair, and only two, none of the others having a suspicion. These two were Freke and Judith.

The knowledge came quickly to Judith. Women can live ages of agony in a moment over these things. Judith, smiling, graceful, waving her large black fan sedately to and fro, by all odds the handsomest as well as the most gifted woman there, felt something tearing at her heart-strings, that she could have screamed aloud with pain. But even Freke, who saw everything nearly, did not see that; he only surmised it. It was nearly ten o'clock before they went back into the drawing-room. Throckmorton gave nobody occasion to say that he devoted himself particularly to any of the four women who were his guests; but his look, his talk, his manner to Jacqueline underwent a subtile change; and when he sat and talked to Judith he thought what a sweet sister she would make, and blessed her for her tenderness to Jacqueline. Judith's color had been gradually fading from the moment she caught Throckmorton's glance at Jacqueline. She was now quite pale, and less animated, less interesting, than Throckmorton ever remembered to have seen her. At something he said to her, she gave an answer so wide of the mark that she felt ashamed and apologized.

"I was thinking of my child at that moment and wondering if he were asleep," she said.

From the moment of that first meaning glance of Throckmorton's at Jacqueline, the evening had spun out interminably to Judith. Mrs. Temple noticed it with secret approval, as a sign of loyalty to her widowhood.

At eleven o'clock a move was made to go, when Throckmorton suddenly remembered that he had not showed them his modest conservatory, which appeared quite imposing to their provincial eyes. He took Judith into the little glass room opening off the hall. It was very hot, very damp, and very close, as such places usually are, and full of a faint, sickly perfume. Freke followed them in. At last he had got his chance. He began to talk in his easy, unconstrained way, and in a minute or two had got the conversation around to something they had been speaking of the night of the party at Turkey Thicket.

"You were saying," said Freke, "something about a bad quarter of an hour you had with that old sorrel horse of yours—"

"Well, I should say it was a bad quarter of an hour," answered Throckmorton. "To be ridden down and knocked off my horse was bad enough, with that strapping fellow pinioning my arms to my side so I couldn't draw my pistol; and old Tartar, perfectly mad with fright—the only time I ever knew him to be so demoralized—tearing at the reins that wouldn't break and that I couldn't loose my arm from, and every time I looked up I saw his fore-feet in the air ready to come down on me—"

"And what sort of a looking fellow was it you say that rode you down?"

"A tall, blonde fellow—an officer evidently.—Good God! Mrs. Beverley, what is the matter?" For the color had dropped out of Judith's face as the mercury drops out of the tube, and she was gazing with wide, wild eyes at Throckmorton. How often had she heard that grewsome story—even that the plunging horse was a sorrel! But at least Freke should not see her break down. She heard herself saying, in a strange, unnatural voice:

"Nothing. I think it is too warm for me in here." Throckmorton took her by the arm and led her back into the hall, and to a small window which he opened. He felt like a brute for mentioning anything connected with the war—of course it must be intensely painful to Judith—but she stopped his earnest apologies with a word.

"Don't blame yourelf—pray, don't. It was very warm—and Freke—oh, how I hate him!"

Throckmorton had been afraid she was going to faint, but the energy with which she brought out her

11

last remark convinced him there was no danger. It brought the blood surging back to her face in a torrent.

Nobody else had known anything of the little scene in the conservatory; and then Throckmorton had to show Jacqueline over it, and Judith caught sight of him, standing in one of his easy and graceful attitudes, leaning over Jacqueline in expressive-pantomime; and then came the general's big, musical voice: "My love, it is now past eleven o'clock; we must not trespass on Throckmorton's hospitality." Throckmorton felt at that moment as if the evening had just begun; while to Judith it seemed as if there was a stretch of years of pain between the dawn and the midnight of that day—a pain secret but consuming.

There was the bustle of departure, during which Judith managed to say to Freke:

"You have had your revenge—perfect but complete."

"That's for calling me a liar," was Freke's reply. It was, moreover, for something that Judith had made him suffer—absurd as it was that any woman could make Temple Freke suffer. But, after what he had seen that night, he reflected that it was perhaps a work of supererogation to build a barrier between Judith and Throckmorton. The major had other views.

Throckmorton handed the ladies into the carriage; and, in spite of the light from the open hall-door, and *not* from the carriage-lamps—for the Barn Elms carriage had long parted with its lamps—he pressed a light kiss on Jacqueline's hand, under General and Mrs. Temple's very eyes, without their seeing it. Judith, however, saw it, and was thankful that it was dark, so that the pallid change, which she knew came over her, was not visible.

Throckmorton went back into the house, shut himself up in his own den, and smoked savagely for an hour. Yes, it was all up with him, he ruefully acknowledged.

CHAPTER VIII.

A DAY or two after this, however, came a snow, deep and lasting, more like a midwinter snow in New England than a December flurry in lower Virginia. For four weeks the sun scarcely shone, and the earth was wrapped in white. The roads were impassable, the river-steamers stopped running, and the mails were delayed for days at a time. The country people were much cut off from each other. Mrs. Temple missed four successive Sundays at church—a thing she had never done in her life before. Nobody could get to Barn Elms except the Throckmortons and Freke, but they came often in the evenings. Throckmorton saw what was before him with Jacqueline, yet held back, as engineers put down the brakes on a wild engine on a down grade—it does not, however, materially alter the result. He sometimes thought, with a sense of the grotesqueness of human affairs, how strange it was that things had not arranged themselves so that Jack had not been Jacqueline's victim, and himself Judith's. For Jack was undeniably fond of Jacqueline, and so far did not in the slightest degree suspect his father's infatuation, as Throckmorton frankly and bitterly acknowledged it to be. As for Judith, Nature leaves no true woman unarmed for suffering like hers. Even Jacqueline, who was sharp-eyed, only noticed that Judith at this time was, if anything, a little sweeter and kinder than before— even a little more gay. Little Beverley found his mother better company than usual, and more ready for a romp than ever before. The child, whom she had thought everything to her before, became now more passionately dear to her. Alone with him, she would take him in her arms and hold him close to her; she felt an actual softening of the pain at her heart when the child's curly head rested over it. Then she would talk to him in a way the child only half understood, as he gazed at her with grave, mystified eyes, and, while laughing at his childish wonder, she would almost smother him with kisses. Judith was positively becoming merry. In her voice was a ring, in her eyes a light that was different from that calm, untroubled composure that had once marked her. Her manner to Throckmorton was perfect; the same gentle gayety, the same graceful dignity. She did not avoid him ; pain wrung no such concession from Judith Temple. But Judith's invincible cheerfulness was strangely antagonized by Jacqueline. Jacqueline, who talked to her own heart in a very primitive, open fashion, was vexed at the notion that, in

order to be mistress of Millenbeck, she would have to
marry Throckmorton.   How much nicer, thought
Jacqueline, with great simplicity, if it were Jack who
gave her those looks, those words, who had pressed
that kiss upon her hand! Throckmorton was too old,
and had too much sense; Jacqueline made no secret
in acknowledging that mature men of sense bored
and restrained her.   It was very hard, she thought,
disconsolately.   Ever since that dinner at Millenbeck,
Barn Elms had appeared shabbier and sorrier than
ever before.   Although Mrs. Temple continued to
have five kinds of bread for breakfast, and had invited a regiment of poor relations to spend the coming summer with her, under the Virginia delusion
that it costs nothing to harbor a garrison for an in-
definite time, things were certainly going very badly
at Barn Elms; a condition of affairs, though, to which
General Temple was perfectly accustomed, and who
knew no other way of paying Peter than by robbing
Paul.   The old carriage went all to pieces just about
that time, and there was no money to buy another one.
As for a new piano, that was an impossible dream;
and there were two splendid new pianos at Millenbeck, and not a soul to touch them! And Jacqueline
wanted a new frock, and endless other things, which
were distinctly out of the question, and the only way
to get them, that she could see, was to encourage
Throckmorton's attentions and be mistress of Millen-

beck. All this was not lost on Freke, who, with his eyes open, began to play with Jacqueline, and like Throckmorton got his wings scorched. The girl certainly had a power of compelling love. Had Judith ever relented toward Freke, Jacqueline would have had cause for jealousy if she loved him. But, in truth, as it came to pass, Freke cast as much of a spell upon Jacqueline as she did upon him. If Freke owned Millenbeck, instead of that wretched old Wareham, that actually was not as good as Barn Elms! So Jacqueline fretted to herself.

The loneliness of those cold, snowy days was killing to Jacqueline. The long afternoons when she sat by the drawing-room fire and dreamed dreams, were almost intolerable to her. When she heard Beverley's shouts, as Judith romped with him in the cold hall, and hid from him in the dusk until the child set up a baby cry, it was the only living cheerful noise about the house. Judith would come to her and say, "Now, Jacky, for a walk in the hall!" Jacqueline would answer fretfully:

"What do I want to walk for?"

"Because it is better than sitting still."

Judith would take her by the waist and run her up and down the long, dusky hall. It was so cold they shivered at first, and the rattling of the great windows let icy gusts of air in upon them; and sometimes the moon would glare in at them in a ghastly way. Presently they would hear Simon Peter bringing in wood for the night by the back way, shaking the snow off his feet, and announcing to Delilah: " I tell you what, ole 'oman, 'tis everlastin' cole an' gwine ter keep so, fer I seed de hosses in de stable kickin' de lef' hine-foots; an' dat's sho' an' suttin sign o' freezin'."

" You better kick dat lef' hine-foot o' yourn, an' stop studyin' 'bout de hosses, fo' mistis come arter you! Ez long ez ole marse holler at you, you doan' min'; but jes' let mistis in dat sof' voice say right fine, ' Simon Peter!' I lay you jes' hop," was Delilah's wifely reply.

General Temple, confined to the house by the weather, drew military maps with great precision, and worked hard upon his History of Temple's Brigade. The fact that he knew much more about the Duke of Marlborough's campaigns, or Prince Eugene's, or anybody's, in fact, than he did about any he had been directly engaged in, in no wise set him back. Mrs. Temple, who thought the general a prodigy of military science, was rejoiced that he had something to divert him through the long wintry days, when Barn Elms was as completely shut in from even the little neighborhood world as if it were in the depths of a Russian forest. Jack Throckmorton, who after a while began to see that the major was certainly singed, as he expressed it to himself, did not carry out his usual tactics of making his vicinity too hot for his father, but when he wished to see Jacqueline went over in the mornings. If the weather was tolerable, they were pretty sure to find their way to the ice-pond. Jack, carrying on his arm a little wooden chair, and putting Jacqueline in it, would push it over the ice before him as he sped along on skates. Then Jacqueline's fresh, young laugh would ring out shrilly —then she was happy. Sometimes Judith and Throckmorton, smiling, would watch them. Jack liked Mrs. Beverley immensely, but he confided to Jacqueline that he was a little afraid of her—just as Jacqueline candidly admitted she was in awe of Major Throckmorton. Throckmorton, watching this childish boy and girl fun, would sometimes laugh inwardly and grimly at himself. How true was it, as Mrs. Sherrard had said, that Jacqueline would make a good play-mate for Jack! And then he would turn to Judith, and try to persuade himself of her sweetness and truth. But love comes not by persuasion.

Jack had been giving Jacqueline glowing accounts of the sleigh-rides he had had in the Northwest. Jacqueline was crazy for a sleigh-ride, but there was no such thing as a sleigh in the county. One evening, after tea, as Jacqueline sat dolefully clasping her knees and looking in the fire, and Judith, with hands locked in her lap, was doing the same; Mrs. Temple knitting placidly by the lamp, while General Temple held forth on certain blunders he had discovered in the Retreat of the Ten Thousand—a strange tinkling sound was heard far—far away—almost as if it were in another world! Jacqueline sat perfectly still and gazed into Judith's eyes. Judith got up and went into the hall. A great patch of moonlight shone through the uncurtained window, and outside it was almost as light as day. The limbs and trunks of the great live-oaks looked preternaturally dark against the white earth and the blue-black, star-lit sky. Suddenly Simon Peter's head appeared cautiously around the corner of the house, and in a minute or two he came up the back way and planted himself at Judith's elbow.

"Gord A'mighty, Miss Judy, what dat ar'? What dem bells ringin' fur? I 'spect de evils is 'broad. I done see two Jack-my-lanterns dis heah night."

Judith fixed her eyes on the long, straight lane bordered with solemn cedars; she saw a dark object moving along, and heard the sharp click of horses' shoes on the frozen snow.

"It's somebody coming," she said, and in a moment, she cried out joyfully:

"O Jacky, come—come! it's a sleigh—I see Jack Throckmorton driving—Major Throckmorton is there —and there are four seats!"

Jacqueline jumped up and ran out. She had never seen a sleigh in her life, and there it was turning into the drive before the house. Jack had the reins, and the major's two thoroughbreds were flying along at a rattling pace, and the bells were jingling loudly and merrily. Jacqueline almost danced with delight. By the time the sleigh drew up at the door, Simon Peter was there to take the reins, and Throckmorton and Jack jumped out and came up the steps. The general and Mrs. Temple were also roused to come out and meet them. As the hall-door swung open, a blast of arctic air entered. Throckmorton's dark eyes looked black under his seal-skin cap. Jack plunged into business at once.

"Now, Mrs. Temple, you must let me take Miss Jacqueline for a spin to-night; never saw better sleighing in my life. The major's along, and you know he is as steady as old Time "—the major at heart did not relish this—" and, if Mrs. Beverley will go, it will be awfully jolly."

Mrs. Temple began some mild protest: it was too cold, or too late, or something; but for once Jacqueline did not hear her, and bounded off up-stairs for her wraps. Even Judith, usually so calm, was a little carried away by the prospect.

"Come, mother, Major Throckmorton and I will take care of them."

Mrs. Temple yielded.

"I will take care of Beverley while you are gone," she said, and Judith blushed. Was she forgetting the child?

In five minutes both of them were ready. Judith had pressed her soft cheeks to Beverley's as she leaned over the sleeping child. Surely nobody could say she was a forgetful mother.

The sleigh was Jack's. He had sent away and bought it, and it had arrived that evening. Jacqueline sat on the front seat with him, her face glowing with smiles on the clear, cold night, as he wrapped the fur robes around her. Throckmorton did the same for Judith. For once she had left off her widow's veil, and for once she forgot that secret pain and determined to be happy. Jack touched up the horses, and off they flew. As for Jacqueline and himself, their pleasure was of that youthful, effervescing sort that never comes after twenty-five; but Throckmorton and Judith began to feel some of the exhilaration and excitement. Throckmorton had lately heard Mrs. Sherrard's views about Judith's marriage, and it had made him feel a very great pity for her.

"Where are we going?" cried Jacqueline, as they dashed along.

"Anywhere—nowhere—to Turkey Thicket!" replied Jack, lightly touching the flying horses with his whip.

"We will frighten Mrs. Sherrard to death!" said Judith, from the back seat, burying her face in her muff.

It was not a time to think about anybody else,

though. The five miles to Turkey Thicket sped away like lightning. When they dashed through the gate and drew up before the house, half a dozen darkies were there gaping; and Mrs. Sherrard, with a shawl thrown over her head, was standing in the doorway, and standing behind her was Freke.

As they all got out, laughing, huddling, and slipping up the stone steps, Mrs. Sherrard greeted them with her characteristic cordiality, demanding that they should take off their wraps before they were half up the steps. She gave Throckmorton a comical look, and whispered to him as he shook hands with her: "Out with the Sister of Charity, hey? Or is it the child Jacky?" Throckmorton laughed rather uneasily. He had never got over that remark of Mrs. Sherrard's about Jacqueline being a playmate for Jack.

They all went trooping into the dining-room, where a huge fire blazed. Mrs. Sherrard called up her factotum, a venerable negro woman, Delilah's double, and in ten minutes they were sitting around the table laughing and eating and drinking. The colored factotum had brought out a large yellow bowl, a big, flat, blue dish, and a rusty bottle. Eggs and milk followed.

"Egg-nog," whispered Jack to Jacqueline.

So it was. Freke broke up the eggs, and Mrs. Sherrard, with a great carving-knife, beat up the whites, while she talked and occasionally flourished the knife uncomfortably near Freke's nose. Throckmorton poured in the rum and brandy with such liberality that Judith with great firmness took both bottles away from him. The egg-nog was a capital brew. Then Freke produced his violin, and saying, " Hang your Brahms and Beethovens !" dashed into waltzes of Strauss and Waldteufel that made the very air vibrate with joy and gayety and rhythm. Jack seized Jacqueline, and, opening the door, they flew out into the half-lighted hall and spun around delightedly. As Freke's superb bow-arm flashed back and forth, and the torrent of melody poured out of the violin, his eyes flashed, too. He did not mean to play always for Jacqueline to dance.

Judith, standing at the door, watched the two young figures whirling merrily around in the half-light to the resounding waltz-music. She was altogether taken by surprise when Throckmorton came up to her, and said, half laughing and half embarrassed :

"My dancing days are over, but that waltz is charming."

Judith did not quite take in what he meant, but without a word he clasped her waist, and she was gliding off with him. Throckmorton would have scorned the characterization of a "dancing man," but nevertheless he danced well, and Judith moved like a breeze. She went around the big hall once—twice

—before the idea that it was inconceivably wicked of her to dance with Throckmorton came to her; not, indeed, until she saw Freke's wide mouth expanded into a smile that was infuriating. And then, what would Mrs. Temple say to her dancing at all?

"Oh, pray, stop!" she cried, blushing furiously. "I can't dance any more; I ought never to have begun. I haven't danced for—for years."

Throckmorton stopped at once, with pity in his eyes. He suspected the sort of angelic dragooning to which she was subject from his dear Mrs. Temple.

"Why shouldn't you dance?" he said. "I see you like it. Come, let's try it again. I'm a little rusty, perhaps, but we got on famously just now." But Judith would not try it again.

Freke now meant to have his innings.

"Do you know this is Twelfth-night—the night for telling fortunes?" he said, laying down his violin.—"Come, Jacky, let me take you out of doors and show you the moon and tell yours."

"In this snow!" screamed Mrs. Sherrard; but by that time Freke had thrown a shawl over Jacqueline's head, and had dragged her out of the room, and the hall-door banged loudly after them.

Outside, in the cold, white moonlight and the snow, Freke pointed to the moon.

"Now make your wish," he said; "but don't wish for Millenbeck."

Jacqueline's face could turn no redder than it was, but she looked at Freke, and answered on impulse, as she always did:

"Millenbeck is finer than Barn Elms—"

"Or Wareham," responded Freke, fixing her attention with a stare out of his bold eyes. "See here, Jacqueline, I know how it is. You think you will be able to put up with Throckmorton for the sake of Millenbeck. My dear, he is old—"

"He is only forty-four," answered Jacqueline, defiantly.

"And you are only twenty-one. You would be happier even at Wareham with me, than at Millenbeck with Throckmorton."

"I couldn't be happy in a five-roomed house," quite truthfully said Jacqueline.

"Yes, you could. I could make you forget whether it had five or ten rooms."

At this, he put two fingers under her chin, and, tilting up her rosy face, kissed her on the mouth. "Come!" cried Freke, after a little while, remembering how time was flying, which Jacqueline had evidently forgotten, and making for the steps; but Jacqueline stopped him with a scared face.

"Aren't you married, Freke?" she asked.

"Not a bit of it," answered Freke, stoutly. "Don't you believe all the old women's tales you hear about me, Jacky. I'm no more married than you are this minute. I have been, I admit, but I slipped my head out of the noose some time ago. Do you believe me?"

"Yes," answered Jacqueline, who could believe anything, "If—if—people can really be divorced."

They had not been gone ten minutes, when they returned, yet Freke saw a danger-signal flying in Judith's cheeks. She did not mean to have any more of this. Mrs. Sherrard, who had become an active partisan of Freke's, asked, as soon as they came in:

"What wish did you make, Jacky?"

Jacqueline started. She had made no wish at all.

"Freke ran me out of the house so fast," she began complainingly, "I was perfectly out of breath."

"And of course couldn't make a wish," said Jack Throckmorton, laughing.

"I wished for everything," replied Jacqueline.

Presently they were driving home through the still, frosty night. Judith felt a complete reaction from the ghost of merriment that had possessed her in going that road before. Even Throckmorton noticed the change. She laughed and talked gayly, but her speaking eyes told another story. Throckmorton could not but smile, and yet felt sorry, too, when Jacqueline, fancying herself unheard, whispered to Judith:

"I won't tell mamma about the waltz."

But Jacqueline was absent-minded too. When
12

they had got home and had gone up-stairs, instead of Jacqueline following Judith to her room, as she usually did when she had anything on her mind, she went straight to her own room, and, locking the door, began to walk up and down, her hands behind her back. How strange, fascinating, overpowering was Freke, after all! Was a divorced man really a married man? Divorces were dreadful things, she had always known —but—suppose, in some other world than that about the Severn neighborhood, it should be considered a venial thing? Jacqueline became so much interested in these puzzling reflections that she unconsciously abandoned the cat-like tread which she had adopted for fear of waking her mother, and stepped out in her own brisk way up and down the big room. Mrs. Temple, hearing this, quietly opened her own chamber-door beneath. That was enough. The walk stopped as if by magic, and in ten minutes Jacqueline was in bed.

CHAPTER IX.

Throckmorton made one short, sharp struggle with himself, and then yielded to Jacqueline's fascination.

Without Freke's keen perceptions, Throckmorton knew enough to doubt whether he ought to congratulate or curse himself if he won Jacqueline; and that he could win her, his own good sense told him soon enough. Jacqueline's nature was so impressionable that a strong determination could conquer her at any time and at any thing for a season. Throckmorton, tramping about the country roads with his gun on his shoulder; having jolly bachelor parties at Millenbeck, which were confined strictly to the Severn neighborhood; in church on Sunday, half-listening to Morford's pyrotechnics in the pulpit; smoking at unearthly hours in his own den; riding hard after the hounds—the thought of Jacqueline was never far away, and never without a suspicion of pain and dissatisfaction. He was not given to paltering with himself, and nothing could utterly blind his strong common sense—a common sense that was so imperative to be heard, so difficult to answer, so impossible to evade. It was not in him to surrender his judgment absolutely. He faced bravely the discrepancy in their ages, but he soon admitted to himself that there were other incongruities deeper and more significant than that. Nevertheless, although Reason might argue and preach, Love carried the day. Throckmorton reminded himself that miracles sometimes happened in love. He did not suffer himself to think what Jacqueline would be twenty years from then. Time is always fatal to women of her type. Even her beauty was essentially the beauty of youth. In twenty years she would be stout and florid Here Throckmorton, in his reflections, unexpectedly went off on Judith. Hers was a beauty that would last—the beauty of expression, of *esprit*. Then his thoughts, with a sort of shock, reverted to Jacqueline

As for Freke, Throckmorton did not once connect him with Jacqueline. Freke was a black sheep, and, as Throckmorton devoutly and thankfully remembered, the daughter of General and Mrs. Temple would not be likely to regard a divorced man as a single man. So, in the course of two or three weeks, Throckmorton had gone through all his phases, and had made up his mind. He could not but laugh at Mrs. Temple's unsuspecting security. She had always regarded Jacqueline as a child, and indeed regarded her very little in any way.

This excellent woman, whose gospel was embodied in her duty to her husband and her children, had always been a singularly unjust mother; but she thought herself the most devoted mother in the world, because she regularly superintended Jacqueline's changes of flannels, and made her take off her shoes when she got her feet wet. Both Mrs. Temple and the general were absolutely incapable of entertaining the idea that Freke was growing fond of Jacqueline; and Freke was not only astute enough to keep them in the dark, but to keep Judith, too, who fondly imagined that she herself had reduced Freke to good behavior as regarded Jacqueline. Freke's estimate of the two young women had not changed in the least—only Jacqueline was come-at-able and Judith was not—and he loved to cross Judith and vex her, and give her pin-sticks as well as stabs in return for the frank hatred she felt for him. She had elected her own position with him—so let her keep it.

It never took Throckmorton long to act on his determinations. Jacqueline saw what was coming. He had a way of looking at her that forced her to look up and then to look down again. He said little things to her, instinct with meaning, that brought the blood to her face. He performed small services for her that were merely conventional, but which were from him to her acts of adoration. And Judith saw it all.

He did not have to wait long for an opportunity. One evening he went to Barn Elms. The general was threatened with a return of his gout, which had got better, and Mrs. Temple had imprisoned him in the " charmber," where she mounted guard over him. Only Jacqueline and Judith, with little Beverley, who had been allowed to stay up until eight o'clock, as a great privilege, were in the drawing-room when he walked in. The boy and Throckmorton were such chums that there was no hope of getting Beverley off under a half-hour. He stood between Throckmorton's knees, perfectly happy to be with him, asking endless questions in a subdued whisper, and frowning out of his expressive eyes when Throckmorton wanted to know when his mother intended to cut off his long, yellow curls, so that he would be a real boy. Judith, sitting in her usual place, smiling and calm, soon settled that the winged word would be spoken that night. What better chance would Throckmorton have than when she should be gone to put the child to bed? She watched the tall clock on the high mantel with a fearful sinking of the heart, that drove the color out of her face. Presently it was half-past eight.

" Come, dearest," she said to the child.

Beverley held back.

" I don't want to go with you," he said. " I want to stay and play."

This childish treason to her at that moment was a stab. She got up with a smile, and opened her arms wide, her eyes shining under her straight brows.

"Come, dear little boy," she said.

The tone was so winning, so compelling, it went to the child's baby heart. He ran to his mother, with wide-open arms, who caught him and held him tight, covering his yellow mop of hair with kisses. Throckmorton looked on surprised and admiring. He had never seen Judith yield to anything emotional like that; she was laughing, blushing, and almost crying, as Beverley swung round her neck. And Throckmorton thought he had never seen her look so handsome as when she ran out of the room, carrying the child, who was a sturdy fellow, in her slender arms, her face deeply flushed. Throckmorton, as he held the door open for her to pass out, gave her a meaning smile; but Judith would not look at him. Up-stairs, Beverley was soon in his little bed. Judith, sitting on the floor, with both arms crossed on the crib, held one of the child's little warm hands in hers; the only real and comforting thing in life then seemed that childish hand.

"I will stay an hour," she said. "Mother will be vexed"—Mrs. Temple had old-fashioned ideas about leaving girls to themselves—"but he shall be happy. I will see that he has his chance." But, like Throckmorton himself, she feared for his happiness. Nobody knew better than she Jacqueline's weakness. She had, indeed, a sort of childish cleverness, which was, however, of no practical good to her; but then, as Judith remembered, Throckmorton's love could transform any woman. "Yes, I shall go through it," she thought, still kneeling on the carpet, and pressing her face to the child's in the crib; "Jacqueline will insist that I shall take off the mourning I wear for the man I never loved, at the wedding of the man I do love. If Throckmorton has any doubts or troubles with Jacqueline, he will certainly come to me. I will help him loyally, and he will need a friend. So far, though, from making me suffer more, the hope of befriending him is the only hope I have left in the world. I wonder how it feels to have one's heart aching and throbbing for another woman's husband—to be counting time by the times one sees him? For assuredly a few words spoken by a priest can not change this." She struck her heart. "And in everything Jacqueline will be blest above me. See how poor and straitened we are, and Jacqueline's life will be free from any care at all! However, to be loved by Throckmorton must mean to be rich and free and happy." And then, with a sort of clear-eyed despair, she began to look into the future, and see all of Jacqueline's and Throckmorton's life spread out before her. "And how unworthy she is!" she almost cried out aloud. She had now risen from the crib and was gazing out of the window at Millenbeck, that was plainly visible across the white stretch of snow between the two places. "Of course, she will love him—no woman could help that—but she can't understand him. She will not have the slightest respect for his habits, and will always be wanting him to alter them for her. She never will understand the reserves of Throckmorton's nature. She will tease him with questions. I would not care if Jacqueline were the one to be unhappy"—for so had pain changed her toward the child that had been to her almost as her own—" but in a few years the spell will have vanished. Throckmorton will find out that she is no companion for him. There can be no real companionship for any man like Throckmorton except with a woman somewhere near his own level—least of all now, when he is no longer young."

Then she came back and took the child out of his little bed, and held him in her arms and wept passionately over him. "At least I have you, darling; I have you!" she cried.

Down-stairs, in the drawing-room, Throckmorton made good use of his time. With very little apprenticeship, he knew how to make love so that any woman would listen to him.

He told Jacqueline that he loved her, in his own straightforward way; and Jacqueline, whose heart beat furiously, who was frightened and half rebellious, suffered him to get a few shy words from her. Throckmorton did not stoop to deny his age, but he condescended to apologize for it. In a dim and nebulous way Jacqueline understood the value of the man who thus offered his manly and unstained heart, but she felt acutely the want of common ground between them.

Throckmorton's love-making was not at all what simple Jacqueline fancied love-making to be. He did not protest—he did not talk poetry, nor abase himself; he made no exaggerated promises, nor did he sue for her love. At the first sign of yielding, he caught her to his heart and devoured her with kisses. Yet, when Jacqueline wanted to escape from him, he let her go. He would not keep her a moment unwillingly. Jacqueline did not understand this masterful way of doing things. She fancied that a lover meant a slave, and apparently Throckmorton considered a lover meant a master.

At the end of an hour, Judith returned to the room. Throckmorton was standing alone on the hearth-rug, in a meditative attitude. In his eyes, as they sought Judith's, was a kind of passionate, troubled joy; he doubted much, but he did not doubt his love for Jacqueline. He went forward and took Judith's hand, who lifted her eyes, strangely bright, to his face. She was smiling, too, and a faint blush glowed in her cheeks. There were no visible signs of tears.

"I am a happy man," said Throckmorton to her. "Jacqueline has promised to marry me."

His words were few, but Judith understood how much was conveyed in his sparing speech.

"I am happy, too," she returned, pressing his hand. "You deserve to be happy, and you will make—Jacqueline happy."

As she said this, she smiled tremulously. Throckmorton was too much absorbed to notice it.

"I will, so help me Heaven!" he answered.

In all his life before, Throckmorton did not remember ever to have felt the desire of communion about his inner thoughts and feelings. Was it because he himself had changed, or that Judith had that delicate and penetrating sympathy that drew him on to speak of what he had never spoken before? Anyway, he sat down by her, and talked to her a long time —talked of all the doubts and pitfalls that had beset him; his plans that Jacqueline might be happy; his confidence that Judith would be his strongest ally with Mrs. Temple, who was by no means a person to be counted on. She might object to Throckmorton's profession, to his being in what she continued to call the Yankee army, to his twenty-odd years' seniority, to his not being a member of the church; as like as not this was the very rock on which Throckmorton's ship would split. Judith, with the same heavenly smile, listened to him; she even made a little whole-

some fun of him ; and when he rose to go, Throckmorton felt, even at that time—and nobody could say that
he was a laggard in love—that he had gained something else besides Jacqueline, in the sweet friendship
of a woman like Judith.   He took her little hand, and
was about to raise it to his lips with tender respect,
when Judith, who had stood as still as a statue, suddenly snatched her hand away and gave Throckmorton a look so strange that he fancied her attacked by
a sudden prudery that was far from becoming to her
or complimentary to him. She slipped past him out
of the door, and he heard her light and rapid footfall
as she sped up the stairs. As there was nobody left
to entertain the newly accepted lover, he put on a bat-
tered blue cap, for which he had a sneaking affection,
and sometimes wore under cover of night, and let
himself out of the front door and went home across
the snow-covered fields, in an ecstasy.

Meanwhile, Jacqueline, as soon as she had heard
the bang of the hall-door after Throckmorton's
quick, soldierly step, stole out of her own room into
Judith's. In answer to her tap, Judith said, " Come
in."

Judith was seated before the old-fashioned dressing-table, her long, rich hair combed out, and was
making a pretense of brushing it, but occasionally
she would stop and gaze with strange eyes at her
own image in the glass. She rose when Jacqueline

entered, and took the girl in her arms as Jacqueline expected.

"Judith," Jacqueline said, "I am to be married to Major Throckmorton. I wonder what Freke will say!"

Judith held her off at arm's length, and looked down at her with eyes full of anger and disdain.

"Don't mention Throckmorton and Freke in the same breath, Jacqueline! What does Freke's opinion count for—what does Freke himself? It is an insult to Throckmorton to—to—"

"But, Judith," said Jacqueline, "Freke talks better than Major Throckmorton—"

"And plays and sings better. Ah! yes. At the same time, Throckmorton's little finger is worth more than a dozen Frekes."

"But it troubles me about Freke. I know Major Throckmorton can manage mamma—he can do anything with her now; and mamma, of course, will manage papa; but nobody can do anything with Freke."

"Jacqueline," said Judith, sitting down and taking Jacqueline in her lap, and changing all at once into the sweetest sisterly persuasion, "no other man on earth must matter to you now but Throckmorton. Let me tell you what a true marriage is. It is to love one man so much that with him is everything—without him is nothing. It is to study what he likes, and to like it too. It is to make his people your people, and his God your God. I think one need not know a great deal in order to be worthy of a man—for his love makes one worthy; but one should know a great deal in order that one may be creditable to him in the eyes of the world. Think how Throckmorton's wife should conduct herself; fancy how frightful the contrast, if she should not in some degree be like him! I tell you, Jacqueline, a woman to sustain Throckmorton's name and credit should be no ordinary woman. If you do not love him, if you do not make him proud and happy to say, 'This is my wife,' you deserve the worst fate—"

One of Jacqueline's fits of acuteness was on her. She looked hard at Judith.

"It seems to me, Judith, that you would make a much more fitting wife for him than I."

"Don't say that!" cried Judith, breathlessly. "Never, never say that again!"

Jacqueline, who knew well enough when to stop, suddenly halted. After a little pause, she began again:

" I know it will be dreadfully lonely at Millenbeck. Major Throckmorton loves to read, and I shall be a great interruption to his evenings. I don't know how I shall treat Jack. Don't you think it would be a good idea to get a companion—somebody who knows French?"

" You musn't think of such a thing. Good heavens! a companion, with Throckmorton? You can learn more from him in one week than all the governesses in creation can teach you."

"I didn't say governess," replied Jacqueline, with much dignity. "I said companion."

Then, as Jacqueline leaned her head on Judith's shoulder, Judith talked to her long and tenderly of the duty, the respect, the love she owed Throckmorton. Jacqueline listened attentively enough. When the little lecture was finished, Jacqueline whispered:

"I feel differently about it now. At first, I could only think of Millenbeck and a new piano, and doing just as I liked; but now, I will try—I will really try —not to vex Major Throckmorton."

That was all that could be got out of her.

Judith went with her to her room, and did not leave it until Jacqueline was tucked in her big fourposter, with the ghastly white tester and dimity hangings. Jacqueline kissed her a dozen times before she went away. Judith, too, was loath to leave. As long as she was doing something for Jacqueline, she was doing something for Throckmorton. For was not Jacqueline Throckmorton's now?

CHAPTER X.

Throckmorton, who was modesty and respectfulness itself in the presence of the woman he loved, was far from being nervous or diffident with her family. Next morning, having devoted all his smoking hours, which comprised the meditative part of his life, to Jacqueline, it occurred to him that he would have to tackle Mrs. Temple. That quite exhilarated and amused him. He knew well enough the Temple tradition, by which the master of the house was the nominal ruler, while the mistress was the actual ruler, and he also knew it would not be repeated at Millenbeck. He was indulgent toward women to the last degree—indulgent of their whims, their foibles, their faults and follies; but it was an indulgence, not a right. Jacqueline would find she had as much liberty as ever her mother had, but it would not be by virtue of a strong will over a weak one, but the free gift of affection. The major was not a person subject to petticoat government. In fact, he did not exactly know what it meant, and the woman did not live who could make him understand it. He rather looked forward to a brush with Mrs. Temple. He knew that Millenbeck and all the worldly advantages of the match would not influence her one iota. The conviction of this, of her entire disinterestedness and integrity, gave him pleasure. He knew that it was he —George Throckmorton—who would be weighed by Mrs. Temple, if not by Jacqueline ; this last an afterthought that came to him unpleasantly.

At breakfast, Throckmorton could not but feel a sense of triumph over Jack, who, unconscious of an impending step-mother, sat opposite his father, and talked in the free, frank way to him that Throckmorton had always encouraged. The young rascal would see, thought Throckmorton, with much satisfaction, that it was possible for a man of forty-four, with more gray hairs than black in his head, to hold his own even against a fellow as fascinating as Jack fancied himself to be. As luck would have it, Jack began to talk about the Temples.

"Major, don't you think Mrs. Beverley a very captivating woman? By George! she looks so pretty in that little black bonnet she wears, if it wasn't for interfering with you, sir, I would be tempted to go in and win myself."

The boy's impudence tickled Throckmorton. He could not but laugh in spite of himself at the idea— Jack, whom Judith treated very much as she did Beverley! But Jack evidently thought his father

13

had designs in that quarter, which misapprehension still further amused the major.

"Mrs. Beverley is indeed a charming woman," he answered.

Jack, however, became serious. In his heart he sincerely admired and revered Judith, and his blessing was ready whenever the major informed him that she would be the future mistress of Millenbeck.

"Mrs. Beverley has more sense and sprightliness than any other woman I know. If she could be persuaded to take off those black things she wraps herself up in, and be *herself*—which she isn't—I should think she would be—great fun."

Jack knew Throckmorton well enough to see that the shot had not hit the bull's-eye. Throckmorton was too ready to praise, discuss, and admire Judith. "What does the old fellow want, anyway?" thought Jack to himself, "if Mrs. Beverley doesn't suit him?" So then and there he entered into a disquisition on women in general and Judith Temple in particular, which caused Throckmorton to ask sarcastically:

"May I ask where you acquired your knowledge of the sex?"

"It would be impossible to associate with you, major, without learning much about them," answered Jack, "you are such a favorite with the ladies. You are a very handsome man, you know, sir—"

Here Throckmorton smiled.

" For your age, that is—"

The major frowned slightly.

" They all like you—even little Jacqueline."

To save his life, Throckmorton could not prevent a flush from rising to his face, which he hated; for the emotions of forty-four are infinitely ridiculous to twenty-two. But it was just as well to have things settled then. A queer glitter, too, showing understanding, had come into Jack's eyes.

" I may say to you," said Throckmorton, after a little pause, " that you would do well to be guarded in your references to Miss Temple. She has promised to marry me."

They had finished breakfast by that time, and were about to separate for the morning. Jack got up, and Throckmorton noticed his handsome young face paled a little. He had not escaped Jacqueline's spell any more than Throckmorton and Freke; but it was not an overmastering spell, and in his heart he loved his father with a manly affection that he never thought of putting into words, but which was stronger than any other emotion. He walked up to Throckmorton and shook hands with him, laughing, but with a nervousness in his laugh, an abashed look on his face, that told the whole story to Throckmorton's keen eye.

" I congratulate you, sir. She is a—a—beautiful girl—and—and—I hope you will be very happy."

" I think I shall," gravely responded Throckmorton. " I can not explain things to you that you can only learn by experience. I have not forgotten—I never can forget—your mother, who made my happiness during our short married life. I have been twenty years recovering from the pain of losing her enough to think of replacing her."

Jack had recovered himself a little while Throckmorton was speaking. The wound was only skin-deep with him.

" And is it to be immediately? " he asked.

" As soon as I can bring it about," replied Throckmorton; " but I have got to bring my dear, obstinate old friend Mrs. Temple round first "—here both of them laughed—" so you will see the necessity of keeping the affair absolutely quiet."

" You had better join the church, sir," said Jack, who was himself again. " That will be your best card to play."

" Very likely," responded Throckmorton, good-humoredly, " but I think I can win the game even without that."

In the bright morning sunshine out-of-doors Throckmorton began to take heart of grace about Jacqueline. Jack did not seem to think it such an unequal match. With love and patience what might not be done with any woman? Throckmorton began to whistle jovially. He went out to the stable lot to take a look at the horses, as he did every morning. Old Tartar, that had carried him during four years' warfare, and was now honorably retired and turned out to grass, came toward him whinnying and ready for his morning pat—all horses, dogs, and children loved Throckmorton. Tartar, who had lost an eye in the service of his country, turned his one remaining orb around so as to see Throckmorton, and rubbed his noble old head against his master's knee. Throckmorton noticed him more than usual—his heart was more tender and pitiful to all creatures that morning.

Toward noon he went over to Barn Elms. The morning was intensely cold, though clear, and the fields and fences and hedges were still white with snow. For the first time Throckmorton noticed the extreme shabbiness of Barn Elms.

"Dear little girl," he said, "she shall have a different home from this."

When he reached the house he was ushered straight into the plain, old-fashioned drawing-room, and in a moment Mrs. Temple appeared, perfectly unsuspicious of what had happened or what was going to happen.

"Good - morning," cried Throckmorton—something in his tone showing triumph and happiness, and in his dark face was a fine red color. "Mrs. Temple, I came over to make a clean breast to you this morning!"

"About what?" asked Mrs. Temple, sedately.

They were both standing up, facing each other.

"About—Jacqueline." Throckmorton spoke her name almost reverently.

A sudden light broke in upon Mrs. Temple. She grew perfectly rigid.

"Jacqueline!" she said, in an undescribable tone.

"Yes, Jacqueline," answered Throckmorton, coolly. "I love her—I think she loves me—and she has promised to marry me. You may depend upon it, I shall make her keep her promise."

Mrs. Temple remained perfectly silent for two or three minutes before recovering her self-possession.

"You are forty-four years old, George Throckmorton."

"I know it. I never lied about my age to anybody."

"You are in the Yankee army!"

"Yes, I am," responded Throckmorton, boldly, "and I shall stay in it."

"And my daughter—"

"For God's sake, Mrs. Temple, let us talk reasonably together! I am not going to take your daughter campaigning."

"It isn't that I mean, George Throckmorton. I mean the uniform you wear—"

"Is the best in the world! Now, my dear old friend—the best friend I ever had—I want your consent and General Temple's—I want it very much, but it isn't absolutely necessary. Jacqueline and I are to be married. We settled that last night."

Mrs. Temple, with whom nobody had ever taken a bold stand before, looked perfectly aghast. Throckmorton saw his advantage, and pressed it hard.

"Have you any objection to me personally? Am I a drunkard, or a gambler, or a cad?"

"You are not," responded Mrs. Temple, after a pause. "I think you are, on the whole, except my husband and my dead son, as much of a man—"

Throckmorton took her hand and pressed it.

"Thank you! thank you!" His gratitude spoke more in his tone than his words. "And now," he cheerfully remarked, "that you have given your consent—"

Mrs. Temple had given no such thing. Nevertheless, within half an hour she had yielded to the inevitable. She had met a stronger will than her own, and was completely vanquished.

Jacqueline came down, and Throckmorton had a half-hour of rapture not unmixed with pain. If only his reason could be silenced, how happy he would have been! He did not see Judith; he had quite forgotten her for the time.

CHAPTER XI.

Throckmorton, who was nothing if not prompt,
had infused so much life and spirit into his love-affair
that at the end of a week it was settled that the wedding should take place the last of February—only a
month off. Jacqueline's trousseau was not likely to
be imposing, and the few, feeble reasons which Mrs.
Temple urged for delay were swept away by Throckmorton's impetuosity. It was not the custom in that
part of the world for engagements to be formally
announced; on the contrary, it was in order to deny
them up to the very last moment, and to regard them
as something surreptitious and to be hid under a
bushel. General Temple had magniloquently given
his consent, when Throckmorton went through the
form of asking it. Mrs. Temple still shook her head
gravely over the matter, particularly over the brief
engagement, which was quite opposed to the leisurely
way in which engagements were usually conducted in
her experience; but Throckmorton seemed to have
mastered everybody at Barn Elms. For himself that
period was one of deep joy, and yet full of harassing

doubts. The more he studied Jacqueline under her
new aspects, the stranger things became. It cut him
to see how little real consequence either her mother
or her father attached to her. Judith seemed to be
the only person who was concerned to make Jacqueline love him; to regard the girl as a woman, and not
as a child. For Jacqueline herself, she was as change-
able as the weather. Had she been steadily indifferent to him, Throckmorton would have thought nothing necessary but a manly fight to win her; but
sometimes she showed devoted fondness for him, and,
without rhyme or reason, she would change into the
coldest indifference or teasing irritability. Throckmorton told himself it was the coyness and fickleness
of a young girl in love; but sometimes a hateful suspicion overcame him that there was in Jacqueline an
innate levity and inconstancy that went to the root of
her nature. The evident delight she took in the luxury and pleasures that were to be hers—the horses,
carriages, pianos, and flowers at Millenbeck — was
rather that of a child dazzled with the fineries of life.
Her love for them was so unthinking and uncalculat-
ing that it did not shock Throckmorton; yet how
could he, with his knowledge, his experience of men,
women, and things, help seeing the differences between them — differences that, had his infatuation
been less complete, would have appalled him? As it
was, just as Judith had predicted to herself, he often

came to her for sympathy and encouragement—not
expressed in words, but in the subtile understanding
between them.   Judith always spoke in praise of Jacqueline; she artfully managed to show Throckmorton
the best of her.   But for Judith the marriage could
never have been hastened on, as Throckmorton desired; for, as soon as she found out Throckmorton's
wish, she went to work on Jacqueline's trousseau with
a sort of desperate energy that carried things through.
Jacqueline could have no fine silk gowns, but she was
to have piles of the daintiest linen, of which the ma-
terial cost little, but the beautiful handiwork lavished
upon it by Judith was worth a little fortune.   Jacqueline herself, spurred on by Judith's industry, sewed
steadily.   As for Judith, the fever of working for
Jacqueline seized her, and never abated.   She even
neglected her child for Jacqueline, until Mrs. Temple,
with stern disapproval, took her to task about it.   Judith, blushing and conscience-stricken, owned to her
fault, although nobody could accuse her of lacking
love for the child.   But still she managed to sew
for Jacqueline, sitting up secretly by night, and
with a pale, fixed face — stitch, stitch, stitching!
Jacqueline could not understand it at all; and when
she asked Judith about it once, she was so suddenly and strangely agitated that Jacqueline, a little
frightened, dropped the subject at once.   But, in
truth, this was to Judith a time of new, strange, and

terrible grief and disappointment. How she had ever permitted Throckmorton to take up her whole heart and mind she did not know any more than she could fathom now how she ever came to mistake an early and immature fancy for a deep and abiding passion, and had suffered herself to be married to Beverley Temple. She endured agonies of remorse for that, and yet hourly excused herself to herself. "How could I know," she asked herself in those long hours of the night when men and women come face to face with their sorrows. But all her remorse was for Beverley. As for the hatred she ought to feel for Throckmorton as the slayer of her husband, she had come to laugh it to scorn in her own mind. But, like all true women, she respected the world—the narrow circle which constituted her world—and she felt oppressed with shame at the idea that the whole story might all one day come out, and then what would they think of her? What would they do to her? She could not say, as she had once said, "I do not believe it." She had heard it from Throckmorton's own mouth. She would have to say, "I knew it, and went to his house, and continued to be friendly with him, and spoke no word when he wished to marry Beverley's sister." She could not divine the reason of Freke's silence, but, torn and harassed and wearied with struggles of heart and conscience, she simply yielded to the fatalism of the wretched, and let things drift. Some-

times in her own room, after she had spent the evening with Throckmorton and Jacqueline, seeing clearly
under his perfectly self-possessed exterior his infatuation for Jacqueline, she would be wroth with him.
Judith, the most modest and unassuming of women,
would say to herself, with scorn of Throckmorton:
"How blind he is! To throw away on Jacqueline,
who in her turn throws it to the wind, what would
make me the proudest creature under heaven! And
am I unworthy of his love, or less worthy than Jacqueline?" To which her keen perceptions would
answer rebelliously, "No, I am more worthy in every
way." She would examine her face carefully in the
glass, holding the candle first one side, then the other.
"This, then, is the face that Throckmorton is indifferent to. It is not babyish, like Jacqueline's; there
are no dimples, but—" Then the grotesqueness of it
all would strike her, and even make her laugh. The
fiercest pain, the most devouring jealousy never wrung
from her the faintest admission that there was anything to be ashamed of in cherishing silently a profound and sacred love for Throckmorton. He was
worthy of it, she thought, proudly. Toward him her
manner never changed—she was mistress of some of
the nobler arts of deception—but sometimes, although
working for Jacqueline, and tending her affectionately, she would be angry and disdainful because Jacqueline did not always render to Throckmorton his

due. She almost laughed to herself when she compared this horror of pain and grief which she now endured with the shock and pity of Beverley's death. She remembered that the joy her child gave her seemed almost wicked in its intensity at that time. What passions of happiness were hers when she would rise stealthily in the night and, taking him from his little crib, would hold him to her throbbing heart; and often, from the next room, she could hear Mrs. Temple pacing her floor, and could imagine the silent wringing of the hands and all the unspoken agonies the elder mother endured for *her* child! Then she would swiftly and guiltily put the child back in his cradle, and, with remorse and self-denial, lie near him without touching him. Often in that long-past time, when she met him in his nurse's arms, she would fly toward him with a merry, dancing step, laughing all the time—she was so happy, so proud to have him — and, looking up, would catch Mrs. Temple's eyes fixed on her with a still reproach she understood well enough. Then she would turn away from him, and, sitting down by Mrs. Temple, would not even let her eyes wander to the child, and would remain silent and unanswering to his baby wail.

But in this first real passion of her life, the child, much as she adored him, was secondary. He was her comfort—she would not, if she could, have let him out of her sight or out of her arms—but he could no more make her forget Throckmorton than anything else; he could only soften the intolerable ache a little, when he leaned his curly head upon her breast; and as for that easy and conventional phrase, the goodness of God, and that ready consolation that had seemed so apt at the time of Beverley's death, she began to substitute, for the mild and merciful Divinity, a merciless and relentless Jehovah, who had condemned her to suffer forever, and who would not be appeased.

At first, the secret of the engagement was well kept. Only Jack Throckmorton, who behaved beautifully about it, and Freke, knew of the impending wedding. Freke's behavior was singular, not to say mysterious. He was so cool and unconcerned that Jacqueline was furiously piqued, and could scarcely keep her mind off her grievance against him for not taking her engagement more to heart, even when Throckmorton was with her. Freke's congratulations were quite perfunctory—as unlike Jack Throckmorton's whole-souled good wishes as could be imagined. One morning, soon after the news had been confided to Freke, he came into the dining-room, where Judith was sewing, with Jacqueline, also sewing, sitting demurely by her side.

"Making wedding finery, eh?" was Freke's remark as he seated himself.

"Yes," answered Judith, quietly, without laying down her work.

"I want to see how much Jacqueline will be changed by marriage—You mustn't flirt with Jack, little Jacky."

He said this quite good-humoredly, and Jacqueline turned a warm color.

"And don't let me see you running after the chickens, as I saw you the other day. That wouldn't be dignified, you know; it would make Major Throckmorton ridiculous. You must do all you can to keep the difference in your ages from becoming too obvious."

Judith felt a rising indignation. Jacqueline's head was bent lower. She dreaded and feared that people would tease her about Throckmorton's age. Freke saw in a moment how it was with her, and kept it up.

"Throckmorton is sensible in one way. His hair is plentifully sprinkled with gray, but he doesn't use art to conceal it."

"I do not think forty-four is old," said Judith, indignant at Jacqueline's tame submission to this sort of talk. "I think, with most women, Major Throckmorton would have the advantage over younger men."

As soon as she said this, she repented. Freke glanced at her with a look so amused and so exasperating that she could have burst into tears of shame on the spot.

"Come, Jacqueline," cried Freke, rising, "let us go for a walk. I don't know whether Throckmorton will permit this after you are married. Marriage, my dear little girl, is more of a yoke than a garland. I am well out of mine, thank Heaven!"

Judith cast a beseeching look at Jacqueline, but Freke had fixed his eyes commandingly on her. That was enough. Jacqueline rose and went out to get her hat.

Judith sat quite silent. She rarely spoke to Freke when she could help it.

"What do you think of this ridiculous marriage?" he asked.

"I, at least, don't think it ridiculous. There are incongruities much worse than a difference in age."

"Yes, I understand," assented Freke, with meaning. "I have found it so. If I were as free as Throckmorton, though, I would be in no hurry to put my head in the noose."

"You said just now you were free."

"Did I? Well, in fact I am free in some States and not in others. You people down here seem to regard me as an escaped felon. That sort of thing doesn't exist any longer in civilized communities." Judith made no reply. She hated Freke with a kind of unreasoning hatred that put a guard upon her lips,

lest she should be tempted to say something rash.
And in a moment Jacqueline was back, and, with a
defiant look at Judith, went off with Freke. Freke
caught a glance from Judith's eyes as they went out.
The fact that it expressed great anger and contempt
for him did not make him overlook that her eyes were
remarkably full of fire and the turn of her head something beautiful.

"Judith is a thoroughbred—there's no mistake
about that," he said to Jacqueline—and kept on talking about Judith until he reduced Jacqueline to a
jealous silence, and almost to tears—when a few
words of praise restored her to complete good humor.
Throckmorton never played off on her like this—it
was quite opposed to his directness and straightfor-
wardness.

Freke was more constantly at Barn Elms than
ever before. It often occurred to Judith that he took
pains to keep secret from Throckmorton all the time
he passed with Jacqueline. Sometimes she even suspected that Jacqueline had some share in keeping
Throckmorton in the dark, so constant was Freke's
presence when Throckmorton was absent, and so unvarying was his absence when Throckmorton was
present.

After a while, though, a hint of the engagement
got abroad in the county, and the people generally,
who had never relaxed in the slightest degree their
14

forbidding exterior to Throckmorton, now somewhat included the Temples in the ban. Throckmorton, engrossed with his own affairs, had ceased to care for himself, being quite content with the few people around him who took him into their homes. But he felt it acutely for Jacqueline, who told him, with childish cruelty, without thinking of the pang she inflicted, of the strange coolness that all at once seemed to have fallen between her and her acquaintances. And Judith was sure that Freke put notions of that kind and of every kind into the girl's head. Once, after one of Freke's daily visits—for, if anything, he came oftener than Throckmorton—Jacqueline said, quite disconsolately, to Judith :

"Freke says I shall never have any more girl friends after I am married. Throckmorton is too old ; and, besides, the people in this county will never, never really recognize him."

"This county is not all the world—and, Jacqueline, pray, pray don't listen to anything Freke has to say."

"I know you don't like Freke."

"I hate him."

Judith, when she said this, looked so handsome and animated that Throckmorton, entering at that moment, paid her a pretty compliment, which she received first with so much confusion and then with so much haughtiness that Throckmorton was as completely puzzled as the night he offered to kiss her hand, and concluded that Judith was as freakish as all women are.

Among the smaller irritations which Throckmorton had to bear, at this strange time, was Jack's sly rallying. Jack assumed his father to be a love-sick octogenarian. Anything less love-sick than Throckmorton's simple and manly affection, or less suggestive of age than his alert and vigorous maturity, would be hard to find. But Jack had always possessed the power of tormenting his father where women were concerned—the natural penalty, perhaps, of having a son so little younger than himself. Jack felt infinite respect for Jacqueline, and never once indulged in a joke calculated to really rouse Throckmorton; but some occasions were too good for him to spare the major. Such conversations as these were frequent:

"Major, are you going over to Barn Elms this evening?"

"No, I was there this morning."

"I understand, sir, that two visits a day, when the young lady is in the immediate neighborhood, is the regulation thing."

"You are at liberty to understand what you please. With youngsters like yourself, probably three visits would hardly be enough."

"I have been told that these things affect all ages alike."

Throckmorton scowled, but scowls were wasted on Jack, whose particular object was to put the major in a bad humor; in which design, however, he rarely succeeded.

In spite of the silence that had been maintained by the Barn Elms people regarding the engagement, Mrs. Sherrard, who had what is vulgarly called a nose for news, found it out by some occult means, and Throckmorton was held up in the road, as he was riding peacefully along, to answer her inquiries.

"I think you and Jacky Temple are going to be married soon, from what I hear," was her first aggressive remark, putting her head out of the window of her ramshackly old carriage.

"Do you?" responded Throckmorton, with laughing eyes. "You must think me a deuced lucky fellow."

Mrs. Sherrard did not speak for a moment or two, and a cold chill struck Throckmorton, while the laugh died out of his eyes.

"That's as may be," she replied, diplomatically; "but the idea of your marching about, thinking you are deceiving *me!*"

"I am young and bashful, you know, Mrs. Sherrard."

"You are not young, but you are younger than you are bashful. You always were one of those quiet dare-devils—the worst kind, to my mind."

"Thank you, ma'am."

"And Jane Temple—ha! ha!"

Throckmorton joined in Mrs. Sherrard's fine, ringing laugh.

"A Yankee son-in-law!" screamed Mrs. Sherrard, still laughing; then she became grave, and beckoned Throckmorton, sitting straight and square in his saddle, to come closer, so the black driver could not hear. "Jane, you know," she said, confidentially, "was always daft about the war after Beverley's death; and, let me tell you, Beverley was a fine, tall, handsome, brave, silly, commonplace fellow as ever lived. Judith has more brains and wit than all the Temple men put together, and most of the women. Hers was as clear a case of a winged thing that can soar married to a Muscovy drake as ever I saw. Luckily, she hadn't an opportunity to wake up to it fully, before he was killed; and then, just like a hot-headed, romantic thing, she wrapped herself in crape, and has given up her whole life to Jane and General Temple, and Jacky."

Throckmorton felt a certain restraint in speaking of Judith to Mrs. Sherrard, who had assumed that it was his duty to fall in love with Judith instead of Jacqueline. So he flicked a fly off his horse's neck and remained silent.

"I do wish," resumed Mrs. Sherrard, pettishly, "that Jane Temple would act like a woman of sense, and send for me over to Barn Elms, and show me Jacky's wedding things."

"Very inconsiderate of Jane, I am sure. If it would relieve your mind at all, you might come to Millenbeck, and I would be delighted to show you my coats and trousers. They are very few. I always have a plenty of shirts and stockings, but my outside wardrobe isn't imposing."

"I don't take the slightest interest in your clothes. You don't dress half as much as Jack does."

"Of course not; I can't afford it."

"One thing is certain. If you have any sort of a wedding at Barn Elms, they'll have to send over and borrow my teaspoons. There hasn't been a party at Barn Elms for forty years, that they haven't done it, and I always borrow Jane Temple's salad-bowl and punch-ladles whenever I have company."

"I don't think there will be any wedding feast there," answered Throckmorton.

"Jacky wants one, *I* know," said Mrs. Sherrard, very knowingly. "Jacky loves a racket."

"Quite naturally—at her age."

"Oh, yes, of course—her age, as you say. I shall tell Edmund Morford to pay you a pastoral visit, as he always does upon the eve of marriages, to instruct you in the duties of the married state."

"Then I shall tell Edmund Morford that I know considerably more about my duties in the premises than he does; and I'll shut him up before he has opened his mouth, as Sweeney would say."

"If anybody *could* shut my nephew up, I believe it is you, George Throckmorton. Has Jane Temple suggested that you should join the church yet?"

"She suggests it to me every time I go to Barn Elms, and whenever I go off for a lover's stroll with Jacqueline, Mrs. Temple tells me I ought to go home and seek salvation."

"And do you mind her?" asked Mrs. Sherrard, quite gravely; at which Throckmorton gave her a look that was dangerously near a wink.

Mrs. Sherrard drove off, triumphant. She had got at the whole thing, in spite of Jane Temple.

The wedding preparations went bravely along; carried on chiefly by Judith. Jacqueline had set her heart on a white silk wedding dress, which for a time eclipsed everything else on her horizon. Mrs. Temple declared that it was extravagant, but Judith, by keen persuasion, succeeded in getting the wedding-gown. She made it with her own hands, and across the front she designed a beautiful and intricate embroidery, to be worked by her.

"Judith, you will kill yourself over that wedding-gown," Mrs. Temple once remarked. "You have drawn such an elaborate design upon it that you will have to work night and day to get it finished."

"I shall simply have to be a little more industrious than usual," replied Judith, with the deep flush that now alternated with extreme paleness.

Jacqueline herself was deeply interested in this gown; more so than in any particular of the coming wedding. Judith had marked off for herself a certain task of work each day upon the embroidery of the gown. Every night, when she stopped at the end of her task, it was as if another stone were laid upon her heart. Throckmorton had noticed her industry, and had admired her handiwork, which she proudly showed him.

"But you are getting white and thin over it," he said. "Wouldn't it be better that Jacqueline should not have such a beautiful frock, than for you to work yourself ill over it? I have a great mind to speak to Mrs. Temple about it."

"No, no, pray don't!" cried Judith, with a kind of breathless eagerness. "It would break my heart not to finish it."

Throckmorton looked at her closely. She was not given to that kind of talk. But suddenly she began telling him a funny story of Mrs. Sherrard coming over to pump Mrs. Temple about the coming event, and then she laughed and made him laugh too. Walking back home that night, he found himself speculating on this development of fun and merriment in Judith—a thing she had always suppressed and kept in abeyance until lately.

"Certainly she is in better spirits—more like what one can see her natural self is in the last month or two," he thought; and then he began to think what a very sweet and natural woman she was, and to hope that, when Jacqueline was her age, she would have developed into something like Judith. But he never liked to look very far into the future with Jacqueline.

As the time drew nearer for the wedding, Freke's continued presence at Barn Elms became more marked. He did not avoid Throckmorton any longer, who thought no more of it than he did of Jack's frequent visits. Jack had quite got over any chagrin or disappointment he might have felt, and was kindness and attention itself to Jacqueline. Throckmorton sometimes felt annoyed and discouraged at seeing how much more Jacqueline had in common with Jack than with himself. They were on the terms of a brother and sister—Jack teasing and joking, yet unvaryingly kind to her, and Jacqueline always overflowing with talk to him, while with Throckmorton she was sometimes at a loss for words. But one glance from her dark eyes—that peculiar witching glance that had fixed Throckmorton's attention on her that very first Sunday in church—could always make amends to him. As for Freke, he came and went with his violin under his arm, and nobody attached any importance to him except Judith, who honored him with the same still, guarded ill-will that Freke perfectly recognized, and did not apparently trouble himself about. His eternal presence in the house was a nightmare to Judith. She wondered if he would keep on that way after Jacqueline was gone —when Jacqueline was mistress of Millenbeck; but she could not dwell on that without a tightening at her heart. At all events, it would soon be over.

Mrs. Temple had at last got interested in the wedding preparations, and everything was going on famously until about two weeks before the wedding, when one day General Temple got a letter. There was to be a reunion of Beverley's old command at Richmond, and it was desired that the Temple family should attend.

Such a request was sacred in the eyes of General and Mrs. Temple. It was at once decided that General Temple must go, and he insisted that Mrs. Temple should go also. She was only too willing. Inconvenient as it might otherwise be to leave home, the idea of having Beverley talked of, eulogized, re-membered, was too near the idolatrous mother's heart to be foregone. The invitation also included Judith, but it was clearly impossible for both Judith and Mrs. Temple to leave Barn Elms at the same time just then; so it was quickly settled, to Judith's infinite relief, that Mrs. Temple should be the one to go. Mrs. Temple was helped to a decision by the reflection that Judith, being young and handsome, it was not impossible that some miscreant might suggest the possibility of her marrying again; and, without uttering this impious thought, it had its influence upon her. So it was fixed that, within a day or two, they were to start, and would be gone probably four days. Throckmorton was vexed at the decision—vexed at the entire readiness to sacrifice Jacqueline's convenience to that of the dead and gone Beverley. But he wisely said nothing; in a little while Jacqueline would have some one that would always consider her first But suddenly Jacqueline raised a tempest by declaring that she wanted to go with her father and mother as far as a certain station on the railroad, near Richmond, and thence to pay a visit to her Aunt Susan Steptoe. Now, Jacqueline had never showed the slightest fondness for this Aunt Steptoe, and, in fact, was singularly lacking in family affection, after the Virginia pattern, which takes in a whole family connection. Consequently, the notion was the more remarkable. When it was first broached, it was simply pooh-poohed by the general, and calmly ignored by Mrs. Temple. Judith looked at her with reproachful eyes.

"You know, Jacqueline, there is no earthly reason for such a whim; and I am sure Major Throckmorton would not like it."

"It's of no consequence what Major Throckmorton thinks about it!" cried Jacqueline, unterrified by a warning light in Judith's eye—it always made Judith angry when Jacqueline spoke slightingly of Throckmorton.

But Jacqueline held to her notion with the most singular and startling pertinacity. Usually a word or two from Judith would bring her back to the basis of common sense; but in this case, nothing Judith could say would alter Jacqueline's determination. She was tired of wedding clothes—tired of Barn Elms—tired of everybody; in fact, she made no secret to Judith of being tired of Throckmorton, and wanting to escape from him for a time, if only for four days. She forced her mother to listen to her, and would take no denial. At last she hit upon the argument to move Mrs. Temple. It was the last request she had to make until she was married, and, if Mrs. Temple could do so much for the dead Beverley, she certainly could not refuse this trifling request from the living Jacqueline. Mrs. Temple turned pale at this; and she faltered out that, childish and unreasonable as the scheme was, she would agree—provided Throckmorton gave his consent.

That night, when Throckmorton came for his usual visit, Jacqueline met him at the hall-door with a tenderness that surprised and charmed him. It was so sweet, he could hardly believe it to be true. But, before the evening was over, Jacqueline demanded payment in the shape of his consent that she should pay this little visit to her Aunt Susan.

"Damn Aunt Susan!" was Throckmorton's inward remark at this; and he managed to convey practically the same idea to Jacqueline. But it did no good. Jacqueline had the scheme in her head, and it must be carried out. It was in vain that Throckmorton reasoned gently with her. He had often heard that weak women were the most intractable in the world, and the recollection made him wince when he saw how dense this lovely young creature was to common sense. But she was so ineffably pretty—she leaned her bright head on his shoulder and pleaded—and, of course, after a while, Throckmorton yielded, ostensibly because Jacqueline asked him so sweetly, but really because she was utterly impervious to reason.

When the consent was at last wheedled out of him, Throckmorton felt sore at heart and humiliated. He also felt, for a brave man, a little frightened. How often was this sort of thing going to happen? It was true that, after he was married, he could use his authority as Jacqueline's husband to prevent her from doing anything particularly foolish, but it did not please him that he should rule his wife as if she were a child. Jacqueline saw nothing of Throckmorton's secret dissatisfaction; but Judith, with the clairvoyance of love, saw it in an instant. For the first time in her life, she followed him out into the hall, where he was getting into his overcoat, with rather a black countenance.

"Don't be troubled about it," she said, in her charming way. "She is so young—she will learn so much from you!"

Throckmorton took Judith's hand in his. She made no resistance this time—that quick inner sense told her instinctively that there was something comforting to him in her gentle and womanly clasp. He looked at her with a somber expression on his face that gradually lightened.

"Do you think she will ever be different?"

"Yes," cried Judith, gayly. "How perfectly ignorant you are of love! I declare you are worse than Jacqueline. It's the greatest reformer in the world—the most cunning teacher as well. It will teach Jacqueline all she ought to know; but it can't do it at once."

"But does she love me?" asked Throckmorton, smiling a little.

"How could she help it?" answered Judith, turning her head archly, and implying that Throckmorton considered himself a lady-killer — which made him laugh, and sent him off home in a little better humor with the world and himself.

Meanwhile, back in the drawing-room, Jacqueline was having a conversation with Simon Peter, who was raking down the fire for the night. General and Mrs.

Temple had left the room. Usually Jacqueline slipped off to bed an hour before they did; but to-night she lingered, standing over the fire with one little foot on the brass fender.

"How does it look to-night, Uncle Simon?" she asked, meaning how did the sky look, and what were the chances for good weather.

"Hit looks mighty cu'rus to me, Miss Jacky," answered Simon Peter, in a queer sort of a voice that made Jacqueline stare at him. "I seed two tuckey-buzzards flyin' ober de house tog'er'r—and dat's a sign—"

"A sign of what?"

"A sign 'tain' gwi' be no weddin' at Barn Elms dis year."

Jacqueline turned a little pale. It had not been a great many years since she had fully believed every one of Simon Peter's signs and omens; and even now, his solemn prophecies sent a chill to her childish heart.

"An'," continued Simon Peter, advancing and raising a prophetic forefinger, "dis heah night I done heah de owls hootin' 'Tu-whoo, tu-whoo, tu-whoo!'—three times, dat ar way—dat doan' means nuttin' but a funeral, when owls hoots dat away."

Jacqueline shuddered.

"O Uncle Simon, hush!"

"I tole you kase you arsk me," replied Simon

Peter, stolidly; and at that moment Delilah came in.

"O mammy," cried Jacqueline, fairly bursting into tears, "you don't know what awful signs and things Uncle Simon has been seeing—funerals, and buzzards, and no wedding!"

"He have, have he!" snapped Delilah, with wrath and menace. "Simon Peter, he su't'ny is de foolishest nigger I ever seed. He ain't never got 'ligion good; he allus wuz a blackslider, an' heah he come skeerin' my little missy ter def wid he buzzards an' he things!"

Simon Peter, who bore this marital assault with meekness, copied from General Temple, only remarked sheepishly:

"I done see de signs; an', Miss Jacky, she arsk me, an' I done tole her 'bout de two buzzards."

"Wid de tails tied tog'er'r, I reckon!" answered Delilah, with withering sarcasm; "an' maybe dey wuz gwi' fly ter Doc Wortley's ter see ef anybody gwi' die soon.—Doan' you min' Simon Peter, honey; jes' come wid mammy up-sty'ars an' she holp you to ondress an' put you in yo' bed."

Jacqueline went off, and in half an hour was tucked snugly in the great four-poster. But she would not let Delilah leave her. She kept her pulling the window-curtains this way and that, then raking down the fire because the light from the blazing logs

hurt her eyes, and then stirring the flames into a blaze
so that she might see the shadows on the wall.   At
last, however, Delilah got out, Jacqueline calling after
her disconsolately:

"O mammy, do you believe in the two buzzards
flying—"

"You jes' shet dat little mouf, an' go ter sleep,
honey," was Delilah's sensible reply, as she went
out.

The next day the whole party got off, General Temple leaving directions enough behind him to last if he
were going to Turkey instead of to Richmond.   Jacqueline at the last seemed loath to part from Judith.
She said good-by half a dozen times, and wept a little
at parting.   There would be no need of letters, as
they would only be gone four days.   Jacqueline was
to stop off at the station, and join her father and
mother there on their return from Richmond, getting
home ten days before the wedding.   There was some
talk of asking Mrs. Sherrard to come over and stay with
Judith during the absence of General and Mrs. Temple, but Judith protested.   With her child she would
not suffer for company, and the work on Jacqueline's
wedding-dress would keep her busily employed, while
Delilah and Simon Peter were protection enough for
her at night.   Besides this, Throckmorton and Jack
would be over every day to look after her.   When it
was all arranged, Judith felt a sensation of gladness.

15

She would have four days in which she would not be compelled to play her silent and desperate part. She could weep all night without the fear that Mrs. Temple's clear eyes would notice how pale and worn she was in the morning; she could relax a little the continual tension on her nerves, her feelings, her expression. So, when they were gone, she came back into the lonely house, and, leaving Beverley with his mammy, went up to her own room, and taking out the white silk wedding-gown went to work on it with a pale, unhappy face; she had dared not show an unhappy face before.

The day passed quickly enough, and the short winter afternoon closed in. Judith would no longer take time for her usual afternoon walk; every moment must be devoted to Jacqueline's gown. About eight o'clock, as she sat in the drawing-room, stitching away, while overhead in her own room Delilah watched the little Beverley as he slept, she heard Throckmorton's step upon the porch. As she heard it, she gave a slight start, and put her hand on her heart—something she always felt an involuntary inclination to do, and which she had to watch herself to prevent. Throckmorton came in, and greeted her with his usual graceful kindness.

"I thought I would come over and see that nobody stole you and Beverley," he said.

"There's no danger for me," answered Judith;

"but for a beautiful boy like my boy—why, he's always in danger of being stolen."

Throckmorton scoffed at this.

In five minutes they were seated together, having the first real *tête-à-tête* of their lives. Judith sat under the mellow gleam of the tall, old-fashioned lamp, the light falling on her chestnut hair and black dress and the billowy expanse of white silk spread over her lap, making high white lights and rich shadows. Throckmorton had often admired her as she sewed. Sewing was a peculiarly gracious and feminine employment, he thought, and Judith's sewing, when he saw it, was always something artistic like what she was now doing. Throckmorton lay back in one corner of the great sofa, his feet stretched out to the fire. They talked occasionally, but there were long stretches of silence when the only sound was the crackling of the wood-fire and the dropping of the embers. Yet the unity was complete; there is no companionship so real as that which admits of perfect silence. Throckmorton, on the whole, though, talked more than usual. Something in Judith always inspired him to speak of things that he rarely mentioned at all. They talked a little of Jacqueline, but there were innumerable subjects on which they found themselves in sympathy. The evening passed quickly for both. When Throckmorton had gone, and the house was shut up for the night, Judith felt that she had passed the evening in a sort of shadowy happiness; it would have been happiness itself, except that in ten days more it would be wrong even to think of Throckmorton.

Two days more passed. Every evening Throckmorton found himself making his way toward Barn Elms. Each evening passed in the same quiet, simple fashion, but yet there was something different to Throckmorton from any evenings he had ever spent in his life. As for Judith, after the first one, she began to look forward with feverish eagerness to the evening. She lived all day in expectation of that two hours' talk with Throckmorton. She dressed for him; she hurried little Beverley to bed that she might be ready for him. Her eyes assumed a new brilliancy, and she became handsomer day by day.

On the day that the general and Mrs. Temple were to leave for home a letter arrived from Mrs. Temple. The general had been seized with an acute attack of gout, and it would probably take two or three days nursing to bring him around, so that they would not be home until the last of the week. Mrs. Temple had written to Jacqueline, and would write again in a day or two, notifying Judith when to send to the river landing for them. The delay was peculiarly inconvenient then, but it was God's will. Mrs. Temple never had any trouble in reconciling herself to God's will, except where Beverley was concerned.

Not a line had been received from Jacqueline. It did not surprise Judith, because Jacqueline hated letter-writing; but Throckmorton admitted, in an embarrassed way, that he had written to her, but she had not answered his letter.

During all this time Freke had not put in an appearance, for which Judith was devoutly thankful.

On the fifth evening that Throckmorton went his way to Barn Elms, it occurred to him that he went there oftener when Jacqueline was away than when she was there, and he was glad there were no gossiping tongues to wag about it. But luckily little Beverley, Delilah, and Simon Peter were the only three persons who knew where Throckmorton spent his evenings, and none of them were either carping or critical.

He found Judith as usual in the drawing-room, and as usual embroidering on the wedding-dress. But there was something strange about her appearance; she looked altogether different from what she usually did—more girlish, more unrestrained. Throckmorton could not make it out for a long time. Then he said, suddenly, " You have left off your widow's cap."

Judith let her hands fall into her lap, and looked at him with glittering eyes.

" Yes," she said, calmly. " I grew intolerably tired of being a hypocrite, and to-night I determined for once to be my true self, so I laid aside my widow's cap. I believe, if I had owned a white gown, I should have put it on."

Throckmorton was so startled that he rose to his feet. Judith rose, too, letting the white silk fall in a heap on the floor.

"Are you surprised?" she asked, with suppressed excitement. "Well, so am I. But I will tell you— what I never dared breathe before—I am no true widow to Beverley Temple's memory. I never loved him. I married him because—because I did not know any better, I suppose. I spent two miserable weeks as his wife. I was beginning to find out— and then he went away, and almost before I realized it, he was killed." She hesitated for a moment; the picture of Throckmorton and Beverley in their life-and-death struggle came quickly before her eyes. Throckmorton was too dazed, astounded, confounded, to open his mouth. He only looked at her as she stood upright, trembling and red and pale by turns.

"I had no friends but General and Mrs. Temple; he was my guardian. You know, I had neither father nor mother, brother nor sister. I felt the most acute remorse for Beverley, and the most intense pity for him, cut off as he was, and I fancied I felt the profoundest grief. One suffers in sympathy, you know, and, when I saw his mother's pitiable sorrow, it made me feel sorry too. The world—*my* world—saw me a broken-hearted widow—a widow while I was almost a bride. Don't you think any woman of feeling would have done as I did—tried to atone to the man I had mistakenly married by being true to his memory? I determined to devote my life to his father and mother; and, in some way I can't explain, except that you know how Mrs. Temple is, I pretended that my heart was broken; but I tell you, Beverley Temple never touched my heart, either in life or death, although I did not know it then. But for—for some time the deceit has lain heavy upon me. I am tired of pretending to be what I am not. I wish for life, for love, for happiness."

She stopped and threw herself into a chair with an *abandon* that Throckmorton had never seen before. Still, he did not utter a word. But Judith knew that he was keenly observing her, feeling for her, and even deeply moved by what she told him.

" So to-night the feeling was so strong upon me, I took off my widow's cap and threw it on the floor; it was a sudden impulse, just as I was leaving my room, and I took Beverley's picture from around my neck, and I didn't have the courage to throw it in the fire as I wanted to; I only "—with a nervous laugh—" put it in my pocket."

She took the picture from her dress and handed it him. Throckmorton received it mechanically, but, the instant his eyes fell upon it, his countenance changed. In a moment or two he said, in an indescribable voice:

"I know this face well; he was killed on the 14th of April. I shall never forget that face to my dying day."

"I know all about it," responded Judith, rising and coming toward him; "Freke told me."

Her excitement was no longer suppressed, and Throckmorton was deeply agitated. He took Judith's hand.

"But did he tell you all? *I* did not fire the shot that killed your husband; it was fired by one of his own men—probably aimed for me. I never succeeded in drawing my pistol at all. The first I knew, in those frightful moments, was when he shrieked and threw up his arms. I thought he would never breathe again."

"But he lived some hours," continued Judith, "and—and—I thought it was you, and I ought to have hated you for it, but I could not; I could not; and now, God is so good!"

She dropped into a chair. Throckmorton felt as if the world were coming to an end, his ideas about Judith were being so quickly and strangely transformed. He was too stupefied to speak, and for five minutes there was a dead silence between them. Then Throckmorton's strong common sense awoke. He went to her and took her hand.

"For your own sake, for your child's sake, be careful. Do not tell any one what you have told me. The penalty of deception is great, and your penalty will be to keep it up a little while longer. When I am married to Jacqueline, you will have a friend, a home. Then, if you want to take off those black garments, to be yourself, you may count on me; but, for the present, be prudent. You are so impulsive."

But Judith now was weeping violently and accusing herself. The reaction had come. Throckmorton felt strangely thrilled by her emotion. He comforted her, he held her hands, and even pressed kisses on them. In a few minutes he had soothed her. The old habits of self-control came back to her. She rallied bravely, and in half an hour she was quite composed. But it was the composure of despair. She remembered, then, had Throckmorton but loved her, the only obstacle between them would have been shown to be imaginary.

Throckmorton stayed late. In spite of Judith's quietness, he felt unhappy about her. She was too quiet, too deathly pale. He felt an intense pity for her, and he feared that she and her child would not much longer find a home under the roof of Barn Elms.

Three days more passed. There was still no word from Jacqueline, and Mrs. Temple wrote that the general's gout bade fair to be a much more serious matter than they had first anticipated. It might be that the wedding—which was to be of the quietest sort—might have to be postponed. But that was nothing to Mrs. Temple and the general, who reveled in the luxury of a meeting where Beverley was remembered, praised, and eulogized as can be done only by Southerners. Nor did it seem to matter to Jacqueline. In fact, Throckmorton and Judith appeared to be the only persons particularly interested in it. As for Freke, he had not been seen by either of them since the day the Barn Elms people left.

Throckmorton continued to spend his evenings at Barn Elms. The idea of Judith sitting solitary and alone in the drawing-room the whole long, dull evening, drew him irresistibly. Not one line had Jacqueline written, either to him or to Judith. Nor had Throckmorton written again to her. He was not the man to give a woman more than one opportunity to snub him. In his heart he was cruelly mortified; his pride, of which he had much, was hurt. He feared that it was a part of that arrogance which first youth shows to maturity.

On the eighth day after Jacqueline's departure something like alarm began to possess Judith. She called it superstition, and tried to put it away from her. The day had been dull and gloomy—a fine, drizzling rain falling. The flat, monotonous landscape looked inexpressibly dreary in the gray mist that hung low over the trees. It was dark long before six o'clock. The night had closed in, and Judith, sitting alone in the drawing-room, had risen to light the lamp, when she heard the front door open softly, and the next instant she recognized Jacqueline's peculiar light step—so light that even Mrs. Temple's keen ears could not always detect it when fits of restlessness seized the girl at night, and she would walk up and down her room over her mother's head. And in a moment Jacqueline came into the room, and up to Judith, and looked at her with strange, agonized eyes.

The surprise, the shock of seeing her at that hour and in that way, was extreme; and Judith's first words as her hands fell on Jacqueline's shoulder were:

"Jacqueline, you are wet through."

"I know it," answered Jacqueline, in a voice as unlike her own as her looks; "I have been out in the rain for hours and hours!"

"What is the matter with you?" cried Judith, taking hold of her. "Something dreadful has happened!"

"Dreadful enough for me!" replied Jacqueline, white and dry-eyed.

"What is it?" Judith was not easily frightened, but she trembled as she spoke.

"Everything!" answered Jacqueline. "In the first place, I have left Freke. That broke my heart!"

"Left Freke!"

"Yes. I didn't go to Aunt Steptoe's. I got off at the station and Freke was there. He took me to a minister's and got him to marry us. The man could hardly read and write, and he said something about a license; but Freke gave him fifty dollars, and he performed the ceremony."

Judith caught hold of her, to see if she were really in the flesh, talking in this way.

"Don't hold me so hard, Judith. I will tell you all I can; but I feel as if I should die, I am so weak and ill—" and she suddenly began to cough violently. Judith ran and got her a glass of wine. The first idea in her mind was, not the poor, deluded child, but Throckmorton.

"But where is Freke—and your father and mother?—O Jacqueline, Jacqueline!"

"Don't reproach me, Judith. But for you I would never have returned. My father and mother know nothing about it. Freke found out they were yet in Richmond. If they had been at Barn Elms, I don't think I ever would have had the courage to come back. The feeling soon came to me that I had committed a great wrong in marrying Freke; and then— and then—he told me perhaps we weren't married at all in Virginia, and so I would have to go with him out to the place—somewhere in the West—and be married to him straight and right."

"If Freke had never committed any other wrong in his whole life, his telling you that made him deserve to be killed!" cried Judith.

"Don't say a word against Freke," said Jacqueline, a new anger blazing up in her eyes. "I love Freke; it almost kills me when I think I may never see him again, for I ran away from him. At first I thought all the time of the trouble I should bring upon you all. I could see my father's gray head sink down in his hands. I could imagine how my mother would shut herself up in her room as she did when Beverley died. They had always thought so little of me that it gave me a kind of triumph when I remembered, 'They'll have to think about me now!'"

"And Throckmorton?"

"I never thought about him at all. As Freke said, he was entirely too old for me. But I will not speak of him. He knew I never loved him—or he ought to have known it. Then, when Freke found out that mamma and papa were still in Richmond, it came to me like a flash that I could get home, and I was sure of one friend, and only one in the world now—yourself. And I thought you were so clever you could manage to keep anybody from finding out where I had been. I seemed to hear your voice calling to me all the time, and every moment it seemed to crush me more and more that Freke was a divorced man, and that, however he might say he was free, he was not. So, we were staying at a little town through which the railroad passed, and Freke had to go into Richmond yesterday to get some money, and my conscience suddenly rose up and tortured me, and I couldn't stay another moment—and, mind you, Judith, I love Freke. So I took the train all alone, and made the boat, and landed at Oak Point about twelve o'clock. I pretended to be surprised that nobody was there to meet me, and said I would walk as far as Turkey Thicket—you know it is only a little way from the landing. But, of course, I did not. Then I was so afraid that some one would see me that, instead of taking the main road, I came through the fields and by-paths. I believe I have walked ten miles instead of six, from Oak Point—and it was raining, too. I was nearly frightened out of my life —frightened by negroes and stray dogs, and afraid that I should see Freke every moment before me, and, if he should overtake me, I knew I should go back with him. I can no more resist him when he is with me than I can stop breathing. Well, with weakness —for I felt ill from the moment I started—and with fear, and being so tired, and the rain, I thought I should die before I reached here. But now I am home—home!—" Jacqueline's voice rose in a piteous cry. She had been weeping all the time, but now she burst into a perfect tempest of sobs and tears that shook her like a leaf.

In her quiet life Judith had never been brought face to face with any terrible emergency, and this one unnerved and horrified her so that for a time she was as helpless as Jacqueline. She walked the floor, struggling with the wild impulse to send for Throckmorton; that he alone could tell them what to do; and else she and the poor child would sink under the horror of the situation, for to her simple and straightforward mind both conscience and the social code were unalterably opposed to considering a divorced man as a single man. But some instinct of common sense saved her—saved her even from calling Delilah, and caused her to face the thing alone. She gave Jacqueline brandy, she rubbed her vigorously; she even got her up-stairs alone and into her bed. By that time the violence of her emotions was spent; Jacqueline lay in the large four-poster perfectly calm and white. After a while even a sense of physical well-being seemed to possess her; warmth and light and stimulation had their effect. She fell into a heavy sleep, but Judith was terrified to notice her pallor give place to a crimson flush on her face, and her icy hands grow burning hot. By that time Judith's composure had partly returned. She called Delilah, who came in wondering, and told her briefly that Jacqueline had come home unexpectedly and was not well, without mentioning how she had come from the river-landing. Delilah, who was not of a curious turn, saw for herself that part of Judith's statement was true, for Jacqueline had a burning fever. It was impossible to get Dr. Wortley before morning, but, like most women who live in the country, Judith could cope with ordinary ailments, and, whenever the doctor was called in, he always found that the proper thing had been done beforehand.

But, besides Jacqueline's undeniable illness, the thought that tormented Judith was how to keep the dreadful thing that had happened from Jacqueline's father and mother and from the world. It must inevitably come out that she had not been near Mrs. Steptoe's, and only the fact that Jacqueline was a poor correspondent had kept it from being known already. On the impulse of the moment, Judith sat down and wrote Mrs. Steptoe a letter, begging her, for General and Mrs. Temple's sake, not to mention until she heard further from Barn Elms, that Jacqueline had not been with her; and as she wrote hurriedly and nervously, she could hear Jacqueline's heavy and fitful breathing. Some simple remedies had been applied, but Judith knew that the best thing for her was to sleep, and so her troubled slumber was undisturbed except by her own feverish mutterings. All the time it hung like a sword over Judith. "What will Throckmorton say?" for, of course, he must be the first one to know it; there could be no mercy in deceiving him. Judith, sitting before the fire, gazing into it with troubled eyes and aching heart, began thinking, pitying, praying for Throckmorton. Yes, it would be a frightful blow to him. There would be no need for the wedding-gown now. As this thought occurred to her, Judith rose and, going softly toward the wardrobe where she kept her dainty work, took out the dress, and, unwrapping it from the white cloth in which she laid it away so carefully every night, spread it over her knees. How much love, despair, and torture had been worked into that embroidery! "It is so pretty, it is a pity it can't be used," she said to herself, absently, turning the silk about in her fingers; and at that moment she heard a choking, gurgling sound from the bed. Jacqueline was half sitting up, her head supported on her arm, and a thin stream of blood was trickling from her lips.

Judith, who for once lost her presence of mind, ran toward the bed, and, supporting Jacqueline's head, called loudly for help. In her haste she had thrown the dress almost across Jacqueline, and a few drops of blood fell upon it.

"Look, look!" gasped Jacqueline; "my dress is being ruined!"

Judith heard Delilah running up the stairs in response to her frightened call, but Jacqueline's eyes had such a strange expression in them that she asked her involuntarily, as she tremblingly supported her:

"Jacqueline, do you know me?"

16

"Perfectly," answered Jacqueline. "I know everything about me."

Delilah, who was a natural-born nurse, was as calm as Judith was agitated.

"T'ain' nuttin' tall, chile; 'scusin' 'tis er leetle speck o' blood fum yo' th'oat. I kin stop it righter way"; and, sure enough, in ten minutes she had applied some simple remedy and the blood ceased to flow. Meanwhile Jacqueline, unable to speak, had motioned eagerly and violently to Judith to remove the white silk dress. Judith threw it on a chair. Jacqueline's eyes filled with tears.

"It is such a pity to have it ruined—and one's wedding-dress, too!"

"Hush—hush! you must not talk," cried Judith.

The flow of blood apparently was a trifle, and in a little while Jacqueline lay back in the great, old-fashioned bed silent, deadly white, but composed.

Judith, with overflowing eyes, folded up the white dress, but she could not prevent some tears falling on it, and the dress, already stained with blood, was also stained with tears. The thought of Jacqueline, though, could not banish the thought of Throckmorton; the more so when Jacqueline, beckoning, brought Judith close to her. Judith thought she wanted something for her comfort.

"*You* must tell him; he will take it better from you."

Jacqueline, lying wide awake in the bed, and Judith, sitting by her, holding her hand, were both expectant of Throckmorton. At last, about half-past eight, his firm step was heard on the porch. Judith's heart leaped into her mouth; she did not exactly take in all the bearings of what Jacqueline had told her, or whether she was or was not married to Freke; and Throckmorton, with his knowledge of affairs, would know all.

She rose silently and went down-stairs, leaving Delilah with Jacqueline. Throckmorton was standing before the fire in the drawing-room. There was something in his determined eye and in his tone as he spoke to her that struck a chill to Judith's heart.

" Jacqueline, has come, you know," she said.

" Yes, Simon Peter told me so at the door. It does not surprise me."

Judith remained silent for a few moments, when Throckmorton, suddenly wheeling toward her, and looking her straight in the face, said, curtly :

" What is all this ? She never was near Mrs. Steptoe's. I found out, by having my letter returned to me by Mrs. Steptoe herself. What has made her ill ? Don't tremble so, but tell me—you know I have a right to know it all."

But Judith continued to be silent and to tremble. She even began to weep; but Throckmorton, taking her hand, said, firmly :

"There must be no concealments."

His own stern composure controlled Judith's agitation.

"All?" she asked, faintly.

"Yes—all!" he answered.

When Throckmorton used an authoritative tone with her, he could always compel her; and so, scarcely knowing how she did it, with tears and sobs, and faint deprecations for Jacqueline, she told him all. She noticed Throckmorton's dark skin growing paler and paler; he began to gnaw his iron-gray mustache—always a sign of extreme agitation with him.

"Now, tell me this—collect your thoughts and don't cry so—does she—does she love that—" He could not bring himself to utter Freke's name.

Judith remained silent. Throckmorton, in his determination to make her answer, seized her arm. It hurt her so that she could have cried out, but she made no sound.

"Tell me!" he said, in a voice and manner so unlike his own gentle courtesy, that Judith could scarcely have recognized it. But Judith was obstinately silent. Nevertheless, she lifted her eyes to his with so eloquent a plea for mercy for Jacqueline, that he was unconsciously softened.

"You will not tell me!" he said, relaxing his fierce hold. "I can't make you answer—you have a spirit like a soldier. But it makes no difference now whether she loves him or not. If she were free to-morrow, I could kill her with my own hands easier than I could marry her!—and yet—I loved her well."

"But," cried Judith, putting her hand on his arm in her eagerness, "something must be done. It must be managed so that people shall not know it, until her father and mother have decided what is to be done." It will almost kill them!"

"Yes. But if you can manage with Mrs. Steptoe—"

"I have already written to her."

"I am no lawyer, but it seems to me that it rests with Jacqueline whether it is a marriage or not. But General and Mrs. Temple would rather see her in her grave than married to any divorced man—and to him!"

"And there is a good deal of doubt about his divorce, I believe," added Judith.

"There is at present nothing to be done. General and Mrs. Temple will no doubt be here as soon as possible; it is hardly worth while to alarm them. Is she very ill, do you think?"

"I don't know—Jacqueline was always delicate. And—what of him—of Freke?" continued Judith, in a trembling voice. "Is there to be no punishment for him?"

Like a woman, Judith could not look at the case in its practical light; but like a man, Throckmorton, in the midst of his horror, grief, and surprise, yet retained his balance.

"Any punishment of him would react on her—to have her name made public with his— Good God! But there is no power on earth to keep General Temple from committing some frightful folly when he knows of it."

This was a new horror to Judith. A painful pause followed. Then Judith said:

"How like Freke it was—how perfectly reckless of consequences! He is unlike any man I ever saw or heard of. I believe, in his strange way, he loves Jacqueline; but what does any one know of such a man!" .

The absence of vindictiveness toward Freke, on Throckmorton's part, surprised Judith; but, in truth, he scarcely thought of Freke: a creature as weak and impressionable as Jacqueline was bound to succumb to the first overmastering influence. Throckmorton himself had never been able to get any real influence over her. Presently Judith said:

"One thing I do know—she wants your forgiveness."

"She has it, poor child!"

Then there was another pause. Throckmorton, after a while, rose to go.

"If you want anything, send for me. I shall be over early in the morning." He hesitated a moment, and then said : " This has been a strange experience for me ; but it is over—" And then, as if checking a confession, went out of the room and out of the house.

When Judith went up-stairs, Jacqueline was still sleeping, but presently she wakened, and turned her lovely, troubled eyes on Judith.

" He is very sorry, Jacqueline, and he forgives you and will trouble you no more," she whispered. A look of relief came into Jacqueline's face. She closed her eyes as if to sleep.

CHAPTER XII.

The next day Jacqueline was better, and about noon General and Mrs. Temple arrived. Mrs. Temple showed no surprise when she heard that Jacqueline had come the day before; and when Judith said, falteringly, that Jacqueline had probably misunderstood their plans, Mrs. Temple accepted it quite naturally. About the same time Dr. Wortley, who had been sent for, came, and pronounced Jacqueline's attack to be nothing but cold and fever, and raised the prohibition against her talking. The first time Mrs. Temple was out of the room, Jacqueline called Judith to her.

"Judith, I have been thinking about this, and I have made up my mind."

This was so unlike Jacqueline that Judith stared.

"If I thought Freke was really a single man, I would give up everybody—even you—for him. But nobody on earth knows what I suffered from my conscience while I was with him! And I believe Freke told the truth when he said we weren't married, after all, in spite of that minister and the fifty dollars.

And now, dear Judith, it seems so easy to keep papa and mamma from knowing it."

" Easy, Jacqueline ?—"

" Yes, easy, if you will only write to Aunt Steptoe; and it would kill me to have to face them ! "

" But, Jacqueline, suppose—suppose Freke should claim you, or you might, in years to come, want to marry some one else ? "

" I will promise you I will not—I will swear it—if I can't marry Freke, you may depend upon it I sha'n't marry anybody else ! But, Judith, will you promise me to say nothing to papa and mamma until you have seen Freke, for he knows what ought to be done ? I know—and I am sure—he will come back in a day or two. He knows well enough where I have run away to."

Judith was loath to making any promise at all, but Jacqueline became so violently agitated and distressed that at last, almost beside herself, Judith promised that for a few days, at least, she would say nothing about it.

Mrs. Temple was so full of Beverley, and the proceedings at Richmond, that she troubled Jacqueline but little with questions; and Judith was amazed at hearing Jacqueline describe to her mother a visit to her aunt, as if it had really been paid. The idea of concealment had taken complete possession of Jacqueline's mind, and she stopped at nothing.

Of course, the wedding had to be postponed; and Jacqueline surprised her mother, after two letters had passed between Throckmorton and herself, by telling her quite calmly one day that the wedding was off, and that Throckmorton would shortly leave the county. General and Mrs. Temple were stunned; and Mrs. Temple, who had secretly thought the marriage preposterous from the start, now suddenly changed front, and was bitterly disappointed at this strange and unaccountable breaking off. Jacqueline would only say, "I found I didn't love him, and couldn't marry him"; and she repeated this with a sort of childish obstinacy — so it seemed to Mrs. Temple. Throckmorton accepted his supposed bad news with the firmness and dignity that always characterized him. He told Mrs. Temple, when she and the general, sitting in solemn conclave in the drawing-room, had sent for him to give him this unalterable determination of Jacqueline's:

"Her happiness should be first always. The difference in our years I always felt; but, when she began to feel it, she was right in breaking with me. It is better that it should come now than later on."

Mrs. Temple was thoroughly puzzled by Throckmorton. She could not make out his quiet acquiescence in Jacqueline's decision—it was so unlike his usual vigorous way of overcoming obstacles. But, before he left, Freke had reappeared, and the dreadful truth had come to him and to Throckmorton and to Judith that, after all, according to the statutes of Virginia, he was not at liberty to marry again. Dreadful it was to Freke, who, light-minded and evil as he was, had really believed himself free, and whose implied doubt to Jacqueline was merely for the purpose of frightening her into submission. Freke went up to Richmond one day and returned the next. Half an hour's interview each with half a dozen lawyers had settled a hypothetical case that covered Freke's exactly: not all the clerks and licenses and ceremonies in Virginia could make his marriage to anybody good as it stood. It was true that there was an excellent chance that in the course of time various defects in the somewhat informal divorce proceedings that Freke had really thought sufficient might be remedied, and he would be a free man; but, for the present, he certainly was not.

Freke, who had thought his courage impeccable, found it failed him when he met Judith, for the first and last time, to settle upon the best course to pursue. Judith had Throckmorton's advice and assistance to back her up. Freke positively cowered under her gaze. It was settled that he was to go to the Northwest immediately, and devote all his energies to straightening out the strange tangle in which he had left his matrimonial affairs there; and, when it was settled, he was to return to Virginia, and then let

Jacqueline decide what was to be done. He swore
—and swore so that Judith believed him—that he
thought himself a free man, and only despised the narrowness of people who believed there was no such
thing as divorce. Why he should have fallen in love
with Jacqueline did not puzzle Judith: had she not,
with those irresistible glances of hers, ensnared a much
stronger man? But one thing was decided as much
by Jacqueline's agony of fear as anything else: nothing was to be said about the terrible complication to
General and Mrs. Temple. Mrs. Steptoe's answer to
Judith's letter gave a promise that nothing should be
said about Jacqueline's non-appearance; and that removed any immediate danger of discovery. And, in
a little while, both Freke and Throckmorton were
gone—Freke, to move heaven and earth to get his divorce in proper shape; and Throckmorton, merely to
be out of the way, and as far out of the way as possible.

To Judith it seemed as if the world were coming
to an end. How a thing so dreadful, so unlike anything she had ever known before, could happen in
their quiet lives, seemed more and more extraordinary.
Here was Jacqueline—last year a child in heart, and
now the first person in a tragedy. Never had she anything to conceal before; and now, with the most perfect art and premeditation, she was concealing, every
day and hour, something that would be even more

overwhelming to her father and mother than Beverley's death, and would convulse the little world in which they lived. As for the innumerable chances that it might be found out any day, Judith was abnormally alive to them. Every morning, when she went down-stairs, she half expected that the disclosure would come; every night she thanked Heaven it had been postponed a day.

Meanwhile Jacqueline, lying in her great four-poster, progressed slowly but gradually toward recovery. One night she called Judith to the bedside. She was fast getting well then.

"Judith," she said, "you know what queer notions I take? Well, I have been lying here thinking, thinking, perhaps you won't be able to keep the whole county from knowing about—"

The haunting fear of this never left Judith, but she could not but try and comfort Jacqueline.

"We will try—O Jacqueline, we will try!"

"And do you know it has troubled me even more than losing Freke; for I feel he is lost to me, even if he were to come to-morrow morning and say he was a free man; the fear that when I get well I shall be avoided; the people will leave me alone at church, and the county people will stop visiting us. That would indeed kill me."

"Dear child, we will hope and pray. I believe it would kill me too."

Jacqueline at this worked herself up into such a violent fit of weeping that Judith was frightened into giving her a great many more assurances of safety than her own anxious heart believed, but Jacqueline at last was quieted. In both of them, so widely unlike, was that profound respect for their neighbors, characteristic of simple and provincial souls. They knew no other world but that little neighborhood around Severn church, and its opinion was life or death.

But it troubled Judith that by degrees visitors began to fall off and inquiries ceased for Jacqueline. The temper and habit of the people were such that Judith knew Jacqueline could never hope for any forgiveness if that week's journey should be known. Jacqueline too, although she was entirely silent afterward upon the subject, was thinking and dreading and fearing. It was the custom for many kindly and neighborly visits to be paid the sick, many flowers and delicacies to be sent them; but after a while Jacqueline ceased to have either flowers or visitors. She was nearly well, though, or at least she protested that she was. But, although Jacqueline declared to Judith that, if Freke were legally free to-morrow, she would not marry him as long as that other woman lived, it was plain that he had completely captivated her imagination. She loved him in her own wild, unreasoning way. Judith was hourly amazed at the sudden self-control, finesse, the power to deceive, that Jacqueline developed regarding him. Usually her composure was perfect, but once in her own room, Jacqueline threw herself on the rug before the fire and wept and sobbed so that Judith was seriously alarmed. But, still trying to keep the burden from the unconscious father and mother, she remained with Jacqueline until a calm had come after the storm.

"I love him! I love him!" was all Jacqueline would say, and Judith believed her.

"You told me how I ought to love Throckmorton," she said that night, with a melancholy smile; "it is exactly how I love Freke. Don't look at me in that indignant way, Judith. It is not my fault."

Jack Throckmorton had remained at Millenbeck when his father left. Throckmorton had briefly announced to him that the wedding was off. Jack came at last to see them, looking very sheepish. Judith suspected that he came in obedience to Throckmorton's wishes. But Jacqueline at once slipped back into her old friendly way, if a little less gay and thoughtless than before. Jack sent her flowers, and would have brought his dog-cart over every day to take her to drive, so much touched was he by Jacqueline's illness, but Judith would not let him. Nevertheless, he was in and out of the house very much as he had been ever since that first night he was there. Judith, who had come to love him for his sweet, bright, boyish nature, he felt was his friend, as indeed everybody at Barn Elms was. The whole affair was intensely puzzling to Jack. He dared not show Throckmorton the awkward sympathy that he was struggling first to express and then to repress ; but Jacqueline was young and ill, and had few pleasures, and he had once been a little gone on her, so it seemed the most natural thing in the world that he should be kind to her.

There were mysterious hints, though, flying about the county regarding Jacqueline's affairs. Mrs. Sherrard was dying with curiosity, and made many visits to Barn Elms for the purpose of gratifying it. But she soon found out that, beyond knowing that Jacqueline had tired of her engagement and had thrown Throckmorton over, neither General nor Mrs. Temple knew anything to communicate. About this time, too, the party-giving fever, which was never long in abeyance with Mrs. Sherrard, seized her. A party she must give. General Temple brought a note to that effect, coupled with a request for Mrs. Temple's salad-bowls and ladles, one day from the post-office. Jacqueline, who had been out-of-doors several times and had quite given up her invalidism, showed the keenest and the most unexpected delight when she heard of the party. She jumped up and down, clapped her hands, and began to dance.

"Oh, how glad I am ! It has been so stupid lately.

I do want to dance again dreadfully. How I wish I could go to a ball every night in the week!"

Judith was surprised at Jacqueline's eagerness about the party. Mrs. Temple had first said decidedly that Jacqueline should not go, at which Jacqueline threw her hands up to her face and burst into such a passion of stormy weeping that Mrs. Temple was completely puzzled, and so was Judith.

"But, my child, you are not strong enough!"

"I am!—I am!" cried Jacqueline. "I will ask Dr. Wortley if I can't go to the party. I am sure I will cry myself ill if I don't go; and I am so well and strong."

Mrs. Temple, who had got a little indulgent to Jacqueline since her illness, agreed to leave it to Dr. Wortley. The next time he came over to pay a friendly visit, Jacqueline took him off to herself, and came back triumphant. Dr. Wortley had agreed. The old doctor had a queer look in his face.

"I consented, madam," he said to Mrs. Temple, "because this young lady promised me that she would make herself ill if she did not go; and I have known young women to keep that promise. She has given me her word she will be very prudent—will not over-exert herself; and Mrs. Beverley is to watch her."

"And I'll come home the instant Judith proposes it!" cried Jacqueline.

Mrs. Temple finally agreed, upon condition that

the weather was fit. For some days before the party
it threatened to be very unfit. Dark clouds overhung
the sky, and a biting March wind swept over the bare
fields and through the somber aspens and Lombardy
poplars, as yet leafless and wintry, around the house.
Jacqueline seemed to have but one idea in her head,
and that was the party. She haunted the windows
where the cutting wind came in through the open
chinks and crannies, until Judith warned her that she
would soon begin to cough again, and worse, if she
did not take care of herself. She pestered Simon
Peter with asking for weather signs. When the
morning broke, cloudy and overcast, Jacqueline was
almost in despair; she could eat no breakfast, but sat
at the table watching the clouds. Presently the sun
came out upon the dreary landscape, and the sun in
Jacqueline's eyes came out too. From the deepest
gloom she passed to the wildest gayety. Her eyes
shone; and taking little Beverley into the great, empty
drawing-room, she waltzed around with him, singing
and capering about until the boy, like herself, was in
a gale of good humor. Judith had never ceased being
puzzled by it. Still another obstacle, though, seemed
to arise in Jacqueline's path. General Temple had a
suspicion of gout, and declared-that the party was out
of the question for him. At this, Jacqueline looked
so pale and disappointed that even Mrs. Temple's
heart melted toward her.

" But I can take care of Jacqueline, mother," said
Judith; "we are safe, you know, with Simon Peter on
the box, and we will come home before twelve o'clock."

Mrs. Temple consented, and for the second time
that day Jacqueline's spirits rose. Toward twilight,
when the fires had been lighted in their rooms for the
two girls to dress, for early hours prevail in the country, Judith went into Jacqueline's room. Jacqueline
was twisting up her beautiful blonde hair into a knot
on top of her head, taking infinite pains; her eyes
were shining, her whole air one of quick expectancy.

" Why are you so anxious about this party, Jacqueline?" asked Judith, to whose lips the question had
often risen during the last week.

" Wait a moment and I will tell you," replied Jacqueline, still intent on her hair.

Judith waited until the last tress was in place, and
Jacqueline came over to the fireplace.

" Because—because, Judith, I have a feeling—I
don't know where it comes from—that everybody
knows about—" She stopped and cast down her eyes
in a troubled way, but without blushing. " And I
thought if I went to this party I would be convinced
that it was all a mistake. I know it is very silly, but
it has kept me awake at night ever since I was first
ill, thinking how the people would eye me at church.
You know how sick people take up those fancies.
Well, I am determined to prove to myself it isn't so.

Jack Throckmorton won't be at the party, but I shall no doubt have a plenty of partners, and this horrible feeling—that I am disgraced in some way—will leave me; I am sure it will. You know mamma's way of treating these notions. 'Just give your secret fears an airing, and see how they will disappear,' that's what I mean to do. Like ghosts, they vanish when you speak to them and try to handle them, and then you are rid of them for good."

Judith said not a word. The same horrible fear had been with her. Freke and Throckmorton were safe—General and Mrs. Temple suspected nothing—it made her sick at heart as she thought about the news traveling over the county.

When Jacqueline was dressed in the same white frock she had worn the evening she had captivated Throckmorton, she preened like a young peacock before the admiring eyes of Delilah and Simon Peter. She whirled round on her toes like a ballet-dancer. She courtesied to the ground, showing them how she would do at the party. She walked away from the little glass on her dressing-table, arching her neck and fluttering her fan.

"I allus did say Marse George Throckmorton wuz too ole fur little Miss Jacky," Simon Peter remarked to Delilah, after the performance. Delilah, who was bound to differ with Simon Peter, promptly took issue.

"Marse George, he ain' ole, he jes' in he prime.
Dat's de way wid you wuffless niggers—call a man ole
in he prime."

"But whar' *he* gwi' be, when she in her prime?
You heah me, 'oman?"

Delilah, for once, had no answer to make. The
reflection had occurred to her.

As Judith and Jacqueline were jolted along the
road, in the darkness, toward Turkey Thicket, both
of them were reminded of that other party there,
when Throckmorton had been present. Neither of
them said anything, though. Judith, as she watched
the shadowy trees slip past, began to think how
strangely things had gone with her since then. Almost
from that time she had felt a steady and ceaseless
pain associated with Throckmorton. She then suffered, she thought, with him, and for him, although
not one word had come from him since he had left
the county, a month ago. Where was he? What was
he doing at that very moment? Then she tried to
fancy how it would have been with her had she seen
daily before her Throckmorton and Jacqueline's married happiness. The sight of it would have been intolerable to her. "And nobody in the world suspects
me of being the most impressionable, emotional, jealous, and miserable woman on earth," she thought
to herself.

Jacqueline sat back in the carriage, occasionally

speculating on who would be at the party, and how often she might dance without breaking Dr. Wortley's orders.

When they drove up to the door and got out, Jacqueline ran lightly up the steps, like her old self. Judith followed her. In Mrs. Sherrard's own comfortable old-fashioned room, where the ladies' wraps were removed, a number of girls about Jacqueline's age were laughing, chattering, getting their wraps off and their slippers on. Jacqueline ran up to them, and was about to join their circle; but by a slight, indescribable motion, they all drew back. It was a mere gesture, but it froze Jacqueline as she stood. She turned a frightened, piteous glance on Judith, who, with a flushed face, walked straight up to the little group.

"How do you do?" she said, calling each one by name, and holding out her hand. If there were any cloud upon the Temple family, she would force them to come out boldly and define it. Her fine nostrils dilated with anger—for not only was it her duty to stand by Jacqueline, but was not she, Judith, a Temple, too? And Judith had one of those proud and self-respecting souls to whom everything and everybody closely connected with her was due a certain deference. Something in her eye and manner commanded civility—then her greetings were answered even more cordially than she had given them.

But there was still an ominous change toward Jacqueline. The color had all dropped out of her face, and she had not recovered the plumpness she had lost during her illness. She looked nearer ugly than at any time in her whole life.

Judith was soon ready to go down-stairs. She no longer wore black dresses, but white ones. They were as severely simple as the black ones, though. She turned with Jacqueline following her, and went slowly out the door, and down the broad, old-fashioned stairs. In the large, uncarpeted hall, dancing was going on. As Judith, tall and stately in her white dress, holding gracefully a large white fan in her hands, passed through the hall, she was greeted with the hearty kindness she had always met with; but Jacqueline at her side, who was wont to run the gantlet of laughter and jokes and merry salutations, was met with a strange and distant politeness that blanched her face, and brought a glitter to Judith's usually soft eyes. She could have borne it better for herself; but for this unthinking child—this young creature Throckmorton loved—it was too much.

Mrs. Sherrard, with her diamond comb shining in her gray hair, and looking as she always did superbly dressed, without anything splendid about her, received them. In her there was no change. She met Jacqueline just as she always did.

"Why, little Jacky," she cried, "how glad I am to

see you out again! You must let me see your little feet tripping about as if you had never been ill."

Jacqueline responded with a faint smile. Suppose she should not be asked to dance?

Judith, taking in at once this universal shyness shown toward Jacqueline, did not move from her side. People came up and spoke to them civilly enough, but chiefly the older people. Out in the hall beyond, the black fiddlers were scraping, and Jacqueline could see a large quadrille forming. But no partner appeared for her. Until the very last she hoped desperately. Never before had Jacqueline, in the few parties she had been to in her short life, failed to be asked to dance—she was so pretty, so undeniably captivating. She turned two despairing dark eyes and two pale cheeks on Judith. It was indeed cruel and heart-breaking. Jacqueline's evident anguish almost took away Judith's self-possession.

"Perhaps you will have better luck next time, dear," she whispered.

"No," replied Jacqueline, trembling, "I feel it. I know what it means. They all know it. Heavens! what do they think I am?"

The quadrille was soon over, but the time seemed interminable to Judith and Jacqueline. Some of the dancers, flushed and excited, were walking around the hall, while others, more indefatigable, whirled around in a waltz. It was all quite plain to Jacqueline, watching them with strange and miserable eyes. Was she then barred out forever from those people, and all for Freke, while even the happiness of being with him was denied her? Mrs. Sherrard, seeing Jacqueline sitting so still and quiet by Judith, came over to them.

"My dear, I see you are not dancing; shall I get you a partner?"

Mrs. Sherrard's sharp eyes saw something was amiss.

"No, please, Mrs. Sherrard," cried Jacqueline, in an eager voice. "I promised Dr. Wortley not to dance much; perhaps I will dance a little after a while."

But she did not. Nobody came near her to ask her; and even to Judith it was plain that people avoided them both. Most of the county people they knew came up and talked a little, but there was a changed atmosphere around them. Judith looked wonderingly at these people. In all the years they had lived in that county there had been nothing but neighborly kindness, good-will, and friendliness; and now, not one among them, seemed to feel the slightest spark of pity or charity for Jacqueline. They had all condemned her unheard. What version of the story had got abroad, she could not tell; but it was enough to blast the friendship of generations.

It was getting on, hour after hour.

"Shall we go home, Jacqueline?" whispered Judith.

"Not yet—not yet!" Jacqueline would answer, with trembling lips. She kept on hoping against hope. By that time everybody in the rooms had seen it all, except Mrs. Sherrard. She supposed she had done her best, coming up and talking to them incessantly; but, Jacqueline having refused a partner when offered one, Mrs. Sherrard naturally supposed she did not dance from preference, and accepted the idea that Dr. Wortley was responsible. It was past midnight before Jacqueline would agree to go. Judith, as stately, if paler and haughtier than ever in her life, went up to Mrs. Sherrard, made her farewells, and walked the whole length of the rooms, holding Jacqueline's hand. The poor child tried to hold her head up, inspired by Judith's courage, but it drooped, and she could not raise her eyes from the floor. A slight thrill of remorse seemed to come over those who saw her, at the piteous sight; but it was now too late. Jacqueline only longed to escape.

The instant they were in the carriage and alone, Jacqueline threw her arms around Judith and began to weep and sob desperately. Judith could only hold her to her heart and say: "Never mind, Jacqueline; if all the world should be against you, I would not be —nor Throckmorton."

But Jacqueline did not cease to sob and weep with

a sort of despair that struck a chill to Judith's heart. She had never seen anybody weep so. When they reached home, Judith got her up-stairs to her room and undressed her, taking off the little chain around her neck that held the pearl pendant Jacqueline only wore on great occasions, uncurling the bright hair she had dressed so carefully, and laying away the simple white dress—Jacqueline's only ball-dress—that she had admired herself in so much. Jacqueline submitted, still sobbing a continual sob, that showed no signs of abatement. Judith put her in bed, turned out the lamp, and kissing her affectionately went out, thinking Jacqueline would soon cry herself to sleep.

An hour afterward Judith, who had keen hearing, fancied she heard a sound from Jacqueline's room. She went in softly. In the ghastly light that came through the closed shutters she saw Jacqueline sitting up in the great, white bed, still weeping.

"My darling," said Judith, taking the girl in her arms, "you will be ill!"

"Ill!" cried Jacqueline; "I am ill now—so ill, I never shall be well again! Judith, I can't live under this. I am going to die; and I am glad of it."

"Hush, hush! what nonsense are you talking?"

"Nonsense or not, those wicked people will see that they have killed me!"

Judith did not leave her any more, nor did Jacqueline sleep one moment, or cease her weeping. She held Judith tightly about the neck, and her warm tears dropped incessantly. Toward daylight Judith began to be alarmed. But nothing was to be done. It would simply break the hearts of the unconscious father and mother if they knew what had happened, and if she roused them they must know. Judith went to her own room and bróught back some brandy, which she forced Jacqueline to take. In a little while it began to show its effect. Jacqueline stopped sobbing, and lay in the great dawn, with her face white and drawn and tear-stained. Judith, again hoping she might sleep, left her.

All that day Jacqueline lay in her bed dumb and motionless. Judith said the child was tired after the ball; perhaps she would get up later on. Mrs. Temple, supposing she was resting after her dissipation, did not go up to see her in the morning. In the afternoon, as Jacqueline showed no signs of getting up, Mrs. Temple went up to her. One look at her pallid face, and Mrs. Temple, calm and self-possessed as she usually was, almost shrieked, Jacqueline was so changed.

"Tell your master to come here at once!" she cried to Delilah.

General Temple came up-stairs, hurried and flurried, and felt for Jacqueline's pulse, but could detect no beating. And then Delilah owned up:

"Dat ar chile ain' tech a mou'ful dis day. I bring

her up nice hot breakfus', an' she jes' tu'n her face
ter de wall an' say, 'Go 'long, mammy, I c'yarn eat.'
Now, huccome she c'yarn eat?"

"My daughter, what is the matter with you?"
asked Mrs. Temple, anxiously.

Of late this half-forgotten child had been steadily
forcing herself upon Mrs. Temple's notice.

"Nothing," answered Jacqueline, quietly.

But Jacqueline would not eat anything to speak
of. In vain Mrs. Temple commanded, General Temple prayed her; Judith also pleaded with her, and
Delilah—even little Beverley, climbing on the bed,
said:

"Jacky, won't you eat a piece o' mammy's ash-
cake if she bake it for you?"

Jacqueline smiled a faint smile that made Judith
almost weep.

"I can't, dear," she said.

It was impossible to force her to eat, and the next
morning Dr. Wortley was sent for. He came up in
his cheery way; he had heard something of the
Turkey Thicket party, but he would say no word to
the anxious father and mother. He talked cheerfully
to Jacqueline, without assuming to doctor her, and
called her attention to the beautiful spring weather.
It was March, but the air was as mild as April.

"All my hyacinths and jonquils are out," he said.
"There is a bed in my garden that is protected on the

north by a hedge and an arbor, and everything in that bed is a week ahead of the rest of the neighborhood. I will bring you everything that is blooming there to-morrow. By the way, what would you fancy to eat, Jacky?"

"I can't eat anything," replied Jacqueline, with quiet obstinacy.

Next day Dr. Wortley came again, with a great bunch of hyacinths and jonquils, and laid them on Jacqueline's bed. Her large and lusterless eyes gazed at them with indifference. Usually they danced with delight at the sight of flowers. Delilah put a spray of pink hyacinths in her hand.

"Doan' you 'member, honey, how you useter like dese heah hy'cints, an' plague yo' mammy when you wuz little ter plant 'em fur you?"

"Yes, I remember," said Jacqueline, calmly.

Judith and Mrs. Temple were present. Dr. Wortley said nothing about Jacqueline's refusing to eat, but talked away, telling all the neighborhood gossip. Then, in a careless way, he felt for Jacqueline's pulse and listened to the beating of her heart. Both were so faint that Dr. Wortley's eyes became grave. After he left the room, he beckoned to Mrs. Temple to follow him. Delilah came, too.

"Marse Doctor, she ain' tech nuthin' but a leetle bit o' toast an' tea since yistiddy, an' it wan' 'nough to keep a bird 'live, let 'lone a human."

Dr. Wortley wheeled round on his old enemy and snapped out:

"If you'll just use some of your persuasive eloquence and stuff her up with jellies and custards as you do your master when he ought to be living on tea and toast, she'll be all right."

Delilah flounced back into Jacqueline's room, her head-handkerchief bobbing about angrily. Mrs. Temple being present, she could not retaliate on Dr. Wortley.

"But, doctor," said Mrs. Temple, trembling strangely, "this is so unlike Jacqueline. I don't know what has been the matter with her lately. She isn't grieving for Throckmorton, but something is on her mind, that is—that is—"

The doctor waited, thinking Mrs. Temple would finish what she was saying. But she did not. This was, indeed, unlike Jacqueline—unlike any instance Dr. Wortley, in his simple experience, had ever known.

"Let her alone for a few days," he said. "We will see."

At the end of a few days Jacqueline had indeed consented to take enough food to keep life in her, but she had lost ground frightfully. Her round, girlish face was sharp and pinched.

Judith tried persuasion, to which Jacqueline responded, "How can I eat anything, when all night

long I cry and cry, thinking of the hard-hearted
people who—”

Then she stopped suddenly.

“ Mise Judy,” said Delilah, after a while, “ I lay on
de pallet by de baid, an’ all night long I heah her cryin’, jes’ cryin’ quiet—she doan’ make no noise. I say:
‘ What de matter, honey? Tell yo’ ole mammy dat
nuss you? an’ she make ’tense den she ’sleep. But I
know she ain’ sleep—she jest distrusted at de way dem
folks treat her at that ungordly party at Tuckey
Thicket.”

General and Mrs. Temple were anxious about Jacqueline, but by no means despairing. Neither of
them thought that anybody could die without having
anything ostensibly the matter. Judith, on the contrary, thought this the most alarming thing about
Jacqueline. There she lay, steadily losing her hold
on life, without any reason in the world that she
should not be up and about—except, indeed, that
sickness of the soul which saps the very foundations
of life. This fear that Jacqueline was slipping
away from them impelled her to write Throckmorton
a few lines—guarded, but without disguising anything.

Meanwhile, the day that was to have been the wed-
ding-day had come and gone. Jacqueline had not
noticed it—she seemed to notice nothing in those days
—but toward noon she said to Judith:

"I want to see my wedding-dress—to see if it is quite ruined."

Judith, without protesting, went and got it. She spread it out on the bed. It was rich and white and soft, and was beautiful with Judith's handiwork; but it was bloodstained in many places.

"That blood, I think, came from my heart," said Jacqueline; her eyes were soft and luminous. "I've been thinking about Throckmorton in the last two or three days—for the first time. I have been so busy with my own sorrow and Freke's that I haven't had time to think about anything else. Now, though, I want to see him—if he can get here in time."

"He will soon be here," answered Judith, folding up the dress. "I wrote him four days ago."

"That is so like you! None of the others know what I want, or will let me have my own way, but you."

And that very day Freke appeared.

The hatred that Judith had always felt for him was now intensified into a horror of him—he was the murderer of the poor child lying on her death-bed up-stairs—and she had thought her heart so hard toward him that nothing could soften it; but, strange as it might seem, she did soften toward him when she saw how acute was his misery.

Remorse was new to him. He had rather gloried
18

in going against the antique notions and prejudices of
the people in that shut-in, provincial place; but that
anything tragic could come of it never really dawned
upon him until he saw the terrible consequences before his eyes. He was, indeed, a free man, legally,
when he came back; but the moral law, the social
prejudice, stood like an everlasting wall between him
and Jacqueline. Moreover, there could be no talk of
marriage with Jacqueline then—she was the bride of
death !

Judith herself told him this. Whether Jacqueline
had ever had any deep hold upon him or not, there
was no doubt of the sincerity of his grief and his remorse. He said but little, but one look at his changed
and agitated face was enough. He asked to see her—
a request Judith could not refuse. But the sight of
him threw Jacqueline into such a paroxysm of agitation, that Judith almost forced him from the room.
There was something a little mysterious, about the
whole thing, to General and Mrs. Temple, but merci-
fully they suspected nothing of the real state of affairs. After one more attempt to see Jacqueline, and
the extreme agitation into which it threw her, it became plain that it could not be repeated. Jacqueline
herself begged that she might not see him.

"Not that I don't love him—don't think that for
a moment, Judith !" she cried; "but the sight of
him nearly kills me. Then I am sorry that I am go-

ing to die—I am so sorry for myself that I feel as if I should cry myself into convulsions."

Judith tried gently to check this sort of talk, but Jacqueline, with a shadowy smile, laughed at her.

" Don't be silly, Judith—*you* know how it is. All that I hope is, that those hard-hearted people will be sorry when they have killed me with their cruelty."

Freke, still coming every day, walked about the lower floor dismally. Jacqueline, whose senses became preternaturally sharp, soon recognized his footsteps. Even that unnerved her. Judith told him so kindly, and afterward he would sit motionless before the dining-room fire, always turning his head away from Jacqueline's little chair. Like Judith, he was clear-sighted about her. Of them all, General and Mrs. Temple were the only ones who would not or could not see that Jacqueline would soon be gone. Mrs. Temple had never seen anybody die without being ill, and could not believe that Jacqueline, who suffered no pain, should go. She had been in truth much frightened at the time of Jacqueline's illness; but, now, there was nothing to prevent her getting well except—except—

" That she is determined to die," Dr. Wortley inwardly remarked when Mrs. Temple talked to him in this way.

Jacqueline began to show a strange eagerness for Throckmorton's arrival. He was somewhere in the Northwest; but Jack, acting on his own responsibility, telegraphed his father, and put him on the track of Judith's letter.

The news of Jacqueline's illness had got abroad in the county, and something like remorse was felt by many who had seen her at the Turkey Thicket party. By degrees the impression that she was indeed in a bad way became general.

If Judith and Jacqueline had never loved Jack Throckmorton before, they would have loved him then. The sweetness, tenderness, and gentleness of the boy came out every day. There had always been an affinity between Jacqueline and him, and, as other ties weakened, this seemed to grow stronger. He never tired or bored or agitated her. Regularly he came twice a day, with flowers, or game, or with a new book. Dr. Wortley encouraged Jacqueline to see him, as it was plainly through her mind that her body must be cured. So every day Mrs. Temple or Judith would take Jack up to Jacqueline's room, and he would sit down by the bed and tell her his droll stories. Sometimes the ghost of a laugh would come from Jacqueline, and when, at parting, Jack would stand over her, holding her hand and saying, " Miss Jacky, I swear this is not to be stood for another day!—I'm coming over to-morrow to take you to drive!" Jacqueline would almost laugh aloud. Jack never mentioned Throckmorton to her, though; but one day, when he had brought her a great bunch of violets and narcissus, which had actually brought a little color to Jacqueline's cheeks, and had induced her to eat a piece of bread about as big as a silver dollar, he turned to Judith as he got out of the room: "The major is coming," he said, with an altogether different look in his handsome, boyish face. "I got a dispatch from him to-day. If he makes connections, he can be here by day after to-morrow."

"How glad I am—and how glad Jacqueline will be!" answered Judith.

For the first time, that day Judith had begun to hope that Jacqueline would get well. She had certainly brightened, and this strange interest in Throckmorton's arrival was encouraging. Perhaps, after all, she cared for him more than she thought—and if he came—

Till that day Jacqueline seemed to be brighter and better. The next day the weather turned suddenly cold and blustering, with violent gusts of snow and sleet. Jacqueline, who could see out of the window from her bed, seemed singularly depressed by the weather, although the pleasant, old-fashioned room was a nest of warmth and comfort.

Delilah sat in the great rush-bottomed chair by the sparkling fire, knitting, while Judith, with some work in her lap, sat close by the bed, and occasionally talked hopefully to Jacqueline.

"How sad it is!" presently said Jacqueline; "the

peach-trees are all in bloom, and the buds will be killed by this snow—and the little hyacinths that are just coming up—all the young growing things will die to-day."

"Not the plants, dear—only the blossoms," replied Judith, cheerfully. "In a week they will have forgotten all about this snow."

"It is very sad," sighed Jacqueline.

All day Jacqueline seemed affected by the weather. Barn Elms, never a cheerful place at any time, was apt to be funereal when winter blasts swept the branches of the melancholy poplars and elms against the sides of the house, and when the wind howled amid the loosely built chimneys. A blackbird had begun building her nest in the tree nearest Jacqueline's window; and often, during the long days when she had lain in her bed, she had watched the bird flying and fluttering back and forth. The wind, which raged fitfully, came on stronger toward the afternoon. It lashed the still bare branches of the trees, beating them frantically about. The nest soon went. The poor bird, flying wildly around the place where it had been, was suddenly caught by a swaying branch, and, numbed with the cold, was dashed against the window. Jacqueline almost shrieked. Judith ran down-stairs, and out bareheaded in the sleet and snow, and found the bird —but it was already dead. When she went back, Jacqueline was crying.

"See how it is, Judith—everything that is young and weak will die in this weather."

A book lay on the bed beside Jacqueline—Jack Throckmorton had brought it over to her a day or two before. Jacqueline, laboriously—for she was very weak—turned over the pages and showed a paragraph to Judith:

"And the fire is lighted and the hall warmed, and it rains and it snows and it storms without. Then cometh in a sparrow and flieth about the hall. It cometh in at one door and goeth out at another. While it is within, it is not touched with the winter storm. *But that is only for a moment, only for the least space.*"

Judith thought that Jacqueline, in her simplicity, had taken it literally; but she had not.

"Once, Throckmorton read some in this book to me. He said that meant human life—that little moment. Why can't people let other people be comfortable in that least space, instead of—of—killing them as—being so unkind to them?" Jacqueline stopped. Her mind was ever working on that deep resentment against her county people. "And Throckmorton, too," she continued, after a pause, "you know, Judith, how noble he is—and see how they have treated him!"

"My dearest," answered Judith, "you don't understand. These people are really kind and tender-hearted; but they move very slowly—and they have queer prejudices—notions—that they will die with, and die for, I think; but don't think about that—think about getting well, and running about again with Beverley. You ought to see him, trotting around down-stairs, saying: ' Where is my Jacky? I want my Jacky.' He was so naughty to-day that Delilah threatened to whip him, and even mother had to take a stand against him. He is getting thoroughly spoiled while I am up here with you."

Jacqueline smiled slightly, but soon returned to watching the gloomy day without. At twilight she would not have the shutters closed, but lay striving to catch the last fading glimpses of the somber day-light. Judith began to feel an intense longing for Throckmorton to come. Jacqueline, too, who had been so strangely forgetful and neglectful of Throck-morton until lately, had asked a dozen times that day, when it was possible for him to get there, and what if he should miss the boat, and many other questions. About seven o'clock Judith went down to tea, leaving Delilah with Jacqueline.

Delilah, sitting up black and solemn, listened to Jacqueline's faint and sorrowful talk.

"Doan' you fret, honey, 'bout dem blackbirds, an' dem peach-blossoms, an' dem little lambs out in de cold. De Lord gwi' teck keer on 'em. He gwi' meck de sun ter shine, an' de win' ter blow; an' He gwi'

down in de rain an' de gloomerin' fur ter fin' de po'
los' sheep. He ain' gwi' lef' 'em out d'yar ter dey-
selves. He gwi' tote 'em home outen' de rain an' de
darkness."

"Do you think so, mammy?"

"I knows hit, chile."

Down-stairs, General and Mrs. Temple, with little
Beverley and Judith, were all that were present around
the table. Not yet even had Mrs. Temple begun to
be alarmed about Jacqueline, who had not had a pain
or an ache.

Jacqueline's vacant chair struck Judith more painfully than usual. Scarcely had she taken her place at
the table, when she saw Delilah peer in at the door, a
queer, ashy tinge over her black face. Judith rose
and went out quietly, Mrs. Temple looking surprised,
but saying nothing. Judith, Mrs. Temple thought,
coddled Jacqueline rather too much for her own
good, so Kitty Sherrard and Dr. Wortley both said.

"Miss Judy," whispered Delilah, "Miss Jacky is
a-gwine—she done start on de road—"

Judith, without a word, flew up-stairs. Jacqueline
lay, scarcely breathing, her face perfectly white, her
dark and beautiful eyes wide open. Judith raised her
up, Jacqueline protesting feebly.

"Judith, it is come! I feel it. I am not at all
frightened. It was those cruel people at Mrs. Sherrard's party—"

"Don't—don't say that, Jacqueline! You are only a little faint and discouraged. Here is Delilah coming."

"Tell Throckmorton I tried to live until he came, but my breath won't hold out any longer, and my heart has scarcely beat at all for a week, it seems to me."

Judith made a sign to Delilah to go for Mrs. Temple. Scarcely was she out of the room, before Jacqueline's head fell back on Judith's shoulder. Judith, brave as she was, began to tremble and to weep.

"I did so want to see Throckmorton, to tell him something. I wanted to say to him—Judith—"

Mrs. Temple came in swiftly, followed by the general. Jacqueline had strength enough left to hold out a thin little hand. A smile like moonlight passed over her face. She gasped once, and all was over.

CHAPTER XIII.

THE next night at midnight there was a solemn stir, a painful and heart-breaking commotion, at Barn Elms. Throckmorton had come. He had indeed missed the boat, and had driven seventy miles rather than wait a day. Mrs. Temple, as when Beverley died, had shut herself up in the " charmber " with General Temple. Most people thought it was to comfort General Temple, but in those two dreadful tragedies of her life it was General Temple who comforted Mrs. Temple. Both parents felt something like remorse in their grief. They had been good parents after their lights, but the wayward, capricious Jacqueline, although their child, was outside of their experience. Her nature had eluded both of them.

"Ole marse," said Delilah, in a solemn whisper to Judith, sitting in Jacqueline's peaceful room, " he set by mistis. He hole her han' an' he read de Bible ter her, an' he tell her she ain' got no reproachments fur ter make. Mistis, she jes' lay in the bed, ez white ez de wall, an' her eyes wide open, a-hole'in ole marse like she wuz drowndin'. It seem like ole marse ain' got no sort o' idee, 'cep 'tis ter comfort mistis. She do grieve so arter her chillen. She ain' got none now."

To Judith, whose grief was poignant and complex, was left the task of watching by Jacqueline. With tender superstition, she got out the wedding-gown—it could be put to no other use—and she and Delilah put it on Jacqueline, deftly hiding the blood-spots.

"My pretty little missy," said Delilah, smoothing down the frock with her hard black hand. "Arter all, you gwi' w'yar dis pretty little frock Miss Judy done wuk for you to git married in."

And to Judith also fell the task of showing Freke into the white and darkened room.

As they looked into each other's eyes, and realized that, after all, they were the chiefest mourners, Judith's old enmity melted away.

"You and I have struggled for this child's soul," he said. "Had you but let me see her—had she but gone with me—she would be alive this day."

"And wretched!" Judith could not help saying.

"No—most happy. I understood her better than anybody else. It was that which gave me my power over her. She wanted nothing in this world except to be loved."

He went in and stayed so long that Judith opened the door softly two or three times. Sometimes, by the dim light, he was kneeling by the bed, holding the cold little hand in his. Again, he sat on a chair, stroking the bright hair that rippled over the forehead. Judith had not the heart to speak to him until midnight, when the sound of Throckmorton's step in the hall told her he had come. She went in and said to Freke hurriedly, but not unkindly, "You must go—Throckmorton is here."

"Then I will go," he said. But with a queer sort of triumph in his voice he added: "She never was Throckmorton's, living or dead. She was mine as far as her heart and her soul and her will went." And so saying, he went down the stairs and out and away, without meeting Throckmorton.

Judith went down into the dining-room, where Throckmorton sat before the decaying fire, with only the light of two tall candles to pierce the darkness. He arose silently and followed her. At the door of the room his courage, which Judith had thought invincible, seemed suddenly to leave him. He, the strong man, turned pale, and clung to the weak woman's arm. Something of the divine pity in Judith's face went to his soul. He stayed only a few minutes. It came to Judith, like a flash, that his grief was not like Freke's. Throckmorton pitied Jacqueline. Freke pitied himself, for the sharp misery of life without her. When Throckmorton came out, Judith went in and resumed her watch.

The day of the funeral was as stormy as the day

of Jacqueline's death. But for that, the whole county would have been at the funeral. Something of the truth had leaked out, and the people were conscience-stricken. Poor Jacqueline, who two weeks before had in vain asked for a little human pity from them, now had her memory deluged with it. But the storm was so violent that but few persons could be present. As Judith stood at the head of the small grave in the wind and the rain, listening to Edmund Morford's rich voice, now touched with real feeling, she glanced toward Freke, standing by himself, with his hands clasped behind his back, his eyes fixed devouringly upon the coffin. As the first damp clods fell resounding on the lid, he said to himself: "Jacqueline! Jacqueline!"

Throckmorton, with folded arms and his iron jaw set, gave no sign of his feelings through his stern composure. Judith's heart was wrenched as if she were burying her own child. When they left the grave, Freke remained standing alone, his hat off, and the sleety rain pelting his bare head. At that sight Judith, for the first time, forgave him from her heart.

CHAPTER XIV.

THROCKMORTON'S year of leave was not up, yet he
went immediately back to his post. Everything that
had happened to him in the last six months had been
so unreal, so out of all his previous experiences, that
he needed the every-day routine of duty to enable him
to get his bearings. He wanted to find out if he himself was changed. There was certainly a change in
him, which everybody saw; but he was not a man to
be questioned. He went about his duty, quietly and
self-containedly. He had always found a plenty to do,
and wondered at the idleness that he sometimes saw
around him; and now he was busier than ever. He
was not a philanthropic meddler, and was as loath
to offer his advice unasked to a soldier as to an
officer, but he earnestly desired, now more than
ever, to be of help to his fellow-men, and Throckmorton's help was always efficient because it never
hurt the self-respect of those who received it. Certain of the non-commissioned officers at his post were
competing for a commission. To his surprise and
gratification, he found them anxious to be instructed

by him. So he turned schoolmaster, and patiently and laboriously, night after night, gave them the advantage of all he knew. Only one got the commission, but all were qualified when Throckmorton got through with them. He was not any less alert and attentive than before, but in all his waking moments, when his mind was not imperatively drawn to other things, he was thinking over those six months at Millenbeck—the hopes with which he went back; the strangeness of finding himself under the ban among his own people; the renewal of the link with Barn Elms, after thirty years' absence; his complete infatuation with Jacqueline—and, out of it all, rose Judith's face. How hard had been her lot; and how strange it was that he had made confidences to her, and that, of all the women he had ever known, she was the only one of whose sympathy he had ever felt the need! He considered his somewhat barren life—his reserved habits—and sometimes thought Heaven was kind to Jacqueline in not giving her to him, for he could not bend his nature to any woman's—the woman must conform to him; and it was not in Jacqueline to be anything but what Nature had made her.

Jack was off at the university, and Millenbeck was shut up, silent and deserted.

Freke was gone. He disappeared apparently from the face of the earth. He wanted neither to see nor hear anything of anybody connected with Jacqueline.

Throckmorton, on the contrary, clung to the ties at Barn Elms.

But to Judith Temple life had become infinitely sadder and poorer than ever before. She had caught one glimpse of paradise, and that had changed the whole face of life for her, and she seemed all at once to be very much alone. But in one sense she was less alone than ever before. Mrs. Temple's will and courage and purpose seemed gone. She changed strangely after Jacqueline's death. She, who had once silently resented the slightest forgetfulness of Beverley, now seemed to feel acutely that the living should not be sacrificed to the dead. She began to urge Judith to go from home; to take off her mourning at the end of a year. Judith gently protested. The truth was that, although Mrs. Temple had at last come out of that strange forgetfulness of Jacqueline and mourned as other mothers do, Jacqueline took nothing out of her life. With Judith it was as if her child had been taken. She could not pass Jacqueline's empty room without remembering how she would waylay her, and draw her in to sit by the fire and dream and romance. She could not sew or read or do anything without feeling the loss of the childish companionship. Even when she laid aside her seriousness for her child and romped and played with the boy, he was apt to say, "I wish Jacky would come back and play with me again."

19

At intervals Mrs. Temple received kind and sympathetic letters from Throckmorton, and replied to them with letters worded with her own simple eloquence. In Throckmorton's letters he spoke of Jacqueline rather as if she had been his child than his promised wife. Among them all Jacqueline's memory was that of a child. Throckmorton sent kind messages to Judith; and Mrs. Temple, when she wrote, conveyed short but expressive replies from Judith.

Two years had passed. So quiet and uneventful had been their lives, that Judith would have had difficulty in persuading herself that the years were slipping by, but for little Beverley, now a handsome, sturdy urchin, whose long, fair hair had been cut off, and who emerged from dainty white frocks into kilts. The grandfather and grandmother daily more adored the child. Judith thought sometimes they were fast forgetting Jacqueline. The grass was quite green over Jacqueline by this, and the head-stone had lost its perfect whiteness. But to Judith there was no forgetting. She had loved the child as if she had been her own, and she loved Throckmorton still. Jack wrote to her at intervals, his letters always containing some allusion to Jacqueline. Judith thought sometimes, with wonder, that Fate should not in the first instance have united those two young creatures, boy and girl.

One night, two winters after Jacqueline had gone

away, Judith, who every night before going to bed went to her window, and, drawing the curtain, looked long toward Millenbeck, saw a bright light shining from the hall-door and two of the lower windows of the house. Every night, as she gazed at it, she had seen it black and tenantless, and utterly deserted; but, now—

"Throckmorton has come!" she said to herself.

Next morning he came over early to see them. He found General Temple the same General Temple —courteous and verbose. His health being very good, he was an Episcopalian for the time being; but, whenever the gout appeared, he had his old way of lapsing into Presbyterianism. Mrs. Temple was the same, and yet not the same. Throckmorton saw a change in her. She, the most unyielding of women, had become easy and indulgent. Simon Peter and Delilah came in to speak to him, and a wifely rebuke, administered in the pantry, was distinctly audible to Throckmorton:

"Huccome you ain' taken off dat ole coat, nigger, an' put on dat one mistis give you, fur ter speak ter Marse George Throckmorton? He sut'ny will think we 'all's po', ef you keep on dat er way."

"We *is* po', but we is first quality, 'ooman!"

Judith, who had great self-command, could control her eyes, her voice, her manner; but happiness, the outlaw, at seeing Throckmorton again, brought the red blood surging to her cheeks. Throckmorton, who was exactly like his old self, was surprised and inwardly agitated at it. They spoke some tender words of Jacqueline, all of them sitting together in the old-fashioned drawing-room. Her little chair was in its old place, but Judith sat in it; and even the ragged footstool on which Jacqueline had toasted her little feet was near it. Throckmorton noticed all these things with tenderness in his dark eyes. He was a little grayer than before, but he was the same erect, soldierly figure; he had the same simple but commanding dignity.

He walked home in a curious state of emotion. In those two years he had not ceased thinking deeply over that short episode, so full of happiness and pain —the happiness a little unreal, and vexed with many pangs; the pain very real, but with strange suggestions that, after all, the happiness held more possibilities of wretchedness. He could think, for Jacqueline's sake, how much better off she was, lying so peacefully in the old grave-yard, than if she had lived, so weak, so captivating, so unthinking. What would life have been to her? And so, at forty-six, after having experienced more than most men, he began the analysis of his own emotions, and realized that all he had known of love was perilously like a mirage. He had entered into a fool's paradise, but he knew that he of all men could least be satisfied there. His

reason, his intellect, always overmastered him in the
end; and what was there in this bewitching child to
satisfy either? Jacqueline, young, was a dream; Jacqueline, old, was a fantasm. All this had come to
him soon after Jacqueline's death, in that period of
self-searching that followed. But, when he had got
thus far, which was some time before his return to
Millenbeck, a great change came upon him. He
began to feel a sort of acute disappointment. He
had loved and suffered much for that which he felt
would not have made him happy had he gained it.
All that love, grief, passion, had been vain; here he
checked himself; the memory of his girl-wife was
sacred from even his own questionings; and so was
that later love, but the necessity for checking himself
told volumes. And then, by slow degrees, the image
of Judith Temple had stolen upon him. It was very
gradual, it was many months in coming, but, when at
last it dawned upon him, it was a sort of glorious
surprise. How stupid, how blind had he been!
Where were his doubts and questionings? Could
anybody doubt Judith Temple's sympathy and understanding? He remembered the quaint words of the
Jewish king, " The heart of her husband doth safely
trust." He had seen enough of the way these weaker
women had striven to bend him, but Judith had the
beautiful charm of bending herself. She could be
whatever the man she loved desired her to be.

Throckmorton at once felt that any man married to Judith Temple would indeed be free, and how sweet would it be to see that proud spirit that yielded but seldom bend to his will! That homage, so rare and precious, was what women of her type paid to the master-passion. Most women that he had ever seen yielded to the predominant influence; but women like Judith Temple bent their heads and smiled and played at humility, but yielded not one inch of their soul's standing - ground until the moment came. Throckmorton, who possessed true masculine courage, admired this kind of feminine bravery. He felt that to conquer such a woman would be like capturing a Roman standard. And how utterly those proud women surrendered when they did surrender! He could fancy Judith's brave pretenses melting away; how charming would be her sweet inexperience! How quickly she would persuade herself that there was nothing so wise, true, just as love! Throckmorton, although he had silenced his discernment, had never strangled it, and he began to study and know Judith. But there was no suspicion in his mind that she cared anything for him; and, when he made up his mind to return to Millenbeck and see her again, he was anything but sanguine. He felt that if he failed it would make infinitely more difference to him than anything that had ever happened to him in life before. He was absolutely afraid, and fear, he knew, when it came to men like him, meant something overmastering. Throckmorton sighed when he realized his want of courage. He knew it would be forthcoming in an emergency; he had felt that in battle, where his first tremors never made him doubt for an instant that when the time came to use his courage it would be there; but it was a new thing to fear his fate at the hands of a woman. But the woman had become much more to him than any other woman had ever been; she was so much to him that it rather appalled him.

Nevertheless, anxieties or no anxieties, he went about winning Judith with the same coolness and deliberation he did everything else. He had two months' leave, and he determined to spend it all at Millenbeck. Judith might break his heart, but she should not defraud him of those months in her society that he had promised himself for a good while before. For a long time past in his pleasant quarters at his post, in his regular round of duty, in the part he took in social life, he had comforted himself with the idea that, whether he was destined to this greater happiness or not, he would at least see this woman of all women; he would hear her soft voice, listen to her talk, seasoned with a dainty, womanly wit. Nobody should deprive him of that. He began to remember with a frown Jack's turpitude about Judith's letters. As soon as Jack found out that his father wanted to see those

friendly, kindly letters, he made great ado about showing them, playing the major very much as he would
a peculiarly game and warlike salmon. The cast in
Throckmorton's eye was apt to come out so savagely
at these times that he was, as Jack said, positively
cross-eyed. But after Jack had worked him up into
a silent rage, he would then produce the letters.
Throckmorton had always taken women's letters as
highly indicative, and Judith's were so refined, so
sparkling in spite of the narrow round in which she
lived, that Throckmorton's countenance immediately
cleared and the cast disappeared from his eye as soon
as he had got hold of one of these cherished epistles,
all of which had been by no means lost on Jack.

Throckmorton went and came between Barn Elms
and Millenbeck in the most natural and neighborly way
in the world. He brought books over to Judith, and
often read aloud at Barn Elms in the evenings. General Temple, still hard at work on the History of Temple's Brigade, which now approached its seventh vol-
ume, found Throckmorton a mine of information. A
soldier from the crown of his head to the sole of his
foot, Throckmorton had a queer diffidence about speaking of his profession, in marked contrast to General
Temple, who declaimed the science of war with same
easy confidence with which Edmund Morford explained
the inscrutable mysteries of religion. As Throckmorton watched General Temple stalking up and down the

quaint old drawing-room, haranguing and expounding, the idea that this man had been intrusted with the fate of battle perfectly staggered him. His sense of humor was keen, and, between his professional horror of General Temple's methods and the utter absurdity of the whole thing, he would be convulsed with silent laughter. Judith, the picture of demureness, would give him a glance that would almost create an explosion. With much simplicity General Temple would add :

"At that time, my dear Throckmorton, I was unfortunately separated from my command. I conceive it to be the duty of the commander of troops to set them an example of personal courage, and so I occupied a slightly exposed position."

Throckmorton did not doubt it in the least. The general's incapacity was only exceeded by his courage.

Throckmorton's native modesty, as well as the fact that he knew a great deal about the war and his profession, kept him comparatively silent; but finding that, when he talked with General Temple about battles and campaigns, Judith's face gradually grew scarlet with suppressed excitement, and that like most women she was easily carried away by the recitals of adventure, he artfully took up the thread of conversation and surprised himself by his own eloquence. It was not like the almost forgotten Freke's polished and charming periods, but it was none the less eloquent for being rather brief and pointed; and once or twice when Judith paid him some little compliment, her speaking eyes conveying more meaning than her words, Throckmorton would be seized with a fit of bashfulness, and clapping his rusty but still cherished blue cap on his head would go home and never say "war" for a week.

Their lives were so quiet, so shut out from even the small world of a provincial neighborhood, that nothing was known or talked of about them.   Judith, who was capable of revenge, felt a deep resentment against the county people.   She, who before Jacqueline's death had been all sweetness and affability, showed a kind of haughtiness to the people who were well enough disposed to make amends to the Barn Elms family. Throckmorton noticed, when she went out of church behind General and Mrs. Temple, holding her boy by the hand, that the father and mother stopped and talked as neighbors in the country do, but Judith made straight for the rickety carriage which Simon Peter still drove.

The two months were nearly over.   Throckmorton and Judith had seen much of each other, but there had been no exchange of intimate thoughts between them but once.   This was one afternoon when they were alone at Barn Elms, that Throckmorton talked openly of Jacqueline.

"It is not treason to her, poor child," he said, "but

—it was—a mistake. I truly loved her. I had thought that love was impossible to me after the loss I suffered so many years ago. But it was a madness; and, however delicious the madness of youth may be, when a man has reached my time of life he knows it to be madness. I have never dared to think what would the ultimate end have been had she lived and married me. The certainty one has of happiness is the life of love; but that certainty I never had. I never knew whether Jacqueline's love would be enough for me, even had it been mine; and I could never shake off a horrible fear that mine would not be enough for her."

Judith, who had listened silently to this, suddenly leaned forward and gazed at him involuntarily. The thought in her mind was, that no ordinary woman would be enough for Throckmorton. He could give much, but he would ask for much. Like all men of commanding sense and character, he was exacting.

Throckmorton could not follow her thought—he only saw her deep and expressive eyes, the pensive droop of her mouth, all the refined beauty of her face. He began to think how she would blossom out under the influence of happiness; what a happy, merry, delightful creature she would be if she loved; and something in his fixed and ardent gaze made Judith draw back, and brought the slight flush to her face, that meant much for her. She trembled a little, and Throckmorton saw it. When he returned to Millenbeck, he

sat up half the night smoking strong cigars—the pro-
saic way in which his agitations always worked themselves off—lost in a delicious reverie of what might be.
Here was a woman who appealed to his pride as much
as to his love. Throckmorton, who was practical as
well as romantic, thought it a very good thing for a
man to marry a woman he could be proud of. Yet,
when the last embers of the library fire had died out,
and the cigars had given out too, and he began to be
chill and stiff, sitting in his great arm-chair, he felt
discouraged, and said almost out aloud, " I don't believe she will marry me."

It grew toward the last days of Throckmorton's
stay. He had gone to but few places in the county.
The temper of the people toward him had changed
since he first came there; every year had brought its
crop of tolerance, but it had ceased to be of importance to him. Indeed, but one thing mattered to him
then—whether Judith would marry him. But he deliberately put off the decisive moment until the very
afternoon before he was to leave. He had in vain
tried to find out whether the friendly regret at his
going that she expressed concealed a deeper feeling,
but Judith was too clever for him. She had gone
through the whole range of feeling since she first
knew him, and now was better armed than she had
ever been before.

He walked over to Barn Elms on that last afternoon, feeling very much as he had done years before, when, after long waiting, with the thunder of cannon in his ears and the smoke of musketry before his eyes, the order had come for him to move forward. It was well enough to think and plan before—but now, it was time to act; and, just as in that time of battle, he became cool and confident as soon as he was brought face to face with danger.

He timed his visit just when he knew Judith would be taking her afternoon walk with little Beverley. Sure enough, she was out. He stayed a little while with General and Mrs. Temple. When he rose to go, he said, quite boldly, to Mrs. Temple:

"I am going to find Judith."

He had never called her by her name before, and did it unconsciously. Mrs. Temple, though, who was acute as most women are about these things, looked at him steadily. Throckmorton colored a little, but his eye had never drooped before any woman's, not even Mrs. Temple's. But she, after a little pause, laid her hand on his shoulder—he was not a tall man, like General Temple, and she could easily reach it—and said: "I hope you—will find Judith, George Throckmorton."

He went forth and struck out toward the belt of fragrant pines, where he knew Judith oftenest walked. It was spring again—April, with the delicious smell of the newly plowed earth in the air, and the faint perfume of the coming leaves—the putting-forth time. The entrancing stillness that all people born and nurtured in the country love so much was upon the soul of Nature. The dreamy and solemn murmur of the pines seemed only to make the greater silence obvious. In a little while he saw Judith's graceful figure coming his way. She wore a pale-gray gown, and a large black hat shaded her face. In her hand she carried a branch of the pale-pink dogwood, that does not grow by open roads and farm-fields, but in the depths of the woods. Beverley, with another branch of dogwood across his shoulder, like a gun, marched sturdily ahead of her. Throckmorton, who had carefully guarded his behavior since he had been home, was quite reckless now. He meant to risk it, and since all depended on the cast of a die, prudence was superfluous. He took Judith's hand and held it until he saw the red blood steal into her face. He looked at her so, that she could not lift her eyes from the ground. Beverley, however, claimed his rights. He and Throckmorton were great friends.

"How you *is?*" he asked, offering his chubby hand and looking up fearlessly into Throckmorton's face. The child had lost his mother's shy, appealing glance. He was a little man, instead of a baby, as he often told her proudly. "I'm going to be a soldier, I am," was his next remark, "and I'm going to be a brave soldier."

"That's right," said Throckmorton, "and, as I'm a soldier, too, perhaps I'll help you along."

"Will you make me a soldier?" asked Beverley, pushing his cap back off his curly head.

"Yes, if you will go immediately home—all by yourself. You see—it isn't far—just along the path and through the gap, to the orchard, and then to the house."

Beverley looked meditatively at the distance. It seemed a perilous way for a six-year old. Judith stood, crimson and helpless. Throckmorton was a masterful man, and, when he took things in his own hands, he was apt to have his own way. She knew at once what he meant, and it gave her a kind of shock —she seemed about to be transported to another world. This sending away of her child was what nobody had ever done before. Throckmorton, smiling, said to the boy, "A soldier shouldn't be afraid."

"I'm not afraid of nothin'," answered Beverley, stoutly. Judith stooped toward him, and the child threw his arms about her and kissed her—a kiss she passionately returned. She felt it to be her farewell to him as the first object of her existence. She knew that he was to be supplanted. The boy trotted off, not looking behind once.

"See how brave he is, for a little fellow," she said, still blushing:

"Yes, very brave. But you are a woman of great courage. You gave some of it to that boy."

Throckmorton was no laggard in love. He lost not a moment. He, who was by nature reticent, became, under the influence of the master-passion, bold and ready of speech. Judith, who was by nature of a sweet and humorous talkativeness, became eloquently silent—her heart seemed to melt into an ineffable softness and yielding. She said one thing, though, as they turned to walk home through the delicious purple twilight:

"I think men can love more than once; but I don't think women can love but once."

Throckmorton perfectly understood her.

When they walked together across the lawn, under the gnarled locusts and poplars, they saw General and Mrs. Temple standing on the steps of the old house, with little Beverley between them. Throckmorton watched Judith jealously to see if there was anything like shame or apology in her look; but she, who could not look him in the face when they were alone in their secret paradise, now held her head up proudly. Nobody could have told, from Throckmorton's quiet self-possession, that anything unusual had occurred; but never before had he known anything like the deep delight that now enthralled him.

THE END.